Crow's Rest

Angelica R. Jackson

SPENCER
HILL
PRESS

Spencer Hill Press

This book is a work of fiction. Names, characters, places, and
incidents are products of the author's imagination or are used
fictitiously. Any resemblance to actual events, locales, or persons,
living or dead, is entirely coincidental.

Contact: Contact: Spencer Hill Press, 27 West 20th Street, Suite
1102, New York, NY 10011

Please visit our website at www.spencerhillpress.com

First Edition: May 2015
Angelica R. Jackson
Crow's Rest/by Angelica R. Jackson—1st ed.
p. cm.

Summary: Sixteen-year-old Avery is determined to reclaim her
almost-boyfriend from the Fae—with the help of the creature who
stole his body in the first place.

The author acknowledges the copyrighted or trademarked status
and trademark owners of the following wordmarks mentioned in
this fiction: AP/Advanced Placement, Amtrak, the Beatles, Buffy,
the Byrds, C-SPAN, Dexter, Disney/Disneyland, Doctor Who,
Doritos, Frisbee, Gandalf, Glee, Google, Groucho Marx, Hogwarts,
Jeopardy!, Kahlua, Kool-Aid, Lassie, Lycra, Old Navy, Peeps,
Photoshop, Pop Rocks, Prius, Punk'd, RAV4, Scooby Doo, Sharpie,
The Simpsons, Skype, Snausages, Trojan, Tweet, Wizard of Oz,
YouTube

Cover design by Kelley York
Interior layout by Errick A. Nunnally

978-1-63392-004-0 (paperback)
978-1-63392-005-7 (e-book)

Printed in the United States of America

For my husband.

He may be quiet, but when he does speak, people listen intently.

Mostly because he mumbles.

But seriously, I really do appreciate and love the guy and couldn't do this without him.

And he seriously does mumble.

Mom woke me as we hit the outskirts of Crow's Rest. "Brace yourself, Avery Girl." She said this every time we visited Uncle Tam's, and it still gave me a shiver.

July air streamed through the car window, coating my tongue with heat and iron-rich dust. *Nearly there...* As we took that last curve on the approach, tree branches arched over the road, blocking our view until...there it stood.

A castle, its ruddy bricks warmed by the afternoon light. Looming over the Gold Rush-era town at its feet, the Wilson School of Industry had reformed bad boys for nearly a century before the state abandoned it to vandals and ghost hunters.

The usual mass of turkey vultures and ravens soared above, sinisterizing the turrets even more. *Makes my shutter finger drool, if that's even possible.* But no need to rummage for my camera—I'd have the whole summer to take pictures for my portfolio.

As the Castle receded in the side mirror, I asked, "Is Uncle Tam going to be home, or does he have lessons at the Hall tonight?"

"He made sure to keep tonight open so we could visit."

I looked at Mom sharply, catching the lines on her brow before she smoothed them into a neutral expression. *Hmm, I smell bull, and it's not coming through the window.*

She'd been acting weird all week, taking hushed phone calls out of the room and kissing the top of my head for no reason.

"Is something wrong with Uncle Tam?" I dropped my feet from the dash and sat up. "He's not sick, is he?"

"No, no, he's fine—no more than the usual aches and pains for a man his age."

"You're sure?" I asked, still suspicious. My hand went to the pendant around my neck, the one he'd given me years ago, as if it could tell me if Mom was lying.

"Yes, I'm sure," she answered. "You don't have to worry about Uncle Tam."

Her attitude said that was all I was getting for now. *Maybe Daniel can tell me if something is going on…* At the thought of Daniel, a warm spot unfurled in the center of my body.

Memory dropped me into that afternoon last summer—nearly a year ago—when we hid from a freak thunderstorm in the barn behind his place. We'd knelt on the hay bales, peering through the cracks in the weathered boards to watch the roiling clouds and light-ning flashes, *ooh*ing and *aah*ing like little kids at a fireworks show.

Until I noticed I was the only one saying anything, and caught Daniel watching me instead of the storm. I could almost see the steam rise off his damp clothes. My own temperature immediately jumped about twenty degrees.

But he shied away once I stared back at him. Like he wasn't sure if kissing me, as he so obviously wanted to do, was such a good idea.

Not a good idea? I'd had a crush on him since he'd moved next door to Uncle Tam's. We only saw each other during the summers and holidays, but I'd always felt like we could make the long-distance romance thing work. That's what texting and Skype were for, right?

Maybe he's finally come around to my way of thinking. About friggin' time. We both startled as thunder shook the barn, and he smiled shakily at me.

"Well?" I dared him, with one eyebrow cocked. But he stayed tongue-tied, and I knew it was up to me. Flush with bravado, I crawled over to his hay bale, and he looked truly terrified as I closed the gap between us. I laughed—a low, husky sound I'd never made before—and leaned in.

Once our lips touched, Daniel's doubts seemed to disappear. He grabbed me like a drowning man, and we toppled from the bale.

"Hey!" I said as my elbow and tailbone hit hard on the floorboards.

"Sorry," he mumbled, untangling our limbs.

"Didn't say you had to stop," I said, pulling him back in. "Just trying to avoid having my ass in a sling."

"My dad will have my ass in a sling if he catches us—" he'd started to reply, but I cut him off with a deep kiss, using plenty of tongue.

After that, our lips were too busy for talking. And were pretty much inseparable over the next few days before I headed home.

It was only after I'd gotten back home to Davis that Daniel's doubts overwhelmed him and he texted: "**mistake? r still friends right**?"

I'd texted back: "**NO MISTAKE! but if u want to cool it 4 awhile, i can wait til u come 2 ur senses**." That last part was a joke, but the joke was on me because he took me up on it. He went back to acting like we were BFFs, like the kissing had never happened.

I spent the next few months analyzing—over-analyzing—where it went wrong. *Maybe for him, taking seven years to get up the nerve to kiss me was moving too fast. Maybe he'd actually been staring at a big spider over my shoulder and what I'd thought was lust in his eyes was really fear.* Or, worst-case scenario, I'd just been someone to practice kissing with, and he'd moved on to other girls.

But it was like the universe was against us working it out in person, what with Mom too busy at work for us to make the trip to Crow's Rest for Christmas or New Year's. And I didn't get my license until May, so I couldn't drive there on my own over spring break. So this weekend, with the Fourth of July holiday and the start of Mom's vacation, was the soonest we could come.

In the meantime, I'd made do with texting and phone calls, and it seemed like Daniel might be willing to pick up where we'd left off, too—until he dropped off the grid about a week ago. Not a peep out of him—not a tweet, not a text.

At first I figured he'd gotten busy with finals, like me, and by the time I'd realized it'd been an eternity since I'd heard from him—*okay, three days*—it was close enough to our trip that I thought it would be way desperate to leave him a bunch of nagging messages. We could sort it out face to face—*or lips to lips, hips to hips...*

"You can unplug your phone from the charger," Mom said, splashing cold water on my thoughts. "We're almost there."

I reached forward and yanked the cord out, stowing it in the messenger bag at my feet. I didn't even need to look up when I heard the crunch of gravel under the tires to know we'd turned into the cemetery.

Uncle Tam did the mowing and trimming here, and kept watch for vandals. Part of his wages included use of a yellow cottage on the cemetery grounds, where we'd been visiting since I was three. Uncle Tam was actually my dad's great-uncle, but somehow Mom and I had gotten custody of him in the divorce. *I'll take the truck, and you get the cantankerous old guy.*

Most of Uncle Tam's income came from fiddle lessons, but he'd been caretaker here for something like thirty years. They probably would have retired him a while ago and hired somebody younger, but since this was an historic graveyard there wasn't much to do. Only the oldest families still had plots here, with space for a few more lucky stiffs.

We pulled up behind Uncle Tam's pickup, and I leaped out the passenger door, my eyes already fixed on the big blue Victorian house up the hill where Daniel and his parents lived.

To drive to it, you had to take another street around instead of going through the cemetery, but their back deck was only steps away from Uncle Tam's and we always grilled together in the summer. Today their house was oddly lifeless—no cars in the driveway and the drapes pulled shut.

Gulp. *Daniel couldn't even be bothered to meet me? What does that mean for our almost-romance?*

"My girls!" Uncle Tam boomed as he emerged from the cottage. He gave my mom a bear hug, and then had one for me—still the same as ever, as far as I could tell. *Gaah, Mom's whackadoo behavior made me worry for nothing.*

Peering at me, Uncle Tam said, "You dyed your hair red, Avery! I like it."

"Henna," I said.

"It suits you, with those freckles," he decided, and mussed my hair. I wrinkled my freckled nose at him, but he winked, unrepentant.

Mom and Uncle Tam each grabbed a box of groceries from the back of the RAV4. I slung a bag over one shoulder and rolled my duffel around to the screened-in back porch that served as my room. Sheets lay stacked on the cot—*mmm, line-dried and stored with lavender.* This scent, along with the smell of fresh-mown grass, meant Uncle Tam's. And summer.

I was heading back to the car to help carry more stuff when a yodeling yelp caught my attention. Over in Daniel's yard, a long brown muzzle protruded between the white pickets before it rose into a howl again.

"Bobbin?" I called. "Are you okay?"

The sound of his name sent the dog into a frenzy, spinning and pogo-ing on the grass. Bobbin was a Corgi mix, all ears and nose with stubby legs, and he could be a spaz, but he was really taking it to the extreme. The Dawes never let him bark for long, so if this commotion didn't draw them out, then the neighbors definitely weren't home.

I leaned over the picket fence and asked, "Where's your ball? Do you wanna play?"

His ears perked, and with a sharp bark he dove into a bush, rooting around for his ball. I came through the gate and sat on the edge of a brick planter so he could bring the ratty tennis ball to me. I threw it a few times and got a closer peek at Bobbin.

Dried clay spotted his back and gave him little red boots on his feet. The expression in his eyes was...desperate. Not at all like the silly puppy he'd been last summer. Daniel treated the dog like his baby, took him everywhere, so why did Bobbin look like a neglected stray?

"Doesn't Daniel brush you anymore?" I asked as I coaxed burrs out of his fur. "Or take you swimming?"

At Daniel's name, the dog sat and cocked his head, oddly intent. I talked to dogs all the time, but I'd never really gotten the feeling we were having a serious conversation before. I stared back, but his gaze didn't slide away like I expected.

Is he going all Lassie on me? Next thing you know, he'll be leading me to a well. Wait, this is Gold Country—more likely an abandoned mine shaft.

I shivered, trying to shed the weirdness like a dog shaking off water.

"Come here, Bobbin!" I patted my leg and he stood, wagging his tail.

Before I knew it, he'd rocketed into me, burying his nose between my legs and sending me sprawling backwards into the planter. As I tried to sit up, I regretted the short skirt I'd worn today as Bobbin took advantage of my helplessness to get a really good snootful of crotch. *So Bobbin's less of a Lassie, and more of a drunken Brian Griffin.*

Oh, God, what if Daniel walks up right this second....? I rocked like a turtle and finally got upright, blocking Bobbin from another assault. "What the hell is wrong with you?"

He hung his head and sank down to crawl on his belly. He made a move to jump into my lap, but I said, "Whoa! You keep all four paws on the ground."

We compromised by letting him put his front paws on the brick border so I could rub his ears. I had just started to relax and trust him again when he darted forward and snatched a hank of my hair in his teeth.

"Damn!" I clapped a hand to my sore head and scrambled to my feet. "If you can't play nice, I'm going home."

He watched me stride to the gate, strands of my hair hanging from his teeth, dangling below his chin like a Mandarin's beard. *Most undoglike.* With one last injured glare, I shut the gate behind me.

Massaging my scalp as I walked back to the car, I met my mom coming out of the house. "What happened to you?" she asked.

Wetness seeped through the back of my skirt—I must have been covered in mud. "Bobbin sounded lonely, so I went over to say hi. He was *really* lonely. Enthusiastically lonely. Doesn't Daniel pay any attention to him anymore?"

"Well, um, probably not lately," Mom said.

"Maybe that's why Bobbin's turned into such a pain." Occupied with trying to blot some of the mud off my skirt with an old towel I found in the back of the car, I didn't register my mom's strained tone of voice right away.

But something about the way she'd said "not lately" caught my attention. When I looked, she had on her bad-news face, like when she'd told me, "Daddy's going to live on his own, and it will be just Avery and Mommy now." And the time we'd had to move to Davis in the middle of my freshman year for my mom's new job as a head nurse in cardiology.

"What is it? What's wrong?" I asked. Tears filled her eyes and now I was truly scared.

"Honey, we have something to tell you. You'd better come in and sit down. Leave the rest of the stuff in the car—I've gotten the groceries, everything else can wait."

I followed her inside to the kitchen, where Uncle Tam waited at the table. A bottle of Scotch, already a quarter gone, sat next to his tea.

"Somebody tell me what's going on," I demanded, voice quavering.

Uncle Tam gestured to an empty chair and waited for me to sit down before he spoke. "Avery, something's happened to Daniel. He's in the hospital."

"Daniel?" I wasn't expecting to hear his name and the word "hospital" in the same sentence—I was still thinking Uncle Tam was going to say he was dying or something. *But Daniel? Daniel's only seventeen.* "What happened? And when will he be coming home?"

Uncle Tam raised a hand so I'd let him answer. "I found him collapsed in his yard, a little over a week ago. Not a mark on him."

"So, he's all right?" *But if he's all right, why are they so serious?* I pushed out of the chair and started pacing. "He's getting better?" I turned to Uncle Tam and my mom, pleading.

"Avery," Mom said, gathering my resistant frame in a hug, "he hasn't woken up. Daniel went into a coma."

"But people come out of comas, don't they? Daniel will, too." I struggled against her, accidentally elbowing her as I rejected her comfort.

Uncle Tam stood to enfold us both in his arms before continuing. "The doctors declared him brain dead this morning, Avery."

I sucked in a breath like I'd been punched in the gut and stumbled backwards. I couldn't even comprehend that "brain dead" comment. *It can't be true.* "But not *dead* dead. There's still hope."

"I'm afraid there's no chance of recovery at this stage," Mom said in her nurse's voice. "The doctors held off on the brain death diagnosis as long as possible, but all the scans never even showed a spark. He's already—"

"Don't say gone!" I yelled, covering my ears. *This isn't supposed to happen in real life, not to someone I know. Not to someone my age.* But their expressions said it all.

Uncle Tam rubbed my back, the lines on his face carved with pain. "Avery, there's one more thing you should know," he said.

Oh God—it gets worse? I shook my head in denial, brushed off their grasping hands with my shaking ones. But Mom continued anyway.

"Daniel's parents have decided to honor his wishes to become an organ donor. They've scheduled the procedure for the day after tomorrow."

woke up later, in the guest bed on the second story. I didn't remember much about how I got there—only that I had collapsed onto the kitchen floor, heaving in some combination of retching and sobbing, until Uncle Tam and Mom each slipped under an arm and helped me up the narrow staircase. Mom pulled up the bedside chair, but I'd said I wanted to be alone, and she'd reluctantly left me to cry myself to sleep.

Now I wished she'd stayed, maybe bathed my face with a cool washcloth like in old movies. Instead I felt thick and hot, and snot crusted my upper lip and one cheek. My necklace lay twisted, the gold chain binding the pendant tight against my neck before I carefully unwound it.

I was still fully dressed. *Great, now I'll have to wash my skirt* and *the quilt.*

What's wrong with me? I just found out Daniel is going to be carved up for his organs—how can I be worrying about laundry? Maybe because I can't really do anything about the Daniel thing?

Helplessness washed over me, and the walls of the room felt too close. *I need to get out of here. To the hospital?*

The thought lit a fire under me and I stumbled down the stairs. Mom and Uncle Tam looked up from the remains of their tea as I clattered into the kitchen.

"I want to go see Daniel," I said. "I want to see him now." I picked up Mom's purse and held it out to her.

Mom set her cup down. "Honey, it's after nine o'clock. Visiting hours are over. We'll have to wait until morning."

"They'll make an exception if you explain," I said. "You're a nurse, you know what to say."

"Unless you're family, nothing I say will make a difference."

If she's going all hospital administrator, no good pushing her. I turned to Uncle Tam. "Please, Uncle Tam. You're like family to the Dawes— they'd let you in, and you could bring me."

But he shook his head. "Mr. and Mrs. Dawes have been staying at the hospital, and if they're managing to get some sleep I don't want to disturb them. The morning will have to do."

"But what if something happens overnight and I don't get to see him before…" I stalled, unable to finish the sentence.

"I know he's your friend, Avery—"

"He's not just some kid I met in summer camp, Mom! We're more than friends." If this coma thing hadn't happened, Daniel and I would have made up. *We could be catching up right now, instead of caught up in this nightmare.* "And why did you guys wait to tell me?"

Uncle Tam glanced at my mom, and I knew it hadn't been his decision to wait.

Heat rushed through me as I yelled, "I could have had more time with him, Mom!"

"You still had your AP chemistry final, plus two others, when Uncle Tam called with the news," she said, oh so reasonably. "I made the decision to postpone telling you until finals were over."

She dropped her gaze to the table, and I gaped at her. *Seriously? She thought it was more important for me to take my finals than to visit Daniel? Who's in a coma, for Chrissake!*

"And then when I talked to Dr. Clark, he made it sound like Daniel could rally at any moment," she continued. "Honestly, I don't understand why doctors give patients and families false hope. If Dr. Clark had told us all the truth earlier—"

"Really? You think this is a good time for your 'cowardly doctors' rant? Why not talk about how you were more concerned about me screwing up my finals and turning out like Dad?"

"Don't you—" Mom started to say, but with an *urrgh* of frustration I cut her off with a chopping hand motion.

She opened her mouth, probably to lecture me again, but narrowed her eyes instead. "Have you taken your pills tonight?"

Behind her, Uncle Tam made a face before he schooled his features. When the doctors had prescribed meds for my ADD and bipolar symptoms, he'd fought my mom about it. But Mom, being Mom, had won, and now I took them twice a day.

"Yes, I have." I rolled my eyes. "Hmm, what are the odds that finding out Daniel is in a coma and on his way to being organ-harvested is a *valid* reason for freaking out? I'd say pretty good." Before she could start in on me again, I stomped out of the kitchen.

As I locked the bathroom door behind me, I heard Uncle Tam's soothing voice. Probably trying to convince Mom to leave me be.

Despite their butting heads over my pills, Uncle Tam had stood by Mom when Dad flaked out just a few credits shy of his degree. Then his flakiness turned into outright abandonment as Dad disappeared for days at a time. Whether it was drugs, booze, or cheating that brought it on, I never knew, but once Dad's absences stretched into weeks Mom filed for divorce.

She grudgingly let me have contact with Dad a few years ago, yet she watched me like a dictator for any signs of impending rebellion. She only encouraged my art because it looked good on college apps, but made it clear I was not going to be a struggling artist like him.

Or anything like him, if she could help it. As if she was the only thing between me and baglady-dom. *Well, her and the pills.*

I splashed water on my face and peered through the droplets for my toiletry bag. *Crap, I bet my stuff's still in the car.* If I went out through the screen porch, I could avoid seeing Mom and Uncle Tam again.

I eased the back door shut soundlessly and crept to the car. Reaching into the backseat through the open window, I grabbed my bag. But as the murmur of Uncle Tam's and Mom's voices floated on the night air, I decided I didn't want to go back inside just yet. I leaned against the hood and sighed.

Overhead, the stars unfolded without the interference of street-lights, and a chorus of summer insects buzzed. I turned my gaze to Daniel's house and saw Bobbin standing with his paws on the fence, watching me silently. Above him, the leaves of the sycamore shifted and rustled. *But—no breeze.* A sound like muffled croaks and squeaks—or whispers—joined the rustling. *Am I more rattled than I thought, or is there really something in that tree?*

I stowed my bag inside the screen door and grabbed the high-powered flashlight Uncle Tam kept for emergencies. The beam played across the leaves and branches, glinting off countless eyes and ruffled feathers. *What the hell?* I caught myself clutching my chest like a B-movie star.

Taking a few steps forward, I squinted to get a better view of whatever was watching me. As the light shone on them again, they snaked their heads in my direction and made rattling sounds in their throats. *Crows.* Like the ones who hung out in the cemetery during the day, dropping walnuts on the street for cars to crush. A barrage of caws and croaks rang out, like I was a red-tailed hawk after their nestlings.

"All right, hush," I called, spreading my hands to show I wasn't threatening them. "If you'll be good neighbors, then I'll be a good neighbor."

The birds quieted instantly, making the hairs rise on my neck and arms. *I know I'm good with animals, but this is beyond weird.* Glinting eyes focused on me with an air of anticipation. Nerve failing me, I turned and ran back to the house with my arms covering my head, half-expecting to feel sharp beaks bloodying my scalp at any moment.

But I made it to the screen porch safely, and hastily drew closed the old sheets that served as drapes. I'd probably stifle in the heat and need to open them again later, but for now I didn't want all those dark eyes trained on me.

I was the first one up the next morning, just before the sun rose. Snores drifted from Uncle Tam's room down the hall, and rhythmic breathing carried from my mom's upstairs. Even though my stomach had clenched tight as a fist with worry since I'd slept through dinner last night (and the fireworks after dark), I knew I'd regret it if I didn't eat breakfast.

Carrying a mug of tea and a pastry, I slipped out the front door and down the path to walk among my old friends, the gravestones. American flags rustled on most of the plots, left by family members on their way to the Fourth of July celebration in town yesterday.

The old-fashioned monuments had tranquil faces—lambs on the graves of little children, angels and cherubs on pillars, the statues of classical-looking women I called "ladystones." Most of these ladies were draped over the raised crypts like they were swooning with grief, or with their serene, faraway gazes trained on Heaven.

I took a seat on the cracked slab beneath the ladystone I'd captioned in photographs as "Smell My Finger." Her upward-rolled eyes were supposed to direct your own gaze heavenward, and if that was too subtle for you, she held her hand with the index finger pointing straight up. But the finger was close enough to her face that it looked like she'd just sniffed it and was offering it to you, saying, "Does this smell like Doritos?"

Mom thought including the cartoon bubble was too irreverent, but I hadn't changed it. The cemetery had been my playground ever since I was little and I'd never really been creeped out by the graves, or the thought of death, for that matter.

Or at least, not my death. Thinking about Daniel's was pretty gruesome. *Will there even be anything left of Daniel to bury, once they've divvied up his parts? Or do they hand you a baggie with some stuff that looks like head cheese?*

A hysterical giggle welled up in my throat and I clapped my hand over my mouth. After a few sucking, whooping breaths, the hysteria turned into sobbing.

I slipped down to the damp grass, curling up in a ball. Bobbin's howls in the distance sounded like *why, why, why*. I didn't have an answer that would make any of this right.

After an eternity, I was able to sit up and noticed Uncle Tam on a bench a few rows over. He didn't say anything, merely watched with me as the sky shaded from pink and orange to a cloudless blue. I stood, finally, and he creaked upright along with me.

As we walked back to the house, he said in an aggrieved tone, "I can't believe they put all those antennae on top of the buildings in town. Now you'll have to Photoshop them out of any pictures you take of the Castle from this direction." Uncle Tam could be obscure when he wanted to be, but this time his subtext spoke loud and clear: *I'm sorry things have changed.*

"Yeah, it sucks," I croaked, and took his gnarled hand.

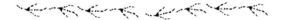

"Brace yourself, Avery Girl," I said under my breath as Mom and I pulled up to the hospital. My insides had dropped through the floor of the car and been left behind at the cottage.

Mom lifted a hand to touch my hair, but I pretended not to see and leaned over to rummage in my bag. But I couldn't miss her stifled sniffle and I relented.

"Mom? Why do you think Daniel wanted to be an organ donor? Not that I'm against it in theory—I'm just having trouble with the idea of bits of Daniel walking around in other people."

"Doesn't surprise me at all he's a donor," she said. "You know he was volunteering in the children's ward, don't you?"

"No, he didn't say. What did he do there?"

"Read them books, played his guitar, spent time with them. They don't keep critical patients here—they transfer them to a bigger hospital, usually, but kids can get chemo and dialysis. It helps to have someone keep their mind off the procedures."

"Oh." *Maybe texts, phone calls, and emails weren't enough to maintain a close, long-distance romance after all.* "He's been doing it for a while?"

"A few months, according to Uncle Tam. He got into it after doing some candy striper work for a school project."

My jaw dropped as I pictured Daniel in one of those sexy candy striper Halloween costumes with a little pink-striped hat nestled on his dark hair, his long, hairy arms and legs emerging from a puffy-sleeved minidress. *Maybe some of those clunky, white nurse Mary Janes on his Sasquatch feet…*

"Are you ready to go in?" Mom asked softly.

"No," I said, but unbuckled my seatbelt and opened the car door anyway.

All hospital lobbies smell the same—a distinct combination of antiseptic and latex—and for a moment I could have fooled myself into believing I was only coming to visit Mom at work. But as we got closer to the Intensive Care Unit where Daniel lay, I struggled to breathe normally.

We stopped at a nurse's station, and the nurse on duty said I'd have to wait while Mom checked with Daniel's parents to see if I could come in. I watched Mom disappear into a doorway down the hall, wishing I was five years old and here to get a shot and a lollipop. *I hate shots, but I'd rather face a needle than what's in there.*

Mom stepped back into the hallway, nodded at the nurse, and beckoned to me. My face scrunched up as I battled tears, trying to compose myself before I stepped inside. Mom stood behind me and put her hands on my shoulders as I took in the sight of Daniel's still form.

He wasn't as bad as I expected, not corpse-y or anything, just… absent. Not like he was sleeping, but the machine making his chest rise and fall meant he didn't look dead, either. From five feet away, this was Daniel's body, but with nobody home.

It's like a soap opera set, from the episode "Boyfriend in a Coma."

My gaze skittered away from the unnerving form in the bed and fell on Daniel's parents. Mr. Dawes stood up and offered me his chair as I came forward to give them a hug and say comforting things like I'd heard people say on TV. When Mrs. Dawes hugged me back, the sadness came off her in waves.

It felt odd at first to be in the room with them and their comatose son, like I was intruding, but after a few moments the silence became more comfortable. We were all here for the same reason—to memorize Daniel before he left us entirely.

I pulled the chair to the bedside and leaned forward for a better look at my almost-boyfriend. The lower half of his face was obscured by the breathing mask and tubes, but around the edges dark stubble roughened his skin. Only a few days' growth, so they must have been shaving Daniel up until...until the brain death diagnosis. *Why bother now?*

His eyes were closed, and I fought the urge to peel back his eyelid. *Would his grey eyes still have a spark, if no one was gazing back at me through them?* I noticed the stutter in the eyebrow hairs above his right eye, from when we were ten and he jumped off the loft, cutting his brow on a hoof pick lost in the hay. And his chicken pox scar, right where a third eye would be, darker than his pale forehead now.

I kissed the pox scar, and my face went hot as I realized I'd just done that in front of his parents, in front of my own mom. But they didn't seem to think it was inappropriate, and Mrs. Dawes reached out to squeeze my hand as I settled back into the chair.

"He was lucky to have a friend like you," Mrs. Dawes said. "If only you could have had more time together. Growing up, I mean—more than the summers and the occasional holidays."

I nodded, not trusting my voice if I tried to speak. *Haven't I already thought the same thing myself a million times in the last few hours?*

Mom and I stayed for another twenty minutes, which were punctuated only by the sound of the machines whooshing and beeping as they kept this body alive. And then Mom said we should go, and the Dawes didn't protest.

I wanted to stay longer. *But what can I do to make a difference? A kiss from me didn't miraculously jar him from his coma.*

I turned at the door and asked Daniel's parents, "Can I come back tomorrow? Or later today?"

They exchanged a glance, and then Mr. Dawes said, "Later today, maybe. Tomorrow's...tomorrow's his last day, and we'd like our privacy."

"You're doing it so soon?" I blurted. "That's it?"

Mr. Dawes winced, but Mrs. Dawes's lips thinned until they almost disappeared.

"I'm sorry," I said. "I only just found out about Daniel, and I'm still getting used to… It's hard for me to think he'll be gone tomorrow."

"He's already gone." Mrs. Dawes said the words I hadn't wanted to hear last night. *Yeah, they don't sound any better today.* Mom led me out of the room, apologizing for my outburst.

Mom asked if I minded one more stop, so while she talked to the chaplain I took a seat in the middle row of the hospital's tiny chapel.

The aforementioned hospital smells mingled with incense and lingering old-lady perfume, but the bustle of the corridors was muted here. Unfortunately, the silence let me think about things I'd been pushing to the back of my brain all day.

Things like picturing masked ghouls carving up Daniel and sending parts of him to their new homes inside other people. His organs could go to some secretive serial killer or child molester, for all I knew. *Someone who seems fine and upstanding from the outside, like Dexter. Do they do background checks on organ recipients?*

My anxieties shifted into overdrive now, and my brain whirred with other scenarios. *How much of Daniel will still be in those parts? Will there be scraps of him or his psyche, trapped and voiceless, while some douchebag goes on a crime spree? Is that what organ rejections actually are—cases where a psychic echo from the donor can't adjust to the new person's life?*

In a welcome interruption to my dark thoughts, sandals slapped the linoleum behind me, accompanied by a clicking sound like toenails. I turned to see a lady dressed in scrubs printed with cartoon dogs, a real dog at her side. Some kind of poodle or doodle wearing a bright yellow vest with "Please pet me!" written on it.

Needing a distraction badly, I obeyed the vest and reached out a hand as they passed. My fingers buried themselves in the dog's shearling fur, and it stopped to lean into me. The lady kept walking until the leash tightened.

"Oh! I'm sorry," she said. "I was coming to see the chaplain."

"She's in her office with my mom," I said, giving the dog a good skritch and already feeling my heartbeat slow. "Is this a therapy dog?"

Not my most scintillating conversational opener, but she smiled and said, "Yes, this is Baxter. We're here three days a week."

She sat in the pew across the aisle, letting Baxter have some slack on his leash so I could continue to pet him.

"Do you ever take him to the children's ward?" I asked. "My friend used to volunteer there. Maybe you know—knew—Daniel Dawes?"

Her lips kept the slight smile, but her eyes clouded. "Yes, I did know him. It's such a shame. Were you close?"

I merely nodded and asked, "Does it really help people, to have a dog visit them in the hospital?"

She focused on Baxter instead of meeting my eyes. "Dogs can get responses from people who the staff can't get through to, like patients with dementia, but they're not miracle workers," she said gently.

"Oh, I know," I said hastily. Though part of me had hoped for some kind of reaction when I'd kissed Daniel… "I thought Daniel's dog might want to come say goodbye, and Bobbin might be a comfort to his parents, too."

"Dogs who come here need special training and certification, they get bathed with special anti-allergy shampoos, and they need permission from the hospital administrator—they don't just let any dog in off the street." She sounded like I'd touched a nerve. Not nearly so friendly now.

"Yeah, that makes sense," I said. "Most hospitals get really… freaked about hygiene." *Almost said "anal" to a complete stranger!* I suppressed a nervous giggle before it could surface.

My mom came out right then, trailed by a woman wearing a gray blouse with a snug white collar. The chaplain came over to tell me how sorry she was about my friend.

It was nice of her, but then she said, "God must have needed an angel to play a harp; that's why He's raising Daniel up. He was such a lovely musician."

I couldn't help it; I snorted in disbelief. *Not unless he improved a lot in the last few months.*

I loved Daniel and his *Glee*-cast good looks, but his guitar playing and songwriting had never been above the level of a mediocre YouTube artist. Not the worst musician, but he wouldn't be making his college money by busking on a corner. *Except now he won't be going to college.*

The thought smothered me, and I just wanted to get out of the hospital and back to Uncle Tam's. *Right now.*

Mom must have picked up on my roller-coaster emotions, because she thanked the chaplain and said her goodbyes. I smiled at the therapy dog lady as I patted Baxter one more time, and then Mom and I left.

We didn't speak much as we drove home, and when we pulled up in the driveway I'd already unbuckled my seatbelt before I realized Mom hadn't switched off the engine.

"Avery," Mom asked, "would you be all right if I go run some errands? I missed two meetings at work and I was going to take my laptop to the library and download them. Get caught up, you know."

"Mr. and Mrs. Dawes said I could come back later—" I started.

"I'll be back in plenty of time," she said. Her smile showed too much teeth, proving how anxious she must be that I'd make a big deal out of this.

The thing is, my mom was the most dedicated, organized person at work. Which was why the other nurses loved her as much as the doctors did. But that dedication came at a price—even when she was outside of the hospital's walls, her attention was still there.

It'd started before my dad left for good; she'd used work as a way to escape problems at home, and she'd never lost the habit. It meant that a lot of the time I felt way down on her list of priorities. Somewhere before finally cleaning out the garage at home, and after getting the car's oil changed.

I gripped the door handle but didn't open it. "You promise? Otherwise, I'll come with you."

"Promise. Why don't you take a nap, and I'll be back before you know it."

The sound of a fiddle, played so badly it must have been one of Uncle Tam's newer students sawing away, floated out the open cottage door.

"Okay," I said, getting out. "See you soon." *What am I supposed to say—"Mom, if you screw this up I'll never forgive you?" She'd damn well better know that.*

The tune behind me changed as Uncle Tam took up his fiddle and added a heartbreaking soundtrack as I watched my mom drive away.

went in the back door so I wouldn't interrupt Uncle Tam's lesson. A heady, familiar scent led me to the kitchen.

The toaster oven glowed faintly on low, and nestled inside lay three crescent-shaped aluminum bundles. *Pasties!* Not the kind strippers wear on their boobs—these were the handheld pies the Cornish miners brought over when they came to the States in the 19th century. They'd caught on with the residents of Crow's Rest, and three shops in town still sold them.

I unwrapped the first one I pulled out—*blecch, beef. That one's Uncle Tam's.* The next one was chicken, my mother's usual request, and the final one was broccoli and cheddar. I held it up to my nose and inhaled the vaguely sulfurous but wholly appetizing scent. I hesitated, then grabbed the chicken one, too. Mom would probably pick up something while she was out, and I was suddenly ravenous enough to eat both pasties.

I was starting to sit at the kitchen table with a mystery novel Uncle Tam had gotten from the library when I heard a howl from Daniel's

ANGELICA R. JACKSON

yard, so I tucked the pasties in a bag and grabbed the leash still hanging by the back door from Uncle Tam's long-dead terrier. *The Daweses probably won't mind if I give Daniel's dog some exercise and attention.*

"Wanna go down to Waller Creek, Bobbin?" I called as I walked toward the fence. He met me at the gate, all wiggles and yelps. "I guess that's a yes."

His warm body against my knee made my sadness feel lighter. But once I fastened the leash, he nearly pulled my arm out of its socket as he lunged across the lawn.

"No, Bobbin!" I said and planted my feet. "The creek is the other way. That's the way to town."

He kept straining, until the brittle leather parted. He shot down the hill through the cemetery, and I followed a few yards behind. *No fair! He has twice as many legs as I do.*

Luckily, he came up against the fence dividing the cemetery from the auto shop below it. Trying to squeeze himself through a hole delayed him long enough to let me tackle him.

"That's enough, Bobbin!" I huffed as he struggled in my arms like a terrified piglet. "I was trying to do something nice for you!"

I held him until we were both wheezing, and he went suddenly limp in defeat. I tied the end of the lead onto his collar and he followed me forlornly up the hill. I relented and stopped at a cemetery bench instead of making him go back into his lonely yard.

"If I share my pasties with you, will you sit here nicely and behave?" I asked.

He jumped on the bench and laid his head on his paws, the picture of innocence. But his nose nudged the air as I unwrapped the now-smushed pasties. They tasted fine despite their pathetic appearance, and I alternated between bites for myself and breaking off pieces for Bobbin.

"Where were you so determined to go, Bobbin?" I asked as I rubbed his full belly after we'd finished eating.

He peered towards town again and whined before pawing my leg urgently. "There's nothing that way but the town and the Castle," I said. And then after a moment's thought, I added, "And the hospital."

At the word "hospital," Bobbin came to attention and stared at me with his head cocked to one side. But "stared" is too weak of a word—his eyes bored into mine, like he was trying to get inside my head, or transmit some thought telepathically.

"B-Bobbin, you're creeping me out again," I stammered. "Stop looking at me like that."

He immediately sat up on his back legs and covered his eyes with his paws. My jaw dropped. *Is this some kind of circus routine or trick Daniel trained him to do?*

I must have slept even worse than I thought I had last night, and now I was hallucinating out of exhaustion and grief. Or, another crazy thought hit me—*what if Bobbin can understand me? Not like a dog understands, but like a person?*

Yeah, right. It's more likely I want someone to understand how I'm feeling, and I'm putting that all on Bobbin. I sighed and said, "It's okay if you're just a dog, Bobbin."

As I had started to speak, Bobbin sat normally and listened again. But when I finished, he met my eyes and gave his head an emphatic shake. *What the—? Did he really shake his head "no?"*

"What's going on?" I asked shakily. "Am I being punk'd? There's some hidden camera or trainer somewhere, right, or you're animatronic?"

Bobbin yawned hugely, giving me a long glimpse down his slick gullet. With gobbets of pastie crust stuck in his teeth, it looked like a real dog's mouth. *Blecch, it even smells like one.* I suddenly spun on the bench, trying to catch some lurking cameraman in the act. No one in the cemetery or the treeline.

I leaned in for a closer examination of Bobbin's collar, scrutinizing it for anything that could be a dogcam. He took advantage of my nearness to snuffle happily behind my ear. *Hmm, that's pretty doglike.* I shoved him off me and wiped a spot of drool off my neck. His doggy grin looked kind of…mischievous.

I narrowed my eyes at him, and he winked back—*winked!* Okay, then, time for an experiment. *Why not start with an obvious question?* "Are you really understanding what I say?"

And he nodded in response. "Right," I said. "Now for the complicated stuff. What is two plus two plus three?"

He barked seven times, nearly startling me straight out of my skin. *So maybe I'm giving him some kind of unconscious clue, and he can't really count? Let's step up the game.*

Clearing my throat to dislodge my heart from where it had leapt, I sang a verse of the "Hokey Pokey" song, changing the lyrics to "paw" and "tail".

Bobbin gyrated as if his life depended on it. When he finished with a scuff-ball-shuffle and a Scooby-Doo grin, I had an attack of the heebie-jeebies as my brain refused to process what my eyes had seen. I ran back towards the house.

I made it to the driveway before he could say "Bark!", but then I remembered Bobbin was tied to the bench. *I can't leave him there in the hot sun, even as unnatural as he is. He'll broil like a mini-mart hot dog.* I trudged back through the cemetery reluctantly, half-expecting him to have untied himself.

But he sat there waiting patiently, and then stood, wagging his tail as I approached. *This is so surreal—if he really is able to communicate with me, what's changed? Is he suddenly able to talk, or am I tuned into dogs?* The more likely explanation was that my meds were off again, but what kid hasn't wished they could talk to animals? For the sake of my eight-year-old self, I decided to go with it.

"We're going to need to come to some sort of agreement," I said as I picked at the flaking knot in the old leather lead to free him. "Even if you're not an average dog, can you at least act a little bit more like one for the sake of my sanity?"

He nodded gravely, but then ruined it with another wink. "Okay, then. So, can you tell me what you wanted when you ran off?"

In answer, he pointed his nose stiffly down the hill again, but didn't say anything. I guessed that was asking too much—although I had just asked him to act more like a dog. "Go ahead and talk if you can. I promise I won't freak too much."

Bobbin gave me a look like, "Are you high? Of course I can't talk." *Back to twenty questions, then.*

"Were you trying to run away?" A shake of the head. "Did you smell something yummy?" Furry head shakes no. "Eww—you weren't trying to get to a…female, were you?"

He rolled his eyes and used his paw again, this time to point towards the Dawes's house and then towards town. "You were searching for your family?" His outstretched paw wobbled, like when you move your hand to say sorta-kinda. "For Daniel?"

He leaped down off the bench and spun in circles, yipping with joy, and then stopped and gave me an "it's about time" look.

"Hey, don't be insulting," I said. "May have taken me a while to figure it out, but I don't see anyone else here trying to help you."

Is that what I'm trying to do, help him? Help him do what?

"So, you need to get to Daniel," I said tentatively. He nodded again, gazing in the direction of the hospital as the crow flies. "Then what?"

His whine had a frustrated edge to it. I laid a comforting hand on him, and the feel of his fur reminded me of my conversation with the therapy dog woman and her claim that dogs can't "work miracles."

But if a dog who can count, who can dance the Hokey Pokey, isn't a miracle, I don't know what is. And if that's possible, is it so farfetched that Daniel could wake up? I mean, if miracles or magic have a place in our world, a dog's love and loyalty have gotta count for something.

"I'm just going to throw this out there," I said. "If I take you to Daniel, do you think you could wake him up?"

Bobbin nodded so enthusiastically that he fell off the bench.

Okay, this is firmly in crazy territory. But if I don't try, I'll always wonder if it would have made a difference. I mused out loud, "I'm not sure if I can get you into the hospital—dogs aren't exactly welcomed in a sterile environment."

In answer to my implied insult, he leaned down and licked where his nutsack used to be.

"Hey!" He peered up innocently and I said, "You can't play all innocent *after* we've established you can understand me, you freak."

At his properly humbled expression, I continued, "Therapy dogs are allowed in, but I don't think you'd pass for one, even if we could find you a little vest. You're not well-behaved enough."

He waggled his tongue at me. The surrealism of it all hit me again, and I finally shrugged. "Let's go up to Uncle Tam's and maybe we'll think of something."

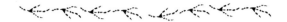

It was Bobbin who hit on a solution, which only made me feel even stupider. He followed me up onto the screen porch and started rooting around my bags on the floor. I left him there while I went to put the foil from the pasties in the recycle bin, and when I came back all my clothes were strewn across the floor. And no sign of Bobbin.

"Damn dog," I muttered as I bent to pick up my underwear. But when I grabbed the side of the duffel bag to shove them back in, Bobbin's head popped out of the bag. As I shrieked and flung my undies at him, he doubled over with what could only be described as wheezing, doggish laughter. "You son of a—" I started to say, then realized this wasn't an insult in his case. *Of course he's the son of a bitch, it's basic biology.*

I gave up. "Fine—stay in there and I'll zip it up and see if I can roll you in it." He obligingly ducked back inside and I rolled him around effortlessly. Then, with a wicked grin, I bumped him down the back steps. A muffled yelp and a growl came out of the bag, but I bumped him right back up the stairs.

I knelt to unzip him, and Uncle Tam appeared in the doorway. I shoved Bobbin's head back into the bag, and he nipped my fingers in indignation.

"What was that screech for, Avery?" Uncle Tam asked. "Big bug?"

"Something like that," I said, trying to block his view of the unzipped doggy bag. "Is Mom back yet?"

"No, but her pastie is gone, so she must have been here," he said as we went into the kitchen.

"Um, I ate both of them." I followed him. "But I left you the beef one."

"Generous of you, considering you don't eat beef," he said.

The big clock in the hallway chimed. *Nearly three—and Mom's not back yet.* I muttered, "I hate it when she does this."

Uncle Tam gave me one of his canny glances. "Your mom late, is she?"

"Yes—she promised to take me back to the hospital."

"Why don't you take my car?" he asked.

"You mean the truck?" If I sounded dubious, there was good reason. His truck was older than me and twice as troublesome.

He grinned as he pulled keys out of his pocket and rattled them at me. "No, I mean the car. You're welcome to use it this summer."

As his words sank in, I probably looked like one of those cartoon wolves when they see the rabbit in a slinky dress. Eyes bugging out and tongue lolling. He tossed me the keys and said, "Let's go see."

He walked to the back door and I raced past him to the old carriage house. *It's probably a Prius, or something equally sensible.*

But I was struck speechless when he pulled open the double doors to reveal a gleaming, steel-gray monster of a car, its chrome bumpers glowing like sunbeams among storm clouds. An iron horse on steroids, it crouched, powerful and bulky, making me understand why these were called muscle cars.

"Whoa," I breathed as I walked slowly around it. After I made a full circle, I reached out a hand—the chassis felt warm against my fingers and seemed to vibrate slightly, even though the engine was turned off. "It's not a stickshift, is it? I can't do stick," I said, suddenly fearful I wouldn't get to drive it today after all.

I leaned in to cup my hands onto the window so I could see the interior. I caught some sort of movement inside the car—*or was it a reflection?*—as Uncle Tam said, "Um, no, it's automatic. What do you think?"

"Are you sure you want me driving this? What if I wreck it?" With the obligatory protest out of the way, I held my breath.

"You'll do fine," he said, waving dismissively. "Why don't you get in and see how he feels?"

I didn't need any more urging and slid into the driver's seat. "He?" I asked. "Aren't cars usually she, like boats?"

"This one is most definitely male."

The steering wheel felt warm, too, and had a little give against my hand, like fine leather. Chrome letters swirled across the center of the wheel. "Nykur? I've never heard of that kind of car. Is it a knockoff?"

"No, this is an original." Uncle Tam chuckled and patted the roof fondly. "Made in Iceland or thereabouts. He'll take good care of you."

"I'll take good care of him, too," I said, climbing out. "I just need to get...my bag." *And then pull off a Miracle Max-style reanimation. No big.*

We walked together back to the house. I started talking way fast, like I always did when I got overexcited. "I can't give you any gas money until my next allowance; I've already spent my last dollar. Is there a full tank right now, or will I need to fill it while I'm out?"

Even a chore like filling the tank had appeal when I could lean against that beast, all cool. Maybe I could change into my vintage romper, the red 1940s one with the Swiss dots.

"Doesn't run on gas," he said. "He runs on alternative fuel."

"Wow, okay, where do I buy that?" I asked. *That'll raise my cachet even more, to be driving an enviro car.*

"Nykur takes—well, it's a form of ethanol. I've got contacts at that distillery they're starting up in the old Skinner place, and they give me the bad batches of whiskey. But you still have to be twenty-one to sign for the casks, so don't worry about fueling him up."

I stopped daydreaming about Daniel waking up and clothes and cachet and gave Uncle Tam my full attention. "Your car runs on whiskey? How is that even possible?"

But Uncle Tam was starting to get impatient with my questions. "Listen, I've got to prepare for my afternoon students. Can you take it from here?"

"Yes, absolutely, and thanks again," I said. *No witnesses to see me zip a dog into a rolling duffel bag suits me fine.*

After Uncle Tam went back in the house, I spotted Bobbin under some bushes. "Now to get you into your bag, and me into some cute clothes, for when Daniel wakes up."

I stopped in my tracks for a second. *Do I really believe that could happen? Or if Bobbin can make it happen?*

"You *promise* you can wake him up? Since you're a magic dog?" I asked, suddenly anxious.

He looked up at me gravely and nodded his head, no trace of teasing in his liquid brown eyes. I nodded back just as gravely, some of the tension easing out of me. At least, some of the Daniel-in-a-coma-related tension eased up—I still had not-crashing-Uncle-Tam's-car, getting-a-dog-into-Daniel's-room, and if-this-doesn't-work-it's-really-goodbye tension to deal with.

The Nykur was surprisingly intuitive to drive, considering it had so much horsepower. I barely had to rotate the steering wheel before it sailed in that direction, and a mere tap of the brakes brought it to a smooth halt.

I took the long way, around the edges of town. Houses flashed by—a few McMansions probably foreclosed on before they'd even been built out, along with the farmhouses from the 1840s and later. Buzzing insects circled the weeds, already drying and brittle under the oaks.

The highlight of the trip was a stop sign near a construction site and seeing every guy there drop what he was doing to stare at the car. I revved the engine, just to give them a thrill. The tires squealed as I pulled away, and a chorus of whistles and catcalls chased us.

But my euphoria started to wear off as I pulled into the hospital parking lot. Once I found a spot in the shade and turned the engine off, I leaned forward and rested my head on the steering wheel.

What if this doesn't work? What if Bobbin isn't magical and I'm actually having some kind of psychotic break because I can't face losing Daniel? I really don't want to end up in a "hospital" room of my own, one with padded walls.

A wet nose invaded my right ear, and I slung my arm around Bobbin. His tail thumped against the seat in a frenzy, and he ducked under my arm to nudge against my boob, smearing me with slobber. "Ugh, Bobbin, you're such a dog," I said, but he'd made me laugh.

I pushed him away and tried to dry off my ear with the neck of my T-shirt. I'd gone with a somber grey shirt and cargo pants (although the pants admittedly hugged my ass pretty tight), figuring a cheery red vintage romper was not appropriate for Daniel's darkened room.

Although maybe the old Hogwarts robes in the closet back home would have been more appropriate for this outing. *And a little wizard hat for the dog.*

Bobbin went into his bag with no fuss, and I rolled him into the hospital and onto the elevator with no problems. I'd forgotten about the nurse's station; since this was an ICU, it was bound to be staffed around the clock.

Without breaking stride, I tried to walk like I belonged there and said, "Change of clothes for the Dawes" as I breezed by. The nurse on the phone raised a finger in my direction, but I pretended I hadn't seen it and continued down the hallway.

It took all my control not to scurry like a cockroach under the bright lights, but I maintained a normal pace and reached the door to Daniel's room without being stopped. I let out the breath I'd been holding in a *whoosh*, and then took another big breath to prepare myself.

"Stay quiet in there, Bobbin, we're not out of the woods yet," I whispered. A slight vibration came through the handle of the rolling duffle as he shifted—or had he nodded again?—and I took it as a promise to behave.

I stepped into Daniel's room, assaulted once again by the wrongness of his still and empty form. *This is stupid—stupid and desperate. How did I ever think bringing Bobbin would cure that? Nothing short of a miracle could help.* Tears welled in my eyes and my shoulders slumped under the weight of defeat.

"Avery," Mrs. Dawes said as she rose from her chair to greet me, "you came back." She hesitated at the sight of my bag. "You weren't planning on spending the night, were you? I'm afraid that won't be possible…"

"Oh, no," I said hastily. "Uncle Tam asked me to drop some stuff off to one of his students on the way home, and I didn't want to leave the instruments in the hot car." This was the story I'd prepared to explain the duffel, but now it sounded lame and unbelievable to my ears.

But Mrs. Dawes must have bought it, because she was visibly relieved. "Well then, please come join us."

I carefully parked the duffel close to my chair, and we sat in uncomfortable silence. Maybe they hadn't been sincere when they'd said I could come back, because it sure seemed like they weren't as welcoming as before. *I should do what I came to do, whether it works or not, and leave them alone to make their peace with their son. I've come this far…*

"Have you two had a break lately?" I blurted, and the Dawes turned startled eyes to me as my voice rang in the quiet room. I dialed back the volume and tried again, "I'd be happy to sit with Daniel if you'd like to go get some coffee or something to eat."

They exchanged glances and Mrs. Dawes seemed on the verge of refusing, but Mr. Dawes said, "It would be nice to stretch our legs. You wouldn't mind?"

"No, I don't mind, take as long as you like," I said, standing up and beaming before I remembered I was in an ICU and nobody grins there. I subdued my face into a more suitable expression and said, "It's the least I could do for you in this difficult time."

Mr. Dawes nodded his thanks and placed his wife's hand in the crook of his arm as he led her from the room. *That gesture is way too old for a couple who were kayaking on the river last summer, and singing embarrassingly enthusiastic karaoke at the bar and grill.* I swallowed around the sudden lump in my throat and watched them until they turned a corner in the corridor.

Then I raced back over to the duffle and pulled it next to the bed, drawing the curtain closed around us all. I unzipped the bag, and Bobbin popped his head out with an eager expression.

"Do I need to do anything?" I whispered, and he shook his head. "Just lift you onto the bed?" He nodded, his impatience clear.

"Okay, here goes." I extracted his rotund body from the duffel, like pulling a Snausage out of a treat bag. I held my breath as I placed him gingerly on the blankets at Daniel's knees. Bobbin wobbled a bit as the mattress gave beneath his weight, but nothing else happened.

Do it, Bobbin. Wake him up.

Then Mrs. Dawes's voice came through the curtain. "I forgot my purse— Avery, why is the curtain closed?"

Quick steps sounded on the linoleum, and with a horrified gasp I lunged at Bobbin, trying to grab him before Mrs. Dawes saw I'd brought a dog into her son's hospital room. But Bobbin bobbed and weaved, easily avoiding me as he threw himself out of my reach. He reached Daniel's shoulder just as Mrs. Dawes swept open the curtain.

Time stopped. I froze while half-crawling on the bed after Bobbin. The dog reached out to touch his nose to Daniel's cheek. And Mrs. Dawes stood with dropped jaw, taking it all in. Then time started up again with a vengeance as Bobbin started barking like mad, and I startled so badly I fell off the bed.

Taking numerous tubes and cords with me.

"What do you think you're doing, Avery Flynn?" Mrs. Dawes hollered.

I regained my feet, disentangling myself from the tubes, and an alarm started beeping from a nearby console. Mrs. Dawes swept towards me and I was glad there was a bed between us, because her eyes were truly murderous.

"I can explain," I tried to say over the barking, the beeping, and my pounding heart. "I thought Daniel might want to say goodbye to Bobbin—"

"Shut that dog up!" she ordered.

I grabbed Bobbin, holding his muzzle shut as he continued to bark with a *mmarf!* sound. "Stop it," I hissed, but the panic in his eyes was far from the intelligence I'd seen there earlier. I faced Mrs. Dawes with the struggling dog in my lap.

"I'm sure the nurse is on her way, and you'd better hope and pray you haven't killed Daniel by pulling out those hoses," Mrs. Dawes ranted. "What was going through your head—"

She stopped as I gave a little shriek and sat up straight, sure I had felt a tentative weight on my back. "Mrs. Dawes——" I tried to say.

I thought I heard a rustle of sheet behind me right before she ripped into me again, "Don't you dare interrupt me, young lady! You are in serious trouble——"

A brush of fingertips on my spine, and this time I was sure. "Mrs. Dawes, will you just listen?" I shouted over her as the nurse ran in.

They both gaped at me in shock before I leapt up and turned to look at Daniel. His hand fell from where it had rested on my back, and a smile touched his lips as he met my gaze. And one eyelid lowered in a wink as his mother dropped in a faint.

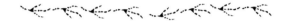

Pure chaos after that, and I was told to leave and take the dog with me. I caught a last glimpse of Daniel, giving me a weak wave over a nurse's shoulder, before the door swung shut and the hush of the hallway enveloped me.

Over the next week and a half, all I got were short texts from Daniel because Mrs. Dawes was being ultra-strict about him not overtiring himself. Wouldn't even allow visitors—especially me, since in her mind it was just a coincidence that Daniel had woken up when I'd smuggled in his dog.

And who was I to argue it was more than coincidence, when Bobbin remained doggish to the *nth* degree no matter how much I bribed him with pasties and treats? *Hard to maintain a belief in Bobbin the Wonder Dog when his favorite activity is rolling in skunk poop.*

The doctors kept Daniel in the hospital for rehabilitation for what seemed like forever—apparently people don't just jump out of bed after being in a coma, like they do on television. He had to get his strength back, and he showed some memory loss. Not full-on amnesia, since he could recognize his family and some friends, but other people and events were blanks to him.

"It's like I can remember how I feel about people and things," he explained in a phone call to let me know he'd come home. "When they brought me tapioca pudding in the hospital, I knew I didn't like it."

Tapioca pudding? That's the best example you can give to the girl that saved you from being head cheese?

But he redeemed himself. "And you, Avery—I can remember things like what your neck smells like, that you love those broccoli pasties even though they give you rank gas, but not what we're talk about when we're together."

Juggling the phone, I dropped my half-eaten broccoli pastie. Then shrugged and picked it up again—*it's not like this is a smellophone*—before answering him. "We just talked about…stuff."

"Not real helpful," he griped. "I've searched through all the texts on my phone, and I guess I deleted everything after a few days, except for a few important ones."

My quick intake of breath sucked pastie crumbs down my windpipe. Through a coughing fit I croaked, "Important texts?"

"Yeah—why did I ask you if we were still friends, and what was the mistake? And you answered back about giving me time to come to my senses."

I lowered my voice so it wouldn't carry into the house from the screen porch, then asked, "You don't remember the barn last summer? And…the kissing?"

Silence on the other end, broken by some quick footsteps and the sound of a door closing. "Sorry, my mom came in my room so I ducked into the bathroom—I'm supposed to be resting. Like I didn't get a week's worth of rest!"

Can we get back to the kissing, please? He hadn't forgotten, though, because he said in a casual voice, "So—we were kissing in a barn last summer? What's so bad about that?"

"It wasn't bad, it was great, but you got all weird afterwards—"

A knock sounded and I jumped, but the knock was on Daniel's end because he hissed, "I've gotta go—meet me in the cemetery early tomorrow?"

I blurted "'Kay!" before he hung up, and I grabbed my pillow to scream into it. *God, as if the aftermath of the kissing wasn't embarrassing enough the first time around, now I'm going to have to rehash it? And maybe that means it was a mistake, if he can't even remember it happening. But my "rank gas" is memorable—what the hell?* I didn't know whether I should punch him or kiss him when I saw him the next day.

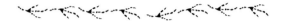

I got up before sunrise and showered, my hair still wet as I sprinted to the cemetery since I didn't know how early "early" was. It had time to dry before the crunch of steps on the gravel drive announced Daniel and Bobbin coming towards me through the lightening gloom.

Once I saw him, it was no contest between punching and kissing. I ran to meet him and jumped into his arms, sending us both toppling over. He made a noise like "cack!" and luckily we rolled onto the grass instead of a curb.

He didn't seem in a hurry to get up as I planted kisses on his face and neck, even though my full weight sprawled across him. His voice rumbled under my ear when he said, "Did you really think it was a good idea to jump a guy recently out of a coma?"

"I thought of that at the last second," I admitted, "but I was already committed. Are you okay?"

"Why wouldn't I be? I've got a gorgeous redhead lying on me, and apparently we spent last summer snogging."

My shoulders started shaking until I couldn't hold it anymore and burst out with a loud guffaw. He jerked beneath me, and said, "What?"

"Snogging? Seriously? Did they have Britcoms on a loop when you were in the hospital or something?"

"No," he said, a wicked grin lighting his face. "I just thought it would help ease the tension to make a joke."

Well, it helped with the awkwardness. But once my gaze met his, a different kind of tension stretched between us. My breath trembled and he was holding his.

But—I've spent months dreaming of this, so why am I feeling like we're skipping a few steps? Or like he's a stranger? Suddenly hyper-aware of all our parts that touched, I sat up—but then I was straddling his lap. *Aaand—hello awkward, my old friend.*

As heat rushed into my face, I scrambled to my feet and offered him my hand. He took it and pulled himself up, keeping my hand in his as we walked over to a nearby bench. We sat and watched Bobbin rolling in the damp grass, sneezing and snorting in ecstasy.

I jumped as Daniel squeezed my fingers, reclaiming my attention. "So, what do you want to do now?" he asked—somehow making it suggestive.

I darted a look at him and blurted, "Hey, this is really weird for me, and it's got to be worse for you. I came to town expecting for us to pick up where we left off, but you don't even know where we left off. How much do you remember? How much have you forgotten?"

He shrugged. "If I've forgotten it, how would I know? And does it matter? I'd rather live in the here-and-now."

I frowned at him, and he said, "What?"

"That was a very un-Daniel-like response," I said. "The Daniel I know would have neuroticized about it for a while before he answered—if he answered at all. But now you're blasé all of a sudden?"

"It sounds like the old Daniel needed a break from the neuroticizing—is neuroticizing even a word? Let's just take this one step at a time." He sat up straighter, and the rising sun hung like a lightbulb over his head. "Hey, why don't we go on a real date? Get all those getting-to-know-you questions out of the way."

"Okay," I said, relaxing a little. "Where should we go?"

"You're asking the guy who couldn't find the cereal this morning? Where do people go on dates?"

"If you want to go into town for dinner, there's Vulcan's for the dress-up crowd, or Alexandre's if you wanted to do takeout and eat by the creek. Oh, and the Italian Picnic is next weekend."

"Hmm—do all your suggestions revolve around food?" he teased.

"Pretty much. All the other stuff involves driving into Sacramento or hitting the karaoke machine at The Hangman. They're opening the Castle for a paranormal night, but I'll be there working the old-timey photo booth at the Crab Feed the day after tomorrow, anyway."

"A paranormal night at the Castle? What's that?"

"A bunch of people wandering in the dark proving they're not scared. No, that's not fair—some people take it seriously. Word is that paranormal activity has stepped up, especially at night. Enough weird stuff happens there during the day that I'll pass."

"Like what weird stuff?"

"You don't remember all the times my equipment has gone haywire—" He tapped his head, and I said, "Oh, yeah, I guess you don't."

"Whenever I'm in the kitchen, where they found that woman's body, the electronics in my lenses go wonky. Like they're trying to focus on a moving target, but I'm the only one in the room."

He slipped his hand out of mine, using it to rub the back of his neck instead. "You're sure you were alone? You never heard anything? Felt anyone?"

Can this really be Daniel the Skeptic, sounding like he half-wants to believe I encountered a ghost?

"Well, yeah, I feel things there all the time. When you're taking pictures in a public place, you kind of have to stretch out your senses so you can tell someone's going to walk into your shot. Even if you're hyper-focusing on what you're doing. So many times I've 'felt' someone coming and waited to hit the shutter, only to have no one walk into frame.

"And I've heard footsteps in a room above me—but the floor fell in years ago, before they fixed the roof, and there was no way anyone could be walking in thin air."

"That's all? That's enough to scare you off going there at night?"

"That kind of stuff, no…" At his raised eyebrows, I said, "You teased me about it when I told you about The Incident before—you even snuck down to the screen porch and scared me one night. You were kind of a jerk about it."

"But I'm different now, remember? More blasé. Tell me," he coaxed.

I couldn't suppress a shiver thinking about The Incident, but I said, "Okay. I was there with the camera club, but alone on one end of the first floor. There's a women's bathroom down some stairs, with a storeroom off of the stairway. I was trying to get a shot from above of the old sink filled with leaves.

"I was balancing the bright light coming in the broken window, but I had this weird feeling. Like this wave of hostility coming from the dark storeroom, as if someone was standing in the shadows glaring at me."

Even a few years later I could still feel that sinisterness washing over my skin, and I shuddered.

"I jokingly said something like, 'Just let me take these last few shots and I'll leave you alone.' I nearly shit myself when a guy's voice said, 'Who do you think you are?'"

I laughed shakily, but Daniel didn't join in. "And I swear I could see light glinting off a pair of eyes in those shadows. It was enough to make a believer out of me."

"I made fun of you for that? I *was* a jerk—that sounds scary." He took my hand again and rubbed his thumb across the palm in comforting circles.

Since he sounded sincere, I went on. "I told the other volunteers about it, but after they added an embellished version of that story to the tours, I've kept any other weirdness to myself. Not all the spooks there are mean, you know? And I don't like it when the ghost hunters come in with an agenda."

"That's understandable," he said. And then he dazzled me with a smile, throwing me out of the dark mood my story had put me in. Twining his fingers in mine, he frowned. "Your hands have gone all cold."

He raised my hand to his lips, blowing on it and chafing the warmth back. My throat caught, heat welling up in me.

As if I'd telegraphed my desire through our hands, he met my eyes with his molten gray gaze. *Oh my god, it's like my head's stuck in a cheesy romance novel*—and he leaned forward and kissed me.

I was expecting him to be the awkward boy from last summer, but Daniel was a pro, making full use of his lips and his tongue and all their exciting combinations. I tried to keep up, but then I just surrendered to his heated breath, the taste of him, his fingers catching in the tangles of my hair. All melding together into a haze of sensation.

The heady fog was pierced by the splintery seat of the bench, scraping my bare back. *What—where did my shirt go? Oh, it's on the ground, there with my bra, and Daniel's shirt... MY BRA????*

My own voice yelling inside my head cleared the mental fog momentarily and my eyes flew fully open. But then the hair on Daniel's bowed head caught the sunlight as his lips moved down my neck, and his hand skimmed across my ribs as I sank again into the daze.

No! Is this really what I want? I struggled to wake up the part of my brain that wasn't wired straight to my crotch. *How far do I want this to go?*

A few more splinters helped me come closer to my senses as Daniel's weight pushed my lower half into the slats of the bench. At least I still had my shorts on—and he had on his. *At this rate, that might not be true a few moments from now.*

"Daniel—wait!" I gasped. "Stop!"

He mumbled something and his lips continued their trek as his fingers found my nipple, almost shattering any control I had. With my last shred of willpower, I yanked him away by the hair. "You have to stop, right now."

"Hmmm?" His grey eyes had darkened almost to a violet. "What?" he said.

"I don't want to do this; get off me." I pushed against his arms and his chest, but it made no difference with the pecs and biceps he'd developed since last summer. *Mmm, wonder if he has a six pack? One little peek won't hurt...* I bit down hard on my own lip, sharpening my focus again.

Instead of trying to push, I wrapped my arms and legs around him and rolled us off the edge before I could change my mind. That did it—the breath whooshed out of both of us on impact, and I crawled over to my clothes. Face flaming, I pulled on my shirt and turned back to check if he was okay.

He sat up, muscles rippling—*oh God, look at those abs, he does kind of have a six pack*—and with an incredulous expression on his face. "How did you—" he stopped himself.

Then, with a real apology in his voice, he said, "Sorry, I got caught up in the moment. I thought you did, too."

"I *was* caught up in it—until I wasn't."

"That's obvious," he said, catching his shirt as I threw it at him. "But what snapped you out of it?"

I couldn't see his expression as he pulled on his shirt.

"Why?" I asked warily. "Planning to try again?"

He emerged from the neck of his shirt wearing a sly grin. "Not unless you ask me to."

I shook my head. *How did I end up like that, well on my way to losing my virginity in a public cemetery?* Even now, the few feet of air separating us crackled with heat, and it wasn't all from the summer sun. He wasn't the boy from the hay bales this time around, though.

Is that what has me so rattled—the thought that he's been practicing kissing some other girl? I mean, before last summer's makeout session, it's not like I was pining for Daniel. I was perfectly willing to take advantage of my own opportunities to improve my technique. Kevin from my algebra class. Dylan, the barely-older-than-me camp counselor who took me nearly all the way.

And I'd been willing to share my grasp of anatomy—*ha!*—with Daniel, only to find he was in an advanced class.

"Daniel, where'd you learn to kiss like that?" I blurted. "Or should I say, *who'd* you learn to kiss like that?"

His brow furrowed. "Uh, oh—we didn't make any promises or anything, did we, after last summer?"

"Well, no," I admitted. *It's hard to make promises when one of you is determined to pretend nothing ever happened.* But then again, he hadn't mentioned a girlfriend in his texts after he'd gone back to being just my BFF. *He didn't mention volunteering in the hospital, either—maybe he's had a whole secret life away from me.* "So, you're saying that while I was gone, you've done enough kissing to go from zero to player?"

"A zero? Really? That hurts." He clutched his hand to his heart, hanging his head but peeping through his long lashes to see if I was laughing.

I didn't feel like laughing. I stood up and swept the grass off my shorts, my bra still balled in my fist. "If you don't want to give me a straight answer, fine. You don't owe me anything."

Bobbin romped around my feet as I turned back to the house, ruining a perfectly good dramatic exit. In spite of me hissing, "Bobbin, this would be a really good time to show your understanding and go away," he slowed me down enough that Daniel was able to catch up in a few strides.

"Avery, wait, I didn't know you cared that much—"

"Daniel, you—you don't need to rub it in. Obviously I—I felt different while we were apart." I hated the way my voice sounded thick, like I was already crying. "I'm just glad you're home safe. Let's just leave it at that."

I ran the rest of the way to Uncle Tam's, ignoring him calling after me. A few minutes later, from where I lay on my bed in the screen porch, I heard the gate in his fence creak open and shut as he went home. Only then did I start sobbing into my pillow, grieving for the way that reunion should have gone.

I mean, when he'd moved me back into the friend zone, I'd thought it was because he wasn't ready for anything more serious yet—a classic "it's not you, it's me" play. All I would need to do was wait him out, and let his maturity catch up. And yeah, in the meantime, it wouldn't be totally unheard of if we both, um, explored other options.

But to find out he'd been with enough girls that he'd been completely cured of any hesitation about getting half-naked on a cemetery bench—how else was I supposed to take that but "it's totally you?"

I tried to go back to sleep, but my phone kept beeping with texts from Daniel. I finally turned it off and wrapped my soggy pillow around my head, only waking up when Mom opened my door.

"Up, Avery Girl—it's after noon," she called. "Don't forget, I'm leaving tomorrow, and if you want my help with your prints, we need to do them today."

I groaned, but I got up. I really did need her help—Mom was a lot more patient with Uncle Tam's finicky old mat cutter than I was. I definitely wouldn't sell any prints with the wobbly bevels I made, and I was hoping to make some spending money off my booth at the Wilson Castle Crab Feed. Taking the old-timey pictures at the fundraiser was just a volunteer position, so it didn't pay.

My first gallery show had been in Davis last spring, pairing my pics with three-line atmospheric poems. It got a write-up in the local paper and some flattering attention, but in spite of spending my savings on frames and mats, I sold a grand total of one photo. To a tourist who said she was buying it because the Stellar's jay was the same blue as her recliner. *Oh, the humanity!*

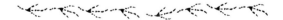

On his break, Uncle Tam came into the ad-hoc framing shop I'd set up in the living room to thumb through the stack of already-matted photos. He peered over my shoulder while I framed a print of the graffiti adorning the Castle's infirmary walls, featuring a bizarre tree with tentacle-like branches.

"Where's that from?" Uncle Tam asked. "It's kind of like Yggdrasill, the Tree of Life."

"That tree of life thing that's all over the T-shirts at the Celtic festivals?" I asked. "This one's in the Castle."

I squinted at the photo, trying to see what had caught Uncle Tam's eye. My picture was from before the repairs, where the drawing seemed more at home among the peeling paint and falling plaster. The construction crew had since tried to paint over the Sharpie during the renovations, but it kept bleeding through the paint in the otherwise stark room. The crazy blue tree, looming over an iron bed with its military-tight sheets and blanket, looked even weirder now. Still, this photo was one of my favorites. "It just caught my eye."

"You have an eye for curious things," Uncle Tam said. "Like your father does."

Uncle Tam hardly ever brought up my father, and in this case it didn't sound like he was paying a compliment.

"Did Dad ever paint the Castle?" I asked. Most of his paintings over the last ten years had been fantastical landscapes straight out of fairy tales, giving weight to my mom's druggie theory.

Instead of answering, Uncle Tam touched a finger to the pendant hanging from the chain around my neck. "Needs cleaning—give it to me after dinner and I'll polish it up."

That was a bit of a conversational leap, Uncle Tam—and here I thought I was the only ADD one in the family. Maybe I'm just the most obvious one. Hey, we could compare notes on which meds work the best without leaving you zombified.

I started to share my joke, but he'd already walked away to get ready for his next student. I shrugged and went back to framing.

Daniel called the house phone twice, and each time I told Uncle Tam to say I'd call him back later. But when Daniel rang again after dinner, Mom handed me the handset without asking.

"Hey," I said, as I walked out of the room with the phone.

"Oh crap, you still sound mad," he said. "I was hoping we could go on our date tomorrow and I could make it up to you. To Vulcan's?"

Seriously? Like I wouldn't be watching every girl in the restaurant, wondering if you've been "snogging" them? Or if you've gotten even further with them than you did with me?

"My mom heads home tomorrow afternoon, so I'm spending the day with her," I said, with what I thought was remarkable restraint.

"What about Sunday?"

"I'm working my booth at the Crab Feed."

"I could come help you—"

"No," I cut him off. "I need to be able to concentrate on customers. Hey, I'll call you when I'm ready, okay?" *Whenever that is.*

Like he'd heard my unspoken thought, he said, "But you *will* call? Or stop by? If I could just see you and explain in person—"

"I said I'll call. Bye, Daniel." I wanted to slam the phone down— *so much for restraint*—but settled for the much less satisfying click of the "talk" button.

Uncle Tam intercepted me on the way to put the handset back on its charger.

"How about that necklace?" he asked, hand outstretched.

Still huffy, I unclasped the chain without a word and gave it to Uncle Tam. Then I tackled the dinner dishes, figuring the activity would help me work out some of my annoyance. But after a few minutes, my gaze drifted up to the blue house. I thought I saw a movement in Daniel's window, but couldn't tell if it was a breeze stirring the curtain or a hand.

Am I being too hard on him? I mean, I'd devoted a lot of brain cells and "alone time" with the shower massager to fantasies of making out with Daniel. He'd given me a chance at some wish fulfillment— was that so bad? *Maybe he deserves a chance to explain.*

Yeah, I should probably go apologize so we can snog and make up.

I dried my hands on a towel and was nearly to the kitchen door when I realized Uncle Tam was calling me.

"That's the third time I said your name—are you all right?" he asked as he strode across the kitchen.

"Yeah, I'm just going out," I said, my hand already on the doorknob.

"Take this, then." Uncle Tam pressed my pendant and chain into my other hand, and I yelped at the heat of it.

"What'd you clean this with, a blowtorch?" I shook the chain so the pendant swung free.

"Why—it felt hot to you just now?" He turned my palm over to look at it.

"Yes," I answered, tentatively poking a fingertip against the gold. "It's fine now—I must have imagined it. Or does gold conduct static electricity?"

"Hmm," he answered unhelpfully. "Avery, were you thinking of anything in particular just before I handed it to you?"

Blood rushed to my face as I remembered. *Only about making up with Daniel and finishing what we started this morning, that's all.*

"No, nothing, I was a total blank." I pushed past Uncle Tam, deciding it was time for a cold shower. "Thanks for cleaning my necklace."

"Avery?" His voice stopped me. "Didn't you say you were going somewhere?"

"I—I changed my mind," I said. And it was true—that urge to go see Daniel, so strong just a minute ago, had vanished. It'd be better to give us both time to think, like I'd originally planned. I was going to shower and spend my valuable time with Mom instead, before she left.

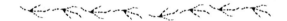

Mom and I watched *Hot Fuzz* for the millionth time that night, giggling like sisters whenever one of us whispered "crusty jugglers." The next day I drove her around to a bunch of the local wineries in the Nykur, so she could buy some wine to take back to her friends and coworkers. Even her snooty doctor friends would be glad to see these bottles, since the entire county was starting to give Napa a run for their winey money.

And yes, I thought of Daniel once or twice, but squashed any romantic feelings towards him right away. Maybe it was the heat cynicizing me, but even when I saw a couple making out in the grass at one of the winery's picnic grounds, all I could think was, *daaang, they are going to be covered in foxtails and ticks by the time they get up.*

Mom cracked open one of the bottles of wine as we made an early dinner, getting jolly enough to jig with Uncle Tam around the kitchen to some Celtic music CDs. Fortunately, her buzz had worn off by the time she left, helped by some doughy pasties to soak up the fumes in her belly. She set off into the sultry night air with a "Be good, Avery Girl," and I came back in to wash up the dishes.

The next morning was a rush of getting my booth set up at the Castle's Crab Feed—it seemed like no matter how well-planned these events were, there were always last-minute snafus. This time, the lamps spotlighting my photos kept blowing the circuit. Each time I heard that "pop" and the lights flickered out, it meant a trip to the Castle's basement to reset the switch.

The buzz of the crowd upstairs faded as I trudged downstairs. Which just made the whispers coming from the disused elevator shaft all the more noticeable in the weighted silence of the basement.

The elevator car and its water-driven engine were long since scrapped, but the Castle still had trouble with people breaking in to steal lengths of the steel cable. Was this another supernatural event, or just plain ol' thievery?

"Hello?" I called, stepping closer. I pulled my radio off my belt, finger at the ready on the transmitter.

The whispering stopped, and a ghastly face glared at me from the dimness between the close walls of the elevator shaft. My heart skipped and I fumbled for the penlight in my pocket—I still hadn't found it when a man emerged into the hallway.

"M-Mr. Forrest?" I stammer-gasped.

The old caretaker nodded, seeming a lot less alarming under the hanging bulb above us. I peered over his shoulder, trying to see if he'd been talking to someone in there, but I saw only shadows. A dank breeze seeped out like an exhalation and I shivered.

Spooked, I asked hastily, "Could you help me with the circuit breakers? They keep popping off in the downstairs dormitory."

His stare held a little too long, then he nodded again and headed to the electrical room. I followed him, frowning. I'd known Mr. Forrest for years—he went to all the same Celtic festivals as Uncle Tam. *What happened to the guy who dresses as a merry leprechaun, the better to show off his wild orange muttonchops and jollity?* He still had the mutton-chops, washed with gray and framing sunken cheeks, but any jolli-ness had vanished from his face.

But his gnarled hands worked as efficiently as ever, and the fuses held for the rest of the day. Business at the old-timey photo booth was brisk, as people put their arms through the costumes that only covered their fronts and transformed into figures from the past. A few of them even lucked out with stray lights or orbs showing up in their pictures—paranormal souvenirs of the day.

Then some of the Red Hat crowd came through and chose to squeeze their wrinkly, spray-tanned torsos into saloon girl corsets. I'd never seen so many liver-spotted thighs and shoulders, and I could quite happily go the rest of my life without seeing them again. Unfor-tunately, they'd burned themselves into my retinas as surely as they'd been recorded on the camera sensor. I could still see spots dancing on the backs of my eyelids when I closed my eyes to try and sleep that night.

So when Daniel's stage whisper sounded outside the screen room, I was awake and ready for a distraction.

"Avery," he called again, "come out and play in the graveyard." And he added a "mwahahaha," too ridiculous to be scary.

I peered at him through the screen door. "What do you want, Daniel?"

"Another chance," he answered. "And look—I brought ice cream."

He waved a pair of big-box-store sundae cones, so tooth-achingly good. In the sticky midnight heat, they were the perfect lure.

"Just don't try to steal my cherry like you did last time," I said as I stepped outside—then nearly fell down the porch steps as my own words echoed in my head. *I did not just say that! Maybe he'll let it slide.*

And he did, but judging by his lipbiting it was a struggle not to say anything as he solemnly handed me one cone.

"Thanks," I muttered, knowing my blush must have been glowing brighter than the sliver of moon in the sky.

The crows in the sycamore tree gave sleepy mumbles as we passed beneath it, and I sidestepped in case they let loose some poop. In companionable silence, Daniel and I found a bench in the cemetery, carefully keeping a space between us as we sat.

Maybe it was the headstones around us, but my mind flashed back to when we all went to the Haunted Mansion at Disneyland one summer. "Hey, if we held up a mirror, do you think there'd be a ghost sitting between us?" I asked, grinning.

But he turned blank eyes my way. "Why—is this bench a ghostly hot spot?"

"No! Well, it could be, I've no idea. But I meant like on the ride at Disneyland, at the end when you pass in front of the big mirrors and it shows a ghost in the car with you. It seemed like we always got the suitcase guy."

It was our favorite part of the ride, so I expected him to show a spark of recognition. But once again, I'd failed to account for coma brain.

He cocked one eyebrow as he licked his cone. "The only parts of that sentence I recognized were 'the,' 'at,' and 'and.' Are you sure you're not remembering some weird dream you had?"

I stood up. "Whoa, whoa, whoa—forgetting school days and boring parts of your life I could understand—" I stopped when it occurred to me I'd just self-included our kiss under the "boring" heading.

Shaking it off, I continued, "But forgetting *Disneyland?* That might be the saddest thing I've ever heard."

"Sadder than almost dying and getting carved up?" The mischief was back in his eyes as he teased me.

"Yes! If you'd died, Heaven would have been a lot like Disneyland—or at least, that's what we thought as kids."

"And Heaven has a place for a haunted mansion with ghosts and mirrors and cars?"

I rolled my eyes. "Of course! Plus all the made-up parts we imagined, like Space Monkey Mountain and Mr. Toad's Sedate Ride."

He nearly spewed melty ice cream on me as he burst out laughing. "Mr. Toad's Sedate Ride? Sounds like a day out for a bunch of medicated mental patients."

I cringed inside at his "medicated mental patients" comment, but rallied with a comeback. "Hey, you're the one who screamed like a

banshee and tried to duck out from under the safety bar when it seemed like we were going to crash into the wall. And then our car rotated like half a second later and you looked like a goob."

"I know what a banshee is—what's a goob?"

"You are! If you looked up 'goob' in the dictionary, it would have your picture," I said, and we both laughed.

I dropped into the seat and it seemed the most natural thing in the world to lean into him, our lips sticking instead of sliding from the ice cream around our mouths. He warmed up my tongue with his own, but this time my brain stayed aware enough to notice the practiced dance of his kisses.

I pulled away. "Daniel, you never really answered me about whether you had…whether you kissed other girls while I was gone. Are you going to tell me? Otherwise, it's always going to be hanging over us."

He cocked his head to one side and said, "I don't suppose you'd believe that I learned it from a Better Kissing video on YouTube?"

But his grin faded when I merely shook my head. His hand cupped my cheek before reaching to comb fingers through my hair. "Avery, the honest answer is that I've kissed other girls, but I've only ever loved one."

I opened my mouth to ask, "And am I that one?" but I couldn't make it come out. *What if he says no? There would be no getting past that—not even back to the land of BFFs.*

When I didn't say anything, he said, "Can't we just use this time to get to know each other? We can skip right to the biblical knowing if it would make you more comfortable."

His randy comment earned him a sock in the arm, but he did have a point with the getting to know each other. *Not in the biblical sense, traitorous loins!* There were still things about this new Daniel that threw me. It was weird to think our relationship was built out of this shared history that only I remembered.

It's like Daniel had forgotten—*okay, it wasn't like he forgot, he actually did forget*—that last summer, he'd never have been able to joke around about sex like this. At least, not without dissolving into a blushing, stammering mess.

While I continued to think things through, he pushed up off the bench and hopped onto a low wall surrounding a nearby family plot. He hummed the Charleston and started doing an exaggerated dance back and forth on the crumbling concrete. Lots of elbow flapping and fancy footwork.

It was so bizarre—*what guy his age even knows the Charleston?*—I had to laugh. That only encouraged him to be more flamboyant and goofy, truly hamming it up. He hadn't done anything this spontaneous since he'd hit junior high and been stricken with terminal self-consciousness. Sure, if we were by ourselves he'd get silly, but if there was even the chance someone might see him make a fool of himself, he'd go quiet. It became my job to light a fire under him occasionally, or he'd just sit on his hands in the corner, watching everything go by.

"Come on, Avery, dance with me." He was breathing hard by the time he held out his hand.

But I stayed on the bench. "Did you pick that up from a Better Charleston video on YouTube?"

He gave me a wicked grin and said, "Cattiness doesn't suit you. Wouldn't you rather join me?"

He demonstrated the steps again, and I played with my pendant, foot tapping to his beat. I'd just about decided to get up and show him how to *really* dance, when Daniel said, "Don't like that dance? How about this one?"

And he started to sing "The Hokey Pokey"—but a roaring in my head nearly drowned out his chorus. Because he wasn't singing the right words; he used the version I'd sung for Bobbin. When Bobbin was acting all freaky and manic, like Daniel was now—like he'd been acting ever since the dog and I woke him from that coma.

The kind of behavior that Bobbin hadn't shown since, no matter how many times I'd tried to talk to him like he'd understand.

I sat there, frozen and speechless, as all these mismatched puzzle pieces whirled round in my mind. Daniel was different—strikingly different. Not a huge shocker, after the mysterious coma and all. I'd just begun to accept that this wasn't the same Daniel I knew, but now an insane leap of logic grabbed me.

What if something happened while he was in that coma? What if this isn't Daniel at all? My hand clenched reflexively on my pendant.

I flashed back to how Daniel had been asking all kinds of questions about ghosts at the Castle. *What if, like the hitchhiking ghosts from the Haunted Mansion, one somehow thumbed a ride from the Castle and into Daniel's body?*

Insane, yes, illogical even, but so many things fit. Or didn't fit, and that was a reason, too. *No, it's just not possible.* This was the kind of delusion that landed you in the loony bin, like that goth kid at school who'd taken his vampire phase a little too far.

Don't end up in the padded room next to the goth boy, Avery. It wasn't just paranoia prompting this fear—a few years back, they'd switched my ADD meds and I'd gone full-blown bipolar. Even been hospitalized briefly, until we got the new pills flushed out of my system. *So, is this more chemical craziness? Or am I dealing with a paranormal creature?*

I stood up so suddenly I nearly fell, grabbing the back of the bench to steady myself. Daniel paused in his song and dance to glance at me.

"Avery? What's wrong? Not to be cliché, but you look like you've seen a ghost."

"I—I—" was all I could get out. *Why would he even say that? Is he a ghost?*

"You're really scared—what is it?" He took a step towards me.

"Don't!" I yelled, scrambling backwards to put the bench between us.

"Don't what?" He stopped. "Avery, you're scaring me. Calm down and tell me what's going on."

"You're—you're not—" But I couldn't say it. If I was wrong, I didn't want to end up in a straitjacket—and if I was right, he couldn't know I knew. I swallowed and said in a shaky voice, "I need to go home."

He took a few more steps towards me.

"By myself!" I said.

"I don't think I should let you go home—"

I gasped involuntarily as he got within an arm's length of me. Whether it was a trick of the moonlight or my heightened imagination, it seemed like his eyes had no whites—just pools of blackness ringed in a violet glow. Our gazes met, and those uncanny eyes widened. He must have recognized the raw fear in mine.

He said hastily, "Avery, I think we should have a talk until you calm down—give me your hand and we'll sit back down on the bench. Together."

So reasonable, so soothing. *So false.*

He raised his hand and I bolted for home, too scared I'd stumble over a headstone if I checked behind me. I barely heard his shout over my pounding heart and ragged breaths, but his voice didn't move any closer.

I'd almost reached the back door when I raced beneath the sycamore tree, flushing all the crows out of its leaves. The rush of wings spurred me onward, whimpering, and I made the screen porch steps in one huge leap.

By the time the screen door slammed behind me, I was already in the house proper, twisting the deadbolt. Hands shaking, I raced to the windows, shutting them as quickly as the old sashes allowed. It had to be two in the morning, but I switched on every light I could find in an effort to chase away the smothering darkness.

Once every nook and cranny of the house was lit up like an airfield, I collapsed onto the sofa in the living room. *Okay, I'm safe now. Nobody in the house but me and sleeping Uncle Tam. He—it—the Daniel-thing didn't even try to follow.*

Or is he planning to wait until I lower my guard? I'd better go check.

I went to a window facing the cemetery and peeked through the curtains, but could only see the reflection of the room behind me.

Duh—Spying 101. If you stand in a backlit window, all it does is reveal you to the enemy. And blow your night vision. I dropped the curtain and went around switching off the lights I'd just turned on.

My skin crawled as I stood waiting for my eyes to adjust, imagining ghostly fingers ready to grab me. *Or worse—what if one of them tries to possess me? What made Daniel vulnerable—the coma?* If it was merely proximity to the Castle, I was doomed as anyone.

All heebie-jeebied again, I crouched by the window and peered out a gap in the curtain. The cemetery lay silent and undisturbed. No horde of ghosts or undead called up by the creature-formerly-known-as-Daniel. Nothing but a few crows winging darkly back to their roost in the sycamore tree.

I followed their progress, darting from window to window until I was on the back side of the cottage again. Standing on an overturned basket, I peeked out the laundry-room window to the sycamore tree.

The crows settled on a low branch and sidled over to a dark shadow near the trunk. A shadow shaped like a person.

I clapped a hand over my mouth to stifle my gasp as Daniel's urgent voice carried to me. *Shit, is he actually talking to those crows? Because they seem to be listening. And nodding in all the appropriate places.*

Wanting to get closer, I used all my skills picked up from stalking wildlife with a camera to sneak onto the screen porch. Daniel was definitely talking, but now that I could hear better it wasn't intelligible. *Not English—some kind of guttural language.* I strained to identify it, and nearly cried out when another voice answered him in the same language.

Who else is out there? I can only see the crows.

I crept over to my bag and pulled out my camera, to attach the high-powered lens. Once I zoomed in on Daniel and the crows, I could see they were definitely going through the motions of a conversation. Daniel would say something, and then that other, croaky voice would start up—in synch with the crow's moving beak.

Okay, Avery—it's dark, you're tired, and it's very possible your brain is misfiring. But it's hard to fool a camera, so take a few pictures and look at them in the morning. And with an extra pill before bed, this'll probably turn out to be nothing.

I pressed the shutter, but forgot I had it on burst. Instead of one tiny click, a sound like a mouse's machine gun rattled in the night air.

Motherfu— I ducked, but Daniel and the crows had already turned to look at where I'd been standing. And through the lens, I could see that all three of them had a violet glow ringing night-dark eyes. My entire body clenched in some primal, innate fear. But I'd already given myself away and I needed proof of Daniel's freakishness.

So I hit the shutter again.

As the burst sounded, Daniel raised his arms, hissing and snaking his head just like the crows had done the night I arrived. Then the shadow of a raven or a crow nearly blotted out his own features. The boy, swallowed by a darkness.

I turned and ran into the house, locking the deadbolt and straining for any sound of footsteps—*wingbeats?*—behind me. But the night was quiet again.

Shiiiiit. Did I really see that?

I thumbed through the pictures in my camera and there was the proof—the crows-and-boy conversation, the eye glow, Daniel caught in the middle of what looked like a defense display. Dimly lit without a flash, but unmistakable.

And not looking like any ghost I'd ever heard of. *So, what is this thing, besides not Daniel? Something worse than a ghost?*

Once I finally got to sleep, freaky images filled my dreams. Daniel with a crow's head poking out of his skull, Bobbin driving the Nykur and trying to lure me into the passenger seat with bite-sized broccoli-cheese pasties. And the one where Daniel and I were making out in the cemetery again, only this time we didn't stop.

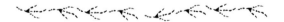

I didn't get out of bed until nearly eleven, when the first of Uncle Tam's fiddle students arrived and started sawing away. An adrenaline hangover from all the drama the night before made my mouth especially dry and putrified-tasting. *First thing on the list is to make a mouthwash cocktail—blech.*

In the cheery, bright bathroom, it seemed farfetched to think that something had taken over Daniel. *Who can believe in the supernatural while science is obviously hard at work blasting at bad breath germs?*

But when I went into the kitchen to make some toast, I heard a scrabbling at the window and turned to see a dark shape fluttering against the screen. I backed into the counter as a crow clung to the window trim, cocking its head so it could watch me closely from one violet-ringed eye. And I knew that it shouldn't be possible with a mostly straight beak, but if a crow could have a wicked grin, this one did.

I reached blindly behind me and grabbed a utensil from the flower pot beside the stove. But the whisk I brandished must have been less than impressive, because the crow made a derisive rasping noise.

A rasping noise that echoed from other parts of the house, too.

Still waving the whisk in front of me, I stepped backward to the arch leading to the hallway and peeked around the corner. Every window I could see from there had at least one crow on duty. If there was a tree or a bush outside, they were perched in its branches. Those without perches clung to the screen or trim, like the first one had. One even hung upside-down from a wire, swinging absurdly.

But none of the crows were overtly threatening; they merely watched me as if I was a particularly ripe piece of fruit.

"Ha, I've seen what you can do to a tree full of ripe plums, piranhas of the skies!" No way was I going to play into their hands—*their claws? wings? ice-pick beaks?*—by venturing out today.

I closed the kitchen window, careful not to make eye contact with that sly, dark gaze only inches away. If "Daniel" (I could hardly think of him without air quotes around his name now) had set them to watch me, to see how much I suspected, he'd only confirmed my intuition that something unnatural was going on. Something supernatural.

But seeing the crows again, plus the dream I'd had with Daniel and the crow in his skull, had knocked an old memory loose. Once upon a time, I'd seen a strange drawing of a bird superimposed on a person.

Where did I see it? In one of Uncle Tam's books? No, I'm remembering it hand-drawn, not printed. Maybe in some of Dad's stuff—that's it! The box of old sketch books he left behind in the divorce, and that Mom brought here. If he never picked them up, Uncle Tam probably would have shelved them with his collection.

I inhaled my cereal and headed into the living room to check. Normally, I took every chance I got to dig through his library, but this time I kept wishing for a search function—Uncle Tam had books all jammed on top of each other and I couldn't see any organization to them. *Why can't he have a computer with Google like a normal person?*

I'd asked him that very question once, and he'd said, "Why should I buy a computer that will likely be out of date as soon as I've paid for it, when I can walk to the library in under five minutes and use theirs for free?"

But obviously that reasoning didn't apply to books, because he kept coming home from book sales with more, organized by some kind of secret system known only to himself.

"Accio sketch book!" I called, but nothing happened. *Curse you, J.K. Rowling, for giving me magical expectations! I guess I'll have to search the old-fashioned way.* I sighed and started checking every book on the floor-to-ceiling shelves, before moving on to those stacked under the chairs and tables. Nothing was there but esoteric books on music, herbology, fairy and folk lore, and the odd mystery novel.

I heard Uncle Tam rattling in the kitchen—was it lunchtime already? *Maybe he's seen the box of Dad's stuff. And I can pick his brain about any weird crow behaviors while I'm at it.*

I stopped still as I realized no crow shapes lurked at the windows. A quick look-see confirmed it—the crows had all left. It might have prompted another doubting-if-I'd-really-seen-anything session, except for the droppings near every window. They'd obviously been staking out the place, but were gone now. *Maybe it's their lunchtime, too.*

I shrugged and went to find Uncle Tam. I made small talk about his lessons until I could slip in, "Hey, Uncle Tam, do you know where that box of Dad's old sketchbooks ended up? We left it here when we moved to Davis."

"I remember. He looked in it last time he was here and said he'd left them for you. They're under your bed."

Dang, they've been in my room all night? Wait—my dad has been here recently? "I thought you don't see Dad anymore."

"We still see each other occasionally, but you're right that he doesn't usually come here. It was during one of his rough patches and I let him stay a few days."

Dad's rough patches seemed to have smoothed out over the last few months. No more scary rants that I wasn't safe and to be on guard against "them." At least, not since I'd established ground rules that I didn't want to hear about stuff like that. Or maybe he'd found some new pharmaceutical cocktail that worked for him.

I kept Uncle Tam company while he ate lunch and then went to look for the box. I found it shoved all the way against the wall, under the far reaches of my narrow bed. I dragged it out, smearing the dust while trying to read the "for Avery" Dad had lettered on the lid.

So Dad really did mean for me to have it. Did he know I might need it? But I still didn't know if it held what I needed.

Shuffling through some pages coming loose from their bindings, faces jumped out at me. Sly creatures, all angles and spikes, grinned at me from gnarled tree branches. And what I thought were some colorful plant studies—until I looked closer and noticed the spindly limbs among the flower petals.

Early versions of the fantasy creatures and landscapes that Dad sold in galleries. Images I'd always thought had sprung from his imagination—but when I found the crow drawing, I wondered.

A picture of a raven or crow overlaid on a boy's face, the eyes of both limned with violet oil pastels. It was labeled with, "Corbin, a minor fae prone to mischief. Crosses into our world by inhabiting lower creatures like birds, dogs, rats. Will take humans when it can."

Is this what happened to Daniel? There's a corbin "inhabiting" him? Or is this some kind of highly specific, hereditary imbalance where Dad and I halluci-nate the same things?

I needed to see if corbin were mentioned in any of the fairy lore in Uncle Tam's library. I pulled down titles until I had a hefty stack. Fairy tale collections, Briggs's *Encyclopedia of Fairies*, *A Compendium of the Faer Folke*, and *The World Guide to Gnomes, Fairies, and Elves*—they were all research at this point. I dug an old composition book out of

Uncle Tam's desk and spread everything out on the kitchen table, intent on making notes on corbin and finding a way to bring Daniel back.

But no matter how much I tried to ignore the scratching and wailing coming from the music room, I wasn't accomplishing much. Uncle Tam's young student screeched his bow across the fiddle strings again and I cringed. *This is getting me nowhere. I'd love to get outside and get away from the noise, but all those crows... If only the Nykur wasn't all the way in the garage, I'd make a run for it.*

I got up to check if the crows had reappeared, only to find them busy with normal, crow-ly things—grooming each other, squabbling over walnuts stolen from the orchard up the street, conversing in soft chuckles and croaks. Almost charming, really.

Until one spotted me and let out a reptilian hiss. *Charming? Yeah, like a Disney villain is charming, but still thinks it's reasonable to make a puppy-fur coat.* I blew a raspberry at the crows and went to check if the sycamore was alive with them, too.

But as I stepped onto the screen porch, I froze in place. The Nykur gleamed in all its chromish glory, its driver-side door just a few short strides—or one wild leap—from the steps. *Didn't I see it in the garage before? Maybe Uncle Tam moved it while I was gathering the fairy books.* You'd think I would have noticed that, but I wasn't going to look a gift car in the mouth. *Or should that be grille?*

I shrugged and bent to pull my rolling duffle from under the bed. Then back to the kitchen to load up all the books, plus a stop by the entryway to get Uncle Tam's umbrella and the car keys. It wasn't until I had my hand on the screen door that I wondered, *how fast could those crows be on me?*

I stepped close to the screen and said, "Remember how we had that talk about being good neighbors? As far as I'm concerned, it's still in effect. I don't have anything against crows, and hopefully you feel the same about me."

No answer but the glittery eyes trained on me. Some rimmed in violet, others not. *I wish there was someone I could ask about that—someone other than the questionable Daniel, that is.*

I opened the screen door tentatively and stepped out, ready to spring back inside. But other than a few birds shifting slightly so they could keep me in their line of sight, no reaction. *Okay, here goes.*

Opening the umbrella as a shield, I dashed to the car, the duffel bag bumping along behind me. Crows exploded into flight above me, and hisses and shrieks filled the air as I pulled open the car door. I threw my bag inside, and myself right after it.

The umbrella bent as I pulled it in behind me, but all my limbs made it safely inside the quiet dimness of the Nykur. Cradled in the plush upholstery, I waited for my heart to slow.

And all the relaxation breathing was working, until a pair of crows slammed into the windshield. A black ball of shedding feathers, they scrabbled and pecked at each other mercilessly. They finally separated, and one of the crows ended up with its face pressed against the glass. It made eye contact, and I shivered at the malevolence in that dark bead, ringed with seething, angry red rather than violet.

The crow gave a garbled croak. *Almost like it's trying to form words...* I leaned closer to the glass. And screeched as thrashing crow bodies almost entirely blotted out the windshield.

But these birds weren't after me—they seemed to be ganging up on the sinister crow, dragging him off the glass and into the air. He gave a furious squawk as they carried him away, and again, I could almost hear words in it. *Just not English words, and I'm pretty sure they'd be written in the funny pages as @&$*!*

In the sycamore tree, the rest of the crows had gone back to doing crowish things. And none of them seemed to have anything weird about their eyes. I watched them suspiciously, but they showed no more supernatural traits than I did.

How friggin' anti-climactic. Well, I was here now, and I might as well follow through with my plan to use the car as a study space.

I drove to the town makeout spot, deserted this time of day but offering a gorgeous overlook of Crow's Rest and the Castle. And obviously I hadn't thought the "crows have wings" thing through, because a pair of them followed me. And these two had the violet eye ring I'd come to associate with odd behavior.

Well, not much I can do about my stakeout team. All the more reason for me to find out more about corbin and rid the town of our infestation.

I cracked open the *Encyclopedia of Fairies* and turned to the back for an index, but found only stubs of missing pages. I couldn't tell if they'd held the index—it stopped at Yeats and picked up again with a "books consulted" section. And no alphabetical entry for corbin, either, between "colt-pixy" and "cowlug sprites."

I sighed and opened the musty pages of *A Compendium of the Faer Folke*. It must have been where Dad got his info for the label on the drawings, because it was pretty much word for word what he'd said. *Score!*

Corbin number among the Fae who are more prone to mischief-making and seduction than Courtly ambitions. They most often enter into our world through the design of inhabiting crows and other simple creatures. When sharing these poor bodies, the corbin's own magic is limited to influence, as well as small conjurings or vanishments.

If a corbin manages to take control of a human body (either by force or by prior arrangement), its magic is constrained only by its knowledge of Fae spells, which may be enacted in our world with a lessened effect... The corbin's abilities are strongest when it crosses into our world in its natural form, where its shape-shifter lineage manifests in bird or human guises and combinations thereof.

And once again, I was following in my Dad's researching footsteps, because the margins of this held notes like "corbin not the only ones," "tell—violet," and "NOT crimson."

Okay, Dad, you know what would be really helpful? Some notes on how to stop a corbin, because there's nothing in here on that. I sighed and flipped through the pages, looking for other places he'd made notes. He'd heavily underlined one section on wyverns:

Wyverns, kin to dragons and serpent-spirits, have held powerful Courtly positions in the past but their viciousness and impulsive natures were their downfall. In Faerie, they are feared warriors and often serve as mercenaries—with those who hire them also taking the risk that the wyvern may turn on them when offered insult or a better contract. They are firmly tied to their dragon-like, winged-serpent form and even when occupying a human there are telltale signs for those with the Sight.

Here, Dad had scribbled "what signs???," and I had to agree it was annoyingly vague. Then the text continued:

The dulling of a wyvern's powers (leaving it to rely on manipulation and force) when taking over a human body is offset by heightened emotions and sensations.

Oh, great—so I guess wyverns can take over people, too? It's like a body-snatching free-for-all with fairies. How do I know which one is in Daniel now? I guess it might be moot, anyway—I still have no idea how to get whatever it is out of him. I continued looking through the compendium, since it was my best source so far.

How funny! There's an entry on a nykur, spelled just like it is on the steering wheel, but it's identified as "similar to corbin in status and ambitions but with an affinity for equine forms." I patted the leather seat. *Too bad—I would have been just as happy to have a horse to use for the summer.*

I struck gold with the end pages, where Dad had filled the blank space with notes on herbs and charms to protect against the Fae. *St. John's wort, bread and salt, wearing bells—this will all come in handy.*

But the part that might do me the most good was the info that burning the "thorn" on a Faerie hill can be useful to recover changelings. Changeling stories were all about humans being taken and a substitute left behind—sometimes the replacement was a Fae, sometimes a block of wood charmed to look like the stolen person. But apparently an impromptu hilltop bonfire was a serious-enough threat to make the Fae rethink their exchange.

So, if burning the thorn would work for changelings, would it work for other Fae "inhabitants" like corbin or wyverns? Maybe it would just piss them off, and it sounds like you really don't want to cross those wyvern creeps. Hmm—I'll keep it in mind as a way to pressure them into giving Daniel back, but maybe I need more. I figured I would start by trying to figure out what "thorn" specifically meant.

I guessed, back in the European countries where these stories originated, "thorn" could mean anything from wild rose to thistles or even gorse (which I'd tangled with on a stretch of northern California coast once, and never wanted to encounter again). We had wild roses here, but the dominant thorny nuisance was the Himalayan blackberry that the Chinese gold miners brought with them.

But no way could every patch of blackberry mark a Faerie Hill, or we'd be ovewhelmed any moment. Left to do their own thing, the blackberry vines had engulfed entire pastures, and even cars or objects left in one place too long.

I remembered that, higher on the hill above Daniel's house, blackberries overran the mouth of an old mineshaft a few years ago. Last time I'd seen it, a ring of barbed wire surrounded the entrance and the shaft itself was capped with iron bars wide enough to let the bats come and go, but narrow enough to keep out curious kids.

If anything resembled the old-school description of a Faerie hill, it was that spot. In fact, I remembered Uncle Tam telling me the mine tunnels used to join the natural caves around Lacuna Cavern, before the mining company deliberately caused a cave-in so people couldn't use the tourist entrance as a way to sneak into the mines.

Then, like the miners had brought a curse down on themselves, the rich veins had petered out. The mine company dissolved, but

Lacuna Cavern was still open for tours, its cool depths popular in the summer heat. Easy to picture the folds and spires of rock as the remnants of decorations in an underground Faerie dance hall.

So, if I wanted to try threatening to burn the thorn, the mine entrance was probably a good bet. I'd want to stock up on some of the protective charms and herbs mentioned, but what if merely threatening didn't do the trick? *Am I willing to actually start a fire?* Fire was not something to play with in these straw-dry hills and fields.

Worst-case scenario, the flames would get out of control and burn the whole town. Uncle Tam might be forgiven for his orneriness most of the time, but no way would the locals forgive him having a firebug great-niece. But if the fire just burned the blackberries, they'd probably throw me a parade. All well and good, but none of that brought me any closer to evicting whatever this creature was and getting Daniel back.

Another scan of the books made it sound like the really effective spells were spoken out loud or sung. But what was I supposed to say? *Body thief, body thief, fly away home—your thorn is on fire and your pixies will burn?* I snorted at my pathetic attempt.

And the few stories I'd found about changelings in the reference books mentioned spells but didn't give actual details. *Ha, because that would be helpful.* In the fairy tales, luck or acts of kindness seemed to play a more important part in defeating fairy magic. But I didn't want to go into this feeling like luck was my only asset.

After all, what has luck gotten me lately? My possible boyfriend in a coma, and the knowledge that his waking up was more like a hijacking.

Where does that leave Daniel, anyway? In Faerie? Or maybe still in his body, helplessly trapped? Any confidence that I could do something to get Daniel back drained right out of me. *This thing in Daniel's going to win, and there's no one to stop it.*

No one but me, anyway, and let's face it—I was winging it. *If I can't do this by myself, who do I ask for help? Is there anyone who would take my story seriously, or would telling just get me a handful of medication and a misdiagnosis?*

I leaned forward onto the steering wheel and put my arms over my head, trying to take calming breaths. I didn't realize I was crying until I felt warm drops falling on my bare knees. Damp spots marked the leather wheel cover, too.

Ugh, don't want to get snot all over the steering wheel. Shoving the despair back behind a mental wall once again, I sat up and scrubbed my eyes.

D'oh, no tissues in my bag. I'd taken everything out when I vacuumed the dog hair a few weeks ago. So I leaned across the passenger seat and popped the glove box. *Jackpot!*

Peeping from beneath some folded papers was one of those purse packs. I pulled out the papers, and then the tissues, before I froze. Gaped.

"Oh. My. God."

In the bottom of the glove box, a stack of my favorite hazelnut chocolate bars gleamed under the orange light bulb. Mom must have stashed them in there for me as a surprise. *They'd have to be melted into oblivion, right?* But no, they were promisingly cool and weighty in my hand.

Tearing through the label and foil inner wrapper, I bit into a bar like I'd been starving for weeks instead of having eaten breakfast a few hours ago. *Sugary, melty goodness*, sang my bloodstream. My mood was chemically lifted already.

I pulled over another stack of books, determined to read them all again. Maybe I'd missed something; I owed it to Daniel to try. But a couple of hours later, I was down three chocolate bars—my eyes practically jittering out of their sockets—and still hadn't found anything.

Maybe it was the sugar high talking but I wondered, *What's stopping me from writing my own spell?* What is a spell but words backed up by intention and ritual? And the bond between Daniel and I would have to be an advantage.

I fumbled through the stack of books for the composition book I'd been taking notes in. Before I found it, I came across the folded pages from the glove box, the ones that had been on top of the tissues and chocolate bar. One edge was ragged like they'd been torn from a book, and sure enough, *An Encyclopedia of Fairies* was labeled at the top. *Why would someone tear out the section on Tam Lin?*

Mystery aside, the text of the Tam Lin story could be helpful for modeling a spell. It didn't include one of its own—Janet wins back her love from the fairies by holding fast to him, even through some terrifying transformations—but the old-fashioned Scottish wording was strange and beautiful:

And ance it fell upon a day,
A cauld day and a snell,
When we were frae the hunting come
That frae my horse I fell;
The Queen o Fairies she caught me,
In yon green hill to dwell.

I might be able to work with that. My spell would need to be something I could actually pronounce, though. *I should concentrate my energies on getting my intentions right, rather than the words. And maybe I'll go with something simpler so there's less chance anything can go wrong*

I spent the next few days gathering items said to protect against fairies. Some were easy enough, like the bread and salt, and the collar of bells I'd bought from the bellydancing store back home. Not like a cat collar—this one was kind of a lacy brass necklace with little clappers strung on it.

I'd have to go without berries since rowan berries and ash berries weren't ripe yet—the book seemed pretty emphatic they had to be red. But St. John's wort grew on the edges of the cemetery, waiting to be picked by the armful.

And in between these field trips to hunt down magical plants, I worked on my poem/spell. At first the spell had intimidated me, but once I started thinking of it as a poem it got easier. After all, I'd been creating poems to go with my pictures for almost as long as I could hold a pencil or a camera.

Granted, I'd never outgrown that habit of making up words which had annoyed my teachers so much. It had started when I was little, with Uncle Tam and his *Unabridged Oxford English Dictionary*.

He'd take me in his lap, along with the book nearly as big as me, and turn to a random page. His finger would land on a word—usually a long one that I'd have to sound out—and then we'd take some guesses on what the word meant. Our guesses would get more wild and farfetched as we tried to outdo each other, and then we'd read the real definition.

But if we liked our definition better, we'd continue to use it over the more widely accepted version. It was fun until I started getting zeroes on my vocabulary sheets—for example, it turned out "scruple" was not the name for a tiny creature that lives inside the armor of a roly-poly bug and keeps it well-oiled.

But now my practice playing with words was serving me well. After reading everything Uncle Tam and the local library had, I'd decided to go with a binding spell. A few samples from Wiccan and Druidic sites online helped me narrow down what might (and might not) work. But I was afraid to try it out ahead of time in case it gave me away and I lost the only chance I might have.

I hoped the spell I created would call Daniel back from wherever he was, and help him stay here while we tried to get rid of the fake Daniel. Fake Daniel had tried to call me so many times on the house phone, and continued to text me. But I told Uncle Tam we'd had a fight and I wasn't ready to make up yet, and he helped me by putting him off.

I'd even seen him once, late at night under the sycamore tree, face turned up toward the crows in the watery light of the half-moon like he was deep in conversation. When they saw I was watching from the screen porch, the crows faded into the darkness and Daniel waved hopefully. But I'd pulled the sheets closed without a word.

When my cell-phone alarm buzzed against my skull in the wee hours of Thursday morning, it was a relief to think that, one way or another, this thing with Daniel would be over soon. If there was actually nothing going on, I'd surrender to my shrink like a good girl and hopefully she could make these crackpot ideas go away.

But if I was right, Daniel could come back and truly start to heal.

I got out of bed, the bell necklace jingling when I moved too fast. My pendant kept getting tangled in all the dangly bits, but I wasn't about to take off either one. My necklace comforted me, and according to the books the bells were great protection.

I strapped on my headlamp and turned it to the lowest setting so I could see in the dim light of daybreak without attracting attention with my bedside lamp. My backpack was already bulging with the other protective items I'd gathered, so I slung it over one shoulder and grabbed the bouquet of daisies from the vase on my bedside table.

Easing the front door shut soundlessly behind me, I headed through the cemetery to the main road. The gravel beneath my shoes crunched like a giant eating jawbreakers, but Uncle Tam's window stayed dark.

As I passed Daniel's driveway, I watched his house carefully for signs of activity. Two crows huddled on the roof peak mumbled sleepily, and one cracked its violet-ringed eyes open long enough to recognize me. It let out a tea-kettle screech.

After a bit of indignant squabbling, they both took wing, circling above and slightly behind me. I hid a smile. *Good—I'll need somebody to carry a warning back to Daniel.*

The birds followed me all the way to the end of the street and over the barrier to the old mine road that was now little more than an overgrown trail. Thistles and thorns caught and pulled at my hoodie and left bloody lines on my bare calves. When it began to feel like I was pushing through the brambles outside Sleeping Beauty's castle, I knew I was on the right track.

And then thinking of Sleeping Beauty made me remember a particularly grisly illustrated edition, with pictures of skeletons and corpses of the knights who had tried to reach the enchanted castle hung up on the brambles. *Thorns piercing their eyes and choking off their breath.* I shuddered and moved with more care, the crows watching my every step.

They didn't make a sound, and all the other birds and bugs were strangely hushed in this emerald tangle. I must've zigzagged a while, lost in the thorn until I stumbled into the remains of a clearing. *That lush mound should be the mine entrance.* I poked a stick into the overgrowth, the satisfying ring of wood on iron answering me.

Right. Let's get this show started. I dropped into a crouch and started weaving sloppy daisy chains, until I had two that were long enough to go over my head. But only one was actually for me—the other was for the Daniel creature, to hold him there long enough for me to try my binding spell. I glanced up at the crows perched in an oak tree nearby—other than a few querulous peeps, they hadn't given up their vigil.

They watched closely as I yanked up the dead grass from an area in front of the mound, scraping it down to the hard red dirt with the iron trowel I'd brought. Then I pulled out a heavy metal Frisbee— Uncle Tam's folding grill. The grill opened like a lotus blossom and nestled on its wire stand.

When I flicked the lighter and lit a few bundles of smudge sage, the crows grew more agitated, shuffling on their branch, bobbing their heads and flicking their wings. I ignored them while I watched to make sure the sage bundles in the barbecue weren't going to die out.

Then I looked up at the crows. *No alarm calls yet—we can't have that.* I stood and spoke directly to them.

"You'd better go get him."

The dark birds cocked their heads and peered at me sidelong, as if they were trying to gauge if I was being serious.

"You'd better go get him—or I'm burning the thorn."

That got a reaction! One almost fell off his perch at my words, voicing soft cries of distress, but the other one met my gaze with his canny violet eyes.

"I mean it," I said, softly but firmly. "Tell him if he's not here in five minutes, the thorn will burn. And all your kin with it."

He nodded his head—I was sure it wasn't a reflexive bob—and nudged the other crow with his wing. They flew off together, straight in the direction of Daniel's house. *As the crow flies—ha!* I watched them disappear into the trees downhill and then set to my other tasks.

I quickly surrounded my dirt patch with a ring of St. John's wort plants, and then disguised them with the grass and weeds I'd pulled up. Once the circle was complete, I didn't step out of its protective border. Checking that the sage was still alight, I blew and was rewarded by lines of bright red on the bundles.

When I glanced up, the blackberries along the path parted and Daniel stepped out, dressed in boxers with a sock monkey print—and nothing else. *This is not the time to notice how hard his pecs are! Or his nipples.*

"Avery?" he asked, tentative. His eyes slid from my face to the smoky grill, and the mineshaft just beyond. "What are you doing?"

"What do you think I'm doing?" I countered.

He looked to the crows—now there were, like, twenty of them—perched in the trees and basking in the sun's rays. He frowned.

Ha—got you there! You can't very well say the crows told you I was threatening to burn the thorn without giving yourself away, can you?

He settled for walking towards me, slowly and with his hands held out like you'd do for an easily spooked horse.

Just a little closer... He was only about five feet away now.

"Avery, you've been acting really weird lately. Are your meds right?"

Now, that planted a doubt. I'd told Daniel about that episode when they switched my medication, but sworn him to secrecy. *So how could anybody but Daniel and my family know about it?*

My confusion must've shown on my face because he stood up a little straighter, stepping with more confidence.

"Is that what this is about?" he asked. "Your pills are making you freak out again?"

His face was completely guileless. And then my gaze dropped lower, to his muscled torso with its farmer's tan. No shirt, no hoodie, no shoes. And yet he'd made it through all those thorns and brambles without a scratch. My own welts still throbbed, so I knew it wasn't possible for him to show up unmarked.

"Daniel," I whispered, to remind myself what—*who*—this was about.

"Yes?" He leaned forward to catch my whisper, his toes only a few inches from the St. John's wort barrier. Bringing him within arm's reach.

I slipped off one of my daisy chains and flung it over him. His face blanched as he tried to duck, but it was too late—it settled on his shoulders like a ringer in horseshoes. And then he went very still.

"Avery, what game is this?" He smiled, but it seemed forced.

No use in being cagey now. "I'm not playing," I said. "I've never been more serious."

He started to speak, but I held up my hand. "Whoever you are, whatever you are, don't bother. Here's what's going to happen— you're going to bring Daniel back, and you're going to go away. And never bother us again, or I'll burn the thorn on the hill."

He shook his head, wearing a crooked, condescending smile. "What is burning the blackberries supposed to accomplish? They're just bushes."

I narrowed my eyes. There was a ring of truth in his words, and one of the advantages the protective herbs were supposed to give was to keep the fairies from tricking you or leading you astray. *What if this really is an ordinary patch of blackberries? Or what if it was a fairy mound, but they've abandoned it?*

"So this isn't a fairy mound?" I asked him directly.

"No," he said. "Can we go now? I'll drive you to the emergency clinic, get your dosage checked."

Again, his denial of the fairy mound was too casual to be a lie. "And I suppose you're not some creature who's taken Daniel's place?" I challenged. "And you could just take off that daisy chain and walk away from here?"

He shrugged, nonchalant. But he made no move to take off the daisies. I knelt by my pack and rummaged for the storage container in it. The lid made a popping sound as I opened it, grabbing a handful before he could see what was inside.

"So these don't bother you at all?" I pelted him with chunks of sourdough I'd rolled in rock salt. He tried to avoid them with some fancy *Matrix* moves, but the pieces that hit home left raised, painful-looking burns. Way more damage than simple bread cubes should cause.

He tottered awkwardly, his bare feet rooted in place. But he caught his balance and held his hands to the burns, hissing through his teeth in pain. *Try to deny that, you fairy bastard!* My triumph was only momentarily tinged with guilt at the oozing sores.

"Now, will you stop this pretending?" I gloated. "I know you're not Daniel, and you'd better bring him back or it's going to get a lot worse for you."

"Or maybe for you," he growled.

At his signal, a multitude of crows shrieked as they dove from the trees. Claws extended and beaks ready to jab, they flew straight at me. I reflexively crouched, my arms over my head. But I heard only some squawks and some thuds, both muffled-sounding.

I peeked from under my arms and saw crows on their backs in the dry grass, flailing indignantly. A few gained their feet and hopped towards me in full aggression mode—wings raised and held out like dark opera capes.

But as soon as they reached the boundary of St. John's wort, the birds bounced off like they'd struck a window. *Or a force field, the kind in every sci-fi TV show ever.*

I stood up carefully. Now that I was looking for it, I could see that the smoke from the sage wasn't drifting away naturally. It was swirling above me like it had hit a glass ceiling. I'd always thought St. John's wort was just a pretty weed, but now I was impressed that it was good for so much more than herbal happy pills.

I stood and folded my arms across my chest, a triumphant smirk pulling one corner of my mouth up. A few of the crows continued to hurl themselves at the barrier, which was so futile it was kind of funny—until I saw the blood.

"Wait," I said. "Are these regular crows, or have they been taken over, too? Are they not-crows, like you're not-Daniel?"

He started to speak, and then clamped his lips shut. He seemed to be struggling to keep himself from answering.

"Answer me!" I ordered. "Are those not-crows?"

Another millisecond of internal struggle before he burst out, "Not entirely crows!"

"Then call them off."

He broke out in a sweat while the injuries continued. One crow held its wing at an odd angle, and another wasn't moving. *If they're even part crow, innocent creatures are getting hurt. And he's using them to get me to stop.*

"You have to do what I say when you're held by that daisy chain, don't you?" I said. "Then. Call. Them. Off." I made doubly sure to make it sound like an order, borrowing a certain tone of voice my mom used when she'd had enough nonsense from patients.

Finally, he gestured and the crows went quiet, blinking and gazing around like they'd just woken. Pathetic, baby bird-like calls came from their panting beaks. I almost went to help them, but remembered my St. John's wort boundary just in time.

"You would have let those birds bash themselves to pieces," I said, seething. "Well, thank you for making this easier on me."

"Making what easier?" he asked.

Oh, now you talk—now that it's your skin on the line. "Since you won't cooperate, I'll bring Daniel back myself. And then we'll send you back to Faerie or wherever you came from."

But now he was all smug again. "And how do you mean to do that? A daisy chain isn't that strong."

"That's okay—I have a spell," I said with bared teeth.

His own smile faded and a worried look replaced it as I pulled out my composition book. I took a moment to concentrate on what I wanted the spell to do. My fingers shook as doubts whether this would actually work nearly overwhelmed me. But I ruthlessly smashed down those voices and took a breath.

Our little clearing filled with an expectant hush as I started:

Thread to me

Twine, twine, betwixt

Pull to thee

Twine, twine, the twain

"Stop!" His cry was so heart-wrenching that I halted in spite of myself.

His eyes seemed unnaturally large for his face—and unnaturally dark. The violet glow was the brightest I'd ever seen it in daylight.

Gone was the smug, rebellious captive. Pure terror was in his voice when he said, "Avery, you don't know what you're doing."

Well, no, I don't, not really. But is he saying that because he's trying to distract me, or because there's some real danger? I thought of Daniel, possibly trapped somewhere, or maybe lost in a space between our world and Faerie, and knew I had to try.

So I continued.

Bind to me

Twine, twine, betwixt

Wed to thee

Twine, twine, the twain

A horrible keening broke my spell. Along with the low wail escaping Daniel's lips, the crows sounded teakettle shrieks. They started piling themselves against him, like they were trying to keep something inside his skin by their sheer mass pressing against it.

And Daniel—the not-Daniel—looked like I was killing him. Or at least causing him agonizing pain. *This isn't how it's supposed to go.* I'd expected resistance, but I pictured it like a movie special effect—the false Daniel would pop out of existence, and the real one would take his place. All in the blink of an eye.

I hadn't foreseen this drawn-out torture. I didn't really want to hurt this imposter, or the crows. Reading the next line, I faltered, and so did the spell. Daniel collapsed forward, bracing his hands on his thighs.

"Avery…" he rasped, "if you do this, Daniel's body will die."

That got my attention. "So, that is Daniel's body? You're not some kind of copy?"

He shook his head. "We had an agreement. He said he'd let me use his body, but at the last minute Daniel got scared." He paused to draw a shaky breath. "He fought the transfer. The shock threw us both out. If your Uncle Tam hadn't called the ambulance so quick, this body would've died."

He stood a little straighter so he could meet my eyes. "Daniel's body was already dying. When you brought me to the hospital, I got there just in time. It won't survive that kind of shock again."

He gave me a moment to absorb what he'd said, and I needed it. "So, Daniel—he knew about you? And made some kind of deal? What was the original plan?"

He shook his head wearily. "Daniel was supposed to spend some time in my world. Learning our music and our ways. I would get to use his body for as long as it took me to…do some things in this world. And then we'd switch back."

"He's in Fairyland, then?"

He winced at the word Fairyland, but answered me, "I honestly don't know. All I know is we were both thrown out, and I grabbed onto the closest living being."

The closest living being? What he'd said a minute ago, about me bringing him to the body in the hospital, clicked suddenly. "Bobbin? You—went into Daniel's dog?"

Daniel—Daniel's body and its hitchhiker, rather—was standing straighter as the effects of my half-spoken spell dissipated. "Yes—but by the time I got some of my strength back, Bobbin was locked in the house and the body was in the hospital. I needed someone to take me there."

"But why me?"

"Because you wanted to believe in a miracle—or magic," he said flatly. And not in a flattering way, but like it made me weak or predictable. He continued, "Hey, I'll answer all your questions without the daisy chain and whatever other charms you have. Just take this off and give me a chance to recover."

I wavered. "No tricks? No crow bombardments? You swear you'll tell me the truth?"

"I swear."

But…can I really trust his promise? What's to stop him from telling me what I want to hear, and then doing what he wants afterwards? Well, the daisy chain seemed like it had made him fess up to stuff before, even when he was visibly doing his best not to. *One more piece of insurance, then.*

"What am I supposed to call you, anyway?" I asked, trying to keep my voice casual. Names were meant to be a powerful hold for fairies.

Again, it looked like some internal storm raged before he spit out, "Lonan!"

"Lonan, huh? And knowing your name gives me power over you, right?"

His shoulders sagged. "Yes."

"Then, *Lonan*, I'm going to take off your daisy chain now, and I'm ordering you not to attack me."

"Okay," he said.

But I paused with my foot lifted and ready to step out of my circle—he'd given in awfully quickly. "And no ordering the crows to attack, or whisking me away to Faerie, or any other tricksy things."

"Wouldn't dream of it," he said.

Wait, is that sarcasm? Or maybe cockiness? I stood there with my foot still raised, considering. But we couldn't stay here like this all day—I already needed to pee. So I scuffed a break into the St. John's wort ring, holding my breath.

Nothing happened. The crows watched as I stepped forward and lifted the daisy chain off Daniel—I mean, Lonan. But as soon as it cleared his hair, he grabbed me round the waist and whirled me in a dizzying circle.

I tried to get a hand on my bell collar, the only charm I had left on me, but I couldn't lift my arms while we were spinning so fast. Much faster than was humanly possible. *Oh my God—is he taking me to*

Fairyland? I was so stupid to trust him! I gave up trying to reach the bells—and any hope of coherent thought—and just screamed Lonan's name.

We stopped so abruptly that I spun right out of his arms and landed in a heap on the ground. I started to cry. Great big, childish, wrenching wails and sobs.

Lonan knelt beside me. "I'm sorry, Avery, I didn't mean to scare you. It just felt so good to have that thing off me—"

He reached his hand out to brush my hair off my forehead, and I knocked it away with a wordless screech.

Apparently I did have something to say, because I burst out with, "You're still not Daniel! You don't get to comfort me."

He rocked back on his heels and kept his distance while I curled into a ball in the prickly weeds. I cried like I had that first night at Uncle Tam's, when I thought I'd lost Daniel forever. I'd only kept it together since then because I thought I could do something about it. But I'd just been shown, in a very real and graphic way, that I had no idea what I was dealing with. *No way to make Lonan bring Daniel back.*

And maybe this time Daniel really is gone forever.

When I finally wound down to hiccupping gasps, Lonan said, "Avery, please stop. It can't be good for you to keep crying like that."

"But—but—I thought I could bring Daniel back," I blubbered. "Only he's still lost, and you—you're still here."

He stood up and paced. "Avery, I need to be here a while longer. Everything depends on me having a body—Daniel will have to wait."

I sat up. "So, you just need a body? It doesn't have to be Daniel's? Take mine, then, and give him back his!"

He stopped in his tracks and stared at me. "You'd really do that?" Then he waggled his eyebrows and said, "As much as I'd like to have free access to your body, no."

Now it was my turn to stare at him, with my mouth hanging open. Finally, I lurched to my feet and started swinging punches. None connected as he dodged, but I yelled, "You asshole! I just about peed myself you scared me so bad, and you want to flirt? I hope being beaten to a bloody pulp turns you on, because I'm going to kick your ass!"

But he stayed just out of my reach, not seeming to get out of breath at all, while I puffed like an asthmatic smoker in downtown Beijing. And then I realized he was laughing. So were the crows, chuckling like water over stones.

I stopped and fell to my knees. "Auuggggh!" One wordless scream of frustration later and I was tired of it. Just plain tired—and probably dehydrated from crying so much. I toppled over, the impact raising a cloud of dust, and didn't even fight when Lonan came over and slipped one arm around my shoulders and one under my knees.

He stepped onto the trail and started for home, the thistles and brambles actually curling out of our way. It was too weird to watch the plant tendrils behaving like they were sentient, so I tucked my head into his shoulder. *He still smells like Daniel.*

Whaddayaknow, I do have some tears left.

When the gentle sway of his steps halted, I lifted my head to see we were by Daniel's driveway.

"Can you walk home from here?" Lonan asked.

"I guess so," I said, and he carefully set me on my feet.

My legs trembled but mostly obeyed me. Lonan was already a few steps up the drive when I called, "Wait! If you think I'm letting you out of my sight for one second—"

"Calm down!" He gestured for me to lower my voice. "Do you want someone to see us together so early in the morning, with me only in my drawers? You know what they'll think."

"Drawers?" I said, and snorted. "Who even says drawers—besides my great-grandma, I mean?" My eyes widened as a thought occurred to me, but I refused to voice it. *I've already had the "I know what you are" moment—no need for the "how long have you been seventeen" conversation right now.*

I shook my head and said, "Fine, you go home—I need a shower, anyway. But we're not done. You owe me some more answers, Lonan."

He nodded, resignation in the set of his shoulders. "Do you want me to come over in an hour or so?"

"Let's meet in the cemetery," I countered. "Neutral ground."

I snuck across our yards and came in through the screen porch. When I peeled off my shirt, it was stiff with dried snot and red dust. My hair reeked of sage smoke until my shampoo vanquished it.

An hour later I joined Lonan under a willow tree in the cemetery. He lounged with Bobbin in the cool clover patch beneath the trailing branches, and his smile made me stumble.

"Don't do that," I said sharply.

"Don't do what?" Lonan asked

"Don't make my heart think you're Daniel, even for a second."

His brow furrowed. "I'm sorry if it upsets you, but that's not exactly fair. There're bound to be similarities—but you already know I'm not Daniel. What gave me away, anyhow?"

I sank to the ground, sitting cross-legged. *Should I let on that I can see that weird violet glow in his eyes? Based on Dad's notes not to trust the Fae, I'll keep that to myself for now.*

"Little things," I said. "Some of your movements weren't quite right, your word choices, dancing the Charleston—but it was the Hokey Pokey that decided me."

He hit himself in the forehead. "I knew it was a mistake as soon as I sang Bobbin's version and saw your face. But I was too cocky…"

He stared at me, and it went on long enough that I squirmed under that intense gaze. And I didn't feel any better when he muttered, "It shouldn't have mattered, though. You should have been firmly under my control."

I sat up straighter. "Under your control?" I asked in an icy voice. "Just what does that mean?"

He glowered resentfully, giving his head a crow-like tilt without answering. His eyes flashed violet for just a second and I said, "And do I need to remind you that you promised to tell me the truth, *Lonan*?"

He jumped when I said his name and growled, "I bespelled you, that first day you got here. Well, I cast the spell that night, but I took your hair earlier."

"You mean Bobbin did, when you were in his body," I said slowly, remembering how the dog had knocked me down. And rooted in my crotch. "Jeez, why didn't you take some pubic hair while you were at it?" Then I clapped my hand over my mouth. *I so did not mean to say that out loud.*

Lonan gaped at me before rolling on the ground, laughing. Even though this was total humiliation, I was kind of relieved he wasn't glaring at me anymore. I didn't like that Lonan.

Finally, he gasped, "You really don't have a censor on that mouth, do you?"

My face felt a thousand degrees, but it wasn't like this was the first time I'd blurted out something embarrassing. I answered him with a curt, "No. You should hear the things I don't say out loud. And nice try on changing the subject—what was this controlling spell?"

After a few stifled guffaws, he sat up. "I needed you to take me to Daniel's body, and I used your hair to forge a connection."

"So you could make me do what you wanted? 'Cause that's not how I remember it."

He leaned forward, all laughter gone now. "That's what's so odd—usually humans are pretty easy targets for this kind of spell. It's more of a game for us, really. It's not strong enough to make you do something you ordinarily wouldn't, like murder someone or kill yourself. But you kept shaking it off—like in the car at the hospital, when you doubted it would work. Later on, when we were kissing on the bench in the cemetery—"

"*What?*" I nearly screeched. "That was from the spell, too? That's as bad as if you slipped me a magical roofie or something."

He had the grace to look shamefaced. "It wasn't all bad—I helped you feel less upset about Daniel being in a coma before that. And anyway, I couldn't make you do something you weren't already thinking about, and let's face it—you think about Daniel that way. *A lot.*"

I struggled to my feet, demanding, "How could you possibly know that?"

"The connection lets me sense your thoughts—that's how I could nudge you in one direction or the other. And you're really hot for Daniel."

My face was burning again, but this time it was anger. "Oh yeah? What am I thinking about doing to you now?" I concentrated on sending images of me strangling him, Homer Simpson-style.

His lips curved up, but he wouldn't meet my gaze. "I can guess. But don't worry, I can't feel your thoughts anymore."

I sank down again in relief. "Since when?"

"Since you pushed me off the bench. Well, the connection was still there, faintly, and I was able to get through briefly later, when you were so upset to think Daniel'd been kissing other girls. I almost roped you back in, but by that evening it was completely gone."

"Good," I said. "I'd rather have a clear head around you."

"Believe it or not, I would rather you did, too," he said, with a new intensity. "I don't understand it, but you seem to be different from other humans. I think you might be able to help me, Avery."

I couldn't help but wonder if he was asking for my help now because he couldn't just force me into it. "Help you do what? And give me one good reason why, while you're at it."

He nodded. "I've been sent here to stop an invasion, and if I fail, you and everyone in your world is in danger."

Some vague threat is supposed to sway me? Boy, he really is used to getting his own way—his powers of persuasion are rusty. "Hmm, I'm going to need more than that. You sound like the plot of every *Doctor Who* episode, but you're no Doctor. Try again—why me and what kind of dangerous invasion?"

He picked some blades of grass, tearing them into shreds as he said, "Okay, I'm going to back up a little here. I've already told you that the crows up by the old Faerie mound were not-entirely-crows—"

"*Old* Faerie mound?" I interrupted. "So it was a Faerie mound once upon a time?" And then I giggled at my accidentally funny wording.

But he glared at me. "Yes, it was, before the miners came with their iron and ruined it for most Fae— Hey, stop distracting me and let me finish. This is important."

I made my eyes real big and mimed buttoning my lips.

"Don't give me any ideas," he muttered.

"You're seriously threatening to button my lips—with a spell—right after you begged me for help? You'd better get back to the not-entirely-crows story before I get mad."

"That's what I was trying to do—" He lay down, took a deep breath, and started again. "Those crows are actually corbin, like me."

Not news to me—but maybe if I play dumb he'll give me more info than I have. "A corbin?"

"Corbin occupy crows when we cross over to your world. That's how I learned your language, by listening outside windows. Overhearing lectures and TV shows and conversations."

That explains his mixed bag of phrases—sometimes he sounds like a professor, and other times like the horndog from a teen movie. "So, if you normally take over crows, why are you stealing Daniel's body?"

He visibly winced. "I told you, I didn't steal it. We had a deal—it's like him subletting an apartment."

"Why couldn't he just rent you a room?"

He banged his head into the ground, raising the scent of crushed grass and clover. *Oops, maybe that was one question too many.*

When I didn't speak again, he said, "It doesn't work that way. When we go into crows—or dogs—there's plenty of 'room' for both of us. The host stays aware the whole time, and they can even override us at will. We're like agreeable traveling companions."

Yeah, sure—agreeable traveling companions who just might steal your organs and leave you to wake up in a bathtub of ice.

"But with people, it's different," he continued. "If we shared the body, the person would go mad—too much going on. All the sensory processing, the conflict between two strong wills and what each wants, leads to an overload. Instead of letting the person get overwhelmed, we make deals with them and send them to our world for a time.

"Everybody wins—we get to experience a human life, however briefly, and they come back with new talents and skills."

I shook my head. "You sound like a parent rationalizing summer camp for a kid who hates it."

That got me a chuckle before he rolled over to look me in the eye. His expression was anxious, but kind of sad, too.

"Seriously, Avery, it's worked this way for thousands of years. But some of the other Fae aren't content with crows, or a few weeks in a human's body. They're not satisfied with a little mischief-making or sensual pleasures.

"They want to come here in their natural forms—with all their terrible powers intact. And without the checks and balances, it means disaster for humans and their civilizations. Sheer blood, death, and chaos."

Now I was serious, too. "You say that like it's happened before."

His face twisted in a wry grimace, or maybe a bitter one, that was utterly unlike any of Daniel's expressions. "Ever hear of the Dark Ages? The fall of Rome? Some of the worst villains in human history—Vlad the Impaler, the Borgias, Cortes, and Pizarro—were all my people."

"And you're supposed to stop that?" I shivered. "What are you—some kind of über-villain, who's even badder than they are?"

"No, I'm one of the good guys—there've been good incursions from my world, too, you know. Gandhi, King Arthur, Mother Teresa."

"You're, like, equal opportunity for possession? That's big of you."

"It only seems like possession." He sat up and ran his hands through his hair, frustrated. People did that around me a lot.

"Let's come at this a different way," he said, visibly trying to gather himself. "You don't like the idea of corbin displacing people, right?"

"Whatever gave you that impression?" The summer air around me grew parched, my voice was so dry.

But he continued like I hadn't spoken. "Imagine tens of thousands of people taken over by creatures who don't care about the hosts' well-being. And these people are trapped while their bodies do unspeakable things—mass murder, rape, torture, incest. Even if they survive it, they're left twisted and maddened."

He grabbed my hand and pulled me closer to him, speaking fiercely into my face. "Does that sound like something you want to happen? Or something you'll help me prevent?" And we might not have had a magical connection anymore, but I felt his fear and desperation.

For once, all my smartass comments dried up. No latching onto an absurdity to distract myself from something scary. Just a horrible, horrifying stream of images in my mind of all the bad things I'd ever seen on the news. *Bodies rotting in mass graves. Lynchings. Animals and children, tortured and abused. Entire villages burned alive.*

I stumbled to my feet, and bent over until I felt a little less dizzy. Lonan got up and rubbed circles on my back.

"I'm sorry," he said. "I need you to understand. This isn't a game, or a joke. These are monsters out of humanity's worst nightmares, and you and I might be the only ones that can stop them."

My stomach gave a lurch. "What can I do against monsters?" I asked incredulously.

"When I confront them and try to seal the breach, they'll attack me with magic. There's a chance they can influence me since I'm weakened in a human body. If you're there, and you're able to shake it off like you did my spell, you can keep me focused. It might be the edge that makes all the difference. Are you in?" he asked.

"Lonan, I gave up babysitting because I couldn't stop a toddler from biting me. What chance do I have against honest-to-God nightmares? I don't have any superpowers, magical or otherwise."

"But you do—that spell you used. Where did it come from? Am I right in thinking you created it? That's really rare, for a human to be able to do that with no training. If I work with you some, just think what you could do."

I bit my lip. "I don't know… You're betting a lot on my abilities. How do we know it wasn't a fluke, that your own spell casting wasn't faulty?"

"Just say you'll try."

"Yes, I'll try," I said.

But I couldn't keep myself from imagining those hellish images. And that begged the question, "Lonan? Are you really from Fairyland, or is it Hell?"

"My world has been called Fairyland, or Faerie, as I prefer. Also Heaven, Hell, a dreamworld—it depends on a person's experience there."

"So, which experience is Daniel getting?" I whispered.

Lonan froze in the midst of brushing grass off the back of his shorts. "If he'd gone there like we'd planned, under my protection, he'd definitely be treated well. And come back all the better for it."

I gripped his arm. "And since he didn't go there under your protection?"

He wouldn't meet my eyes as he said, "Then he's fair game. Anything goes."

I sank to my knees. "Fresh meat."

Lonan nodded miserably.

"Is he even—is Daniel still alive?"

"As long as his body is alive, there's a chance his consciousness can find its way back."

I didn't respond when Lonan offered his hand to help me up. After standing there for a moment, he turned towards home.

66WW**99** ait," I said, scrambling to my feet. "What are we going to do about Daniel? Bringing him back, I mean?"

He waited for me to catch up to him. "I told you—it's complicated. I have no idea where he is. Finding him would take time, attention, and resources away from my mission."

He started walking again, obviously thinking the whole thing was settled. *Ha—he really doesn't know me if he thinks I'll give up that easily.* We stopped under the sycamore tree, and I eyed the few birds in its branches warily.

"What do we need to get ready, then? And when are we attacking?"

He rubbed a hand over his face, as if he'd already run over the steps a million times in his head. "I need to gather some herbs and supplies—and to learn the spell. It's more complex than anything I've tried before. Going to take a lot of mental preparation and practice."

"So, how long do *we* have to prepare?" I asked. *A lot of "I" statements in that list, for someone who begged for my help.*

"'Til the blue moon—they'll try to break through then. That's also our best chance of stopping them, when my spell will be at its most powerful."

"So, a week?" I asked.

"Eight days."

"Oh, plenty of time, then."

He laughed bitterly. "It doesn't feel like it to me. Not when I've lost so much ground to the coma. I'd rather I had the three weeks I'd planned."

"Duh," I said. "I meant plenty of time to rescue Daniel first."

He stared at me a long moment, like he was waiting for the punchline to my joke. Only, I wasn't joking, in spite of the grin on my face.

"Not going to happen, Avery," he finally said.

"Oh, yes, it is, *Lonan*." He nearly vibrated at the emphasis on his name. "If you want my help, that's the condition. We have to save Daniel."

"I don't need your help that badly." He turned and stalked away, but stopped at my next words.

"And did I mention I'm not giving you a moment's peace until Daniel's back home? I'll interrupt your spell practice sessions, and burn the ingredients you gather. Speak your name when you're trying to rest. Maybe put another daisy chain on you and practice some spells of my own."

"You'd really put your world at risk for your own selfish desires?" he hissed. "I thought you understood the stakes."

I stalked over to him, getting right in his face. "You think I'm doing this for me? Even if bringing Daniel back meant I'd never see him again, I'd still do it. To make this right. He deserves a chance."

"It's not that simple!"

"It is to me. And if you want to prove to me that you're one of the good guys, that you deserve my help, you'll do this."

He shook his head in disgust and opened the gate into his yard. He froze when I called after him.

"Lonan." I wasn't grinning now. "I meant every word I said. If you want to be able to complete your mission, you're going to have to find a way for Daniel to come back."

Lonan turned his head enough to sneer at me, and waved dismissively as he disappeared into the house.

Ha, just try to dismiss me! And to help you make the right decision, your night is about to get a lot more interesting, buddy. Good thing Uncle Tam has a gig in Nevada City and is staying overnight—all the better for me to wreak some havoc.

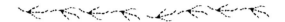

The poor guy didn't stand a chance. I was doing a cha-cha in the kitchen the next morning, drying dishes to the tune of, "Lo-nan, Lo-nan, LO-nan!" when my phone rang.

"Why, Lonan, so good to hear from you!" I cooed.

"Cut the shite, sister."

I laughed at his speakeasy slang. "Is an Irish mobster there with you?"

"Just meet me by the tree." And then a dial tone.

I took my time drying the dishes before I went outside. He'd pulverized the brittle summer grass under the sycamore with his pacing.

"A truce, then?" he called as I approached.

"Truce? No, I think the word you're looking for is 'capitulation.' I remember the definition from a middle school spelling bee, and I'm quite sure that's it."

"Fine—as long as you turn off that blasted alarm. I wrapped that thing in three blankets and I can still hear it."

Wearing an evil grin, I pulled out my phone. After I entered a code, the muffled shrieks audible through his bedroom window stopped.

"Daniel and I traded codes for the 'Find My Device' feature on our laptops. I knew you wouldn't have it," I said smugly.

"And was making Bobbin howl all night really necessary?" he asked. "The neighbors called to complain six times last night."

"That dog loved the attention. Besides, if you'd answered my texts, Bobbin and I wouldn't have had our little singing contest."

"You mean all two hundred and forty-three texts saying, **Are we there yet**? Must be hell to take road trips with you."

"You'll find out, won't you?" At his confused look, I added, "I assume you called to say we're going to get Daniel. I made it clear that's the only way I'll let up." I held up my phone, ready to trigger some kind of mayhem again.

He said hastily, "I've asked a few trusted corbin back home to keep an eye out for him. If we go blundering around, or put out word he's vulnerable, it might attract the wrong kind of attention to him. You don't want that, do you?"

"No," I admitted. *Maaaan, I was all amped up for a rescue mission.* "How long before you hear back?"

"It's hard to say. I told you, time works differently there. Could be hours, could be days."

"Well, lucky you, you'll have the pleasure of my constant companionship until we hear."

He cowered like I'd shaken a fist at him. "You're not…you're not going to sing again, are you?"

"What?" My face heated. "Bobbin only howled because he likes to, not because I'm an awful singer."

But he laughed. "Got you back. So, is it a truce or not?"

"You think you got me back with that weak shit? I just kept you up all night without hardly trying. Game on."

"Not a truce? Please?" He looked truly alarmed. And sleep-deprived.

"Maybe a cease fire." I punched him in the arm. "Starting now."

He rolled his eyes at me as he rubbed his shoulder, but I asked, "What are we doing for the rest of the day? Spellicizing stuff?"

"I'll work on that later," he said. "First I need to go down to the community pool."

"Why, is it a hellgate or something?"

"No, but Daniel wants to try out for the water-polo team this fall. In our original bargain, I agreed to keep up with his training. I don't want him to think I've been neglecting his workouts."

Ah, that explains all the new, delicious muscle tone. Maybe if I helped him practice I could get my hands on those abs again. In a non-creepy way.

"Why would you go in the community pee pool when I have access to a private one?" I asked.

"What private pool?"

"Just go get your stuff and meet me here in fifteen minutes." *Crap, I might need to do some personal grooming if I'm going to be seen in a suit.* "Make that twenty-five."

He nodded, and I dashed back into the cottage to get ready.

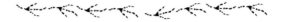

Lonan wasn't under the tree when I came out, but I spotted him leaning against Daniel's hatchback in his driveway.

"No way," I called. "We're taking the Nykur."

He picked up his bag and walked slowly over.

"You're riding shotgun today," I said as I opened the driver's door. "Bicycling is practically a cult back in Davis, and I'm driving every chance I get while I'm here. Are you scared I'm a bad driver?"

"Nooo—it's just that I'm not entirely sure I trust a Nykur," he said and tried to pull the passenger door open. It refused to budge.

"Looks like the distrust is mutual." I leaned across and popped the handle from the inside.

Lonan slid into the seat gingerly, sitting so stiffly his back didn't make contact with the leather. When he felt me watching, he made a show of relaxing into the upholstery and fastening his seatbelt. I rolled my eyes—*it's just a car!*

"Ready?" I asked, starting the engine at his nod.

Music blared from the speakers and we both jumped. We reached for the volume knob simultaneously.

"That's so weird!" I said. "Every other time I've started the car, it's been 'Black Horse and the Cherry Tree' playing. Never The Beatles singing 'Blackbird.'"

"Hmm," Lonan said helpfully.

"And the totally bizarre part is that the Black Horse song isn't on a CD stuck in the dash or something—it's just always tuned to whatever radio station happens to be playing it. I had no idea that song still got that much play."

"Yeah," he said impatiently. "So, where are we going?"

His change of subject was like a neon sign flashing OBVIOUS, but I couldn't figure out if he was hiding something or just bored with my chatter.

"You'll see."

We rode in silence for a few minutes, until I asked, "So, how will your corbin friends pass on the information about Daniel? Do they have inter-dimensional texting or something?"

He snorted. "I wish, but they'll have to do it the old-fashioned way. Occupy a crow and come find me."

When I turned onto Palmyra, Lonan sat bolt upright again. "Why are we— This street ends at the Castle."

"Good thing, cause that's where we're going," I said. "I have the keys, so I can help document the restoration with photos."

"I didn't agree to this," he said, and fumbled with the door handle.

"Hey! Car's still moving, Lonan." Thankfully, the lock wasn't working for him again.

I stopped the Nykur in front of the closed iron gates. "What's your deal with the Castle? Do you have some kind of history or something?"

He was silent a long while before he said, "Yes, I do. I spent some time here during the nineteen-thirties."

I gaped at him. "Seriously? You're that old?"

"I've told you, time is different—"

"—in your world," I finished. *So he's like a spaceman, traveling at a different speed and aging differently?* "Were you an *inmate?*"

"Wards, not inmates. I switched places with a boy after he'd already been sent up. He was glad to get away for a while."

How cool is it that Lonan actually spent time here when the school was operational? I may have tiny-squealed. "Tell me what it was like! I demand stories with lots of drama."

"I don't really want to talk about it."

"But I want to hear about it!"

He had been staring at his clenched hands, but now he looked up. Such sadness and desolation in his eyes. *Wounded* was the word that came to mind.

"You want me to air my mistakes for your amusement?" he asked softly.

"N—no. Of course—of course not," I stammered, my cheeks coloring with shame. *Wow, callous much, Avery?* "We can leave. I'll take you to the city pool."

I started to put the car into reverse, but he placed his hand on mine. "Wait. Maybe it's time I came back here. Faced some demons."

"Are you sure? And, um, we're not talking actual demons, are we? I don't know if I'm ready for that yet. I mean, Buffy at least got some training and ass-kicking abilities."

He smiled sadly. "No, only metaphorical demons this time out, as far as I know. Sometimes those are just as bad."

I parked on the gravel by the old fire station and turned to Lonan. "Are you sure you want to do this? I wouldn't have brought you here if I knew this place had such bad memories."

He shook his head. "Let's just go inside."

Did I have that same mixture of dread and longing on my face when I first visited Daniel in the hospital? Like you're not sure what you're going to find, but you're trying to prepare for it being different or even unrecognizable. *But no one can really prepare for what they can't imagine.*

"Brace yourself, Lonan," I said under my breath.

I fumbled with finding the right key before it turned in the creaky antique lock, then opened the door. He stepped into the room beyond, not really a proper foyer. The sunlight haloed him in swirling dust motes.

"This is the door new arrivals used," he said softly. "Can't you feel the echoes of emotions? Fear and defiance. So scared, those boys, but trying to look tough so they weren't targets for the truly hard ones."

I stood just behind him, the better to hear, but didn't say anything.

"They went there next." He pointed to the room off to the left, empty now but for some rotting shelving and a heavy, angular sink on one wall. I'd photographed that sink countless times, with its picturesque garlands of cobwebs and drifts of dust.

"We hoped we'd get away with a quick whore's bath in the sink, but instead we were run through the pool like sheep in dip."

I don't think he was even aware he'd switched from "they" to "we." His voice was rougher around the edges, too, an accent creeping in. *A brogue? A Southern flavor?* A blend of the two, maybe.

"And down that hallway on the right is—is Mariah's kitchen. My Mariah."

The last part was so soft I almost didn't catch it.

"*Your* Mariah? You knew the girl who was killed here?"

He didn't answer me—he may have forgotten I was there. But if he'd been here in the thirties, it was possible he'd been around at the time of the unsolved murder. When Mariah Cole's bludgeoned body had been found crammed into the alcove under the stairs. In the room off the kitchen, where my camera and lenses always went haywire.

Lonan walked down the hallway, hesitating before turning through the wide archway into the kitchen. I hung back and his footsteps halted. *I should give him some privacy. He might want some time to commune with her spirit or something.* I held out as long as I could, but when a dull thump sounded I craned my head around the crumbling trim.

He knelt on the age-darkened linoleum, a smile on his upturned face. *So not what I was expecting.*

"Lonan?" I called.

He turned his smile my way. "It's okay. She's not here." His smile faded and he looked towards *that* room. "Those are just echoes, psychic echoes of the trauma and horror, in there. Not Mariah."

"You can tell the difference? Are you sensitive to ghosts?"

"Ghosts and spirits are just symptoms of a crack between this world and the next. I recognize them as fellow travelers."

"I always thought they were leftovers, the parts that won't let go of their lives."

He shook his head. "They tend to return when they feel something is unfinished, yes, but that's not all they are."

He stood up and went into the pantry off the kitchen. "I can almost hear her singing. She had a lovely voice."

"Visitors have said they heard singing in here. But then again, one of the paranormal shows claimed Mariah possessed the host during a truly ludicrous episode, so you can't believe all the reports."

Lonan was smiling again. "I'm glad I came, Avery. It's a weight off my conscience."

"Glad to help," I said. "How did you know her?" *What did he mean about his conscience?*

"I helped out in the kitchen—or Louis did, the boy I took over—and we met there. She wasn't much older than the wards." He drew something in the dust on the pantry countertop, two swift opposite curves. *A heart?*

Something about his wistful tone made me think of something he'd said, back when I still thought he was Daniel: "I've kissed other girls, but I've only ever loved one." *Had Mariah been that one?*

"Were you—" I couldn't bring myself to ask if he'd been in love with the dead girl, and changed it to, "Were you around when they found her?"

"No—but I should have been." He came out of the pantry and the set of his jaw warned me that was the last question he'd be answering on the subject. "I thought you wanted to go swimming?"

"Yeah—it's this way." I led him across the hall.

He guffawed when he saw the rippling water. "Seriously? This is where they made us run through the delousing bath. You go *swimming* here?"

"Hey, it works just fine," I retorted. "One of the local Baptist churches keeps it up, in exchange for holding their baptisms here. They added a filter after a caretaker secretly cleaned out all the trash and made it into an indoor pool for his wife and kids in the seventies.

Except when debris and spiders and gunk rain down on you from the floors above, it's pretty cool. Like a private country club pool, if you don't count the three floors of owl droppings and dry rot above it."

"They should put that in the brochure," he said dryly, dipping a toe in. "How am I going to explain to Daniel about catching leprosy?"

"Shut up and get in!" I snapped him with the towel from around my neck.

He laughed and pulled off his shirt in one swift motion. When Lonan caught me staring, he hooked his thumbs in the elastic of his shorts. "Clothing optional, right?"

"No!" I gasped as he shimmied them down to reveal a pair of skin-tight Lycra trunks, like bicycle shorts. My breath rushed out in a relieved laugh.

"Are those the boy-shorts I had when I was twelve?" I teased, hoping he wouldn't notice my bright red cheeks. "My Ken doll had some just like— Hey, *did* you steal those from Ken?" I realized I was staring again.

Oh my God, I think I can see his—I mean Daniel's— I turned to fumble in my bag. *That's got to be the most anatomically accurate Ken doll I've ever seen.*

A chuckle from behind me, and then a splash. "You can look now. I'm safely under the water, lest I offend your maidenly gaze."

"Just start doing your exercises or training or whatever," I said. I slipped off my sandals, delaying the big reveal when I took off my dress. Sneaking a glance over my shoulder, I saw Lonan was treading water, watching me.

Don't let him rattle you, Avery Girl. I'd put on my vintage-style two-piece, a cute little sailor girl number. *It's not like it's a G-string— nothing to feel self-conscious about, it covers all my naughty bits just fine.*

Deciding to bluff my way through my nervousness, I took a deep breath and peeled off my dress. Then I faced him and struck a pinup girl pose.

A low whistle answered me. "I remember when girls started wearing bikinis—even the good girls. Best invention since stockings and garter belts."

"Wow, you really are ancient," I said as I stepped into the pool. "I should have taken you to the sauna at the senior center. You could hang with all the naked old guys and talk about how there'll never be another looker like Betty Grable."

"Give me Bettie Page over Grable any day," he said with a wicked grin. "And come over here. I'll show you how old I am."

"Eww, you know that's kind of creepy when you do that, right?"

"Do what?" he asked, all innocence.

"You know—get all lech-y. Does coming on so strong ever work?"

"It works often enough." He winked at me. "And let's not forget that the first time we met, you jumped me in the cemetery and ended up with your top off."

"Nuh, uh! The first time we met, you were a pervy dog with a tendency to shove your nose up my skirt. I was kissing Daniel that other time—not you. And you cheated by using magic."

"No magic now—just us." He frog-kicked closer to me.

"Not gonna happen, Lonan," I said, backstroking away. "Get to work."

He shrugged and dropped his feet to the bottom. The water was only about five feet deep and didn't even come up to the tile trim, since it hadn't really been meant for swimming. Laps were only maybe ten strokes the length of the pool, and I did a leisurely paddle while Lonan did a series of jumping, thrusting, calisthenic moves. They didn't look too hard, but judging by how hard he started breathing, and how much water sloshed out of the pool, they were more difficult than they looked.

Finally, he said, "Come here, Avery, and let me throw you—it's more of a dynamic workout."

"Throw me?" If I sounded dubious, that's because I was.

He gestured for me to let him show me. I came up close, facing him, but he turned me around by the shoulders. He placed his hands carefully around my waist, just above my hipbones.

I stiffened, expecting him to get handsy, but all he said was, "Ready?"

When I nodded, he launched me into the air. I shrieked as the ceiling approached way too fast, just missing the top of my head before I fell.

"Sorry, misjudged the distance." He caught me lightly and threw me again, this time adding a spin so I was doing a horizontal quadruple axel in the air. The world jarred back into focus as I landed in his hands, and I barely had time for a breath before I was flying once more. If I'd been able to breathe, I would have been alternating between laughing and shrieking as we fell into a rhythm of tossing and spinning.

When he eventually stopped and put me on my feet, I sank bonelessly beneath the water. He pulled me up and I grabbed him around the neck.

"Ugh, this is like when I had a bad ear infection and got vertigo," I groaned. "I can't tell if I'm still moving, or if it's the room."

"But it was fun, right?"

"Yeah! But how did you do that? I didn't think Daniel was that strong." *Plus, Daniel probably would have made me wear a hardhat and safety harness or something.*

"So I used a little magic," Lonan said.

The room had started to settle at last, and so did the water in the pool. One final wave surged and my body bumped against his. Our exposed skin slipped and slid, catching in interesting places.

"I want—Take me to the stairs so I can sit down," I said, not trusting my legs yet.

He placed me on the top step and braced his arms on either side of me in case I flopped over.

"I—I think I'm okay now," I said. "You don't have to hover."

He didn't say anything, but leaned in a little closer. I held my breath, and when his lips were only a few inches from mine, I said, "Lonan—"

"I'm not going to kiss you," he said.

Is that disappointment or relief I'm feeling? Whoa—is he going to use magic right now, to use my leftover lusty feelings for Daniel to "influence" me?

Before I could examine my emotions any closer, he said, "I just want to show you something."

He chuckled when my eyes involuntarily darted lower. My face heated so much that I was sure all the water droplets on it instantly vaporized.

"What—" I had to clear my throat before trying again. "What do you want to show me?"

"Possibilities."

He closed the distance between our lips, but at the last millimeter turned aside. And went for my left earlobe.

I'd never been much of an earlobe girl, but as his lips settled on it and started biting, sucking, I dissolved into a quivering, moaning puddle of burning lust. Made a noise like *guhhnnh-ooo-ahhh*, which couldn't have been sexy, but it was all I could manage. Fireworks and cliché rocket takeoffs followed.

When he stopped, I did fall over on the step and he had to prop me up against the concrete.

"Whaa—" I had to wipe the saliva off my chin before continuing. "What the *hell* was that?"

He moved to my ear again, and my traitorous body thrummed in anticipation. But all he did was whisper, "I told you. If I can do that with only your earlobe, think of the possibilities."

He planted a chaste kiss on my cheek as he stood and got out of the pool.

I followed his water-slicked form with my eyes as he bent to pick up his clothes and towel, then slipped on his shoes.

"I'll be out by the car whenever you're ready," Lonan said with a last wink.

I didn't trust myself to speak, and merely nodded. *No way will my legs cooperate now, after that little demonstration.*

When I finally made it out to the car, Lonan reclined in the passenger seat, dozing with his mouth hanging open. Relief swept over me. *If he's asleep, we won't have to talk about what happened in the pool. Or squirm through the kind of silence that makes it obvious we're both thinking about it, even if we aren't talking about it.*

I put my bag through the open window of the backseat and stealthily opened the driver's door. The keys jangled as I pulled them out of my pocket, but I clenched my fingers tight around them. It took all my attention and patience to slide into my seat, close the door, and start the engine without unnecessary sounds.

With the engine idling softly, I eased the car into reverse and looked over my right shoulder to back up. And met Lonan's slitted gaze, alive with suppressed amusement. My foot reflexively hit the gas pedal, and the Nykur leapt backwards like a startled hare.

Before we could careen onto the Castle's front steps, Lonan's hand yanked the emergency brake between us. The car halted so suddenly that we whipped back and forth like crash test dummies before slamming to a complete stop.

I took a breath with a near-hysterical laugh to it and said, "Oh. You're awake." *Wow. Could I sound any lamer?* "Are your hands always that fast?" *Oh yeah, way to raise the lameness bar, Avery.*

"Not always," he said dryly. After a loooong moment, he added, "Is there something else you wanted to do before we go home? Because Daniel's mom is expecting me for dinner."

I realized I'd been staring at the corner of his mouth, where it turned up as he tried to keep a straight face. "Yes—no—I mean, yes, let's go home." The roots of my hair must have been roasting, my face felt so hot. And putting the car in drive—but failing to take off the emergency brake so it squealed horribly when I tried to go—didn't help.

When we pulled into Uncle Tam's driveway, I blurted, "Lonan, I—I don't want you to expect anything after—whatever that was back there. Daniel is still my priority."

There might have been a flash of disappointment in his eyes before they were crackling with mischief again.

"No worries," he said as he got out of the car and headed home. "I knew that going in."

So how did I let myself forget it, in one hormone-fueled moment? Were my defenses down because of the scrambling my nerves took when Lonan tossed me in the air? I shook my head and went inside to rinse off the chlorine and confusion.

Turned out my herbal body wash only worked on the chlorine. I was so conflicted about Lonan that I didn't follow through with my threat of "constant companionship." I couldn't even say whether it was him or myself I didn't trust.

As a distraction, I spent the rest of the afternoon processing a bunch of photos of the Castle I'd been meaning to catch up on. But

I couldn't look at the Castle rooms the same way. Instead of suggesting history and arrested decay, genuinely tragic stories saturated those peeling walls. The murder wasn't just a gimmick that made the Halloween Haunt more thrilling—Mariah had been a real person, loved and missed.

Out of an admittedly morbid curiosity, I looked up Mariah's background in the docent training manual. The much-photocopied picture reduced her features to a mass of dark curls and elfin-sharp cheekbones and chin. *For all I know, there were elves somewhere in her bloodline.*

The playful tilt to her smile didn't quite fit her sad story. She'd been the sixth of eleven children in a desperately poor Chicago family, and spent a few years with an order of nuns before deciding she hadn't been Called after all. The growing social reform movement led her to Wilson Castle, to help give the boys a feeling of home. By all accounts, she'd been mother, sister, or boyhood crush to the wards, softening the military-strict school.

So her murder had been a shock, and remained unsolved in spite of the best efforts of police and private investigators. Oh, there was a suspect all right, but nothing that they could pin on the boy. When he attacked a mother and daughter in another town a few years after his release, and then killed himself, it was all the proof the townspeople needed to condemn him.

But knowing Lonan had been around, now I wondered if corbin or other Fae had been involved somehow. *Had the murderer been acting under his own power when he bludgeoned Mariah? Or was one of Lonan's dark kin responsible?* I squashed down the inner voice that tried to ask if Lonan himself could be the killer.

The training binder closed with a final-sounding snap. I wouldn't find any real answers in there, and it was time to go make dinner for Uncle Tam and me.

Hmm, speaking of Uncle Tam… I did some quick math in my head— nope, he wasn't old enough to have been around at the time of the murder. Too bad—he might have been able to offer some insights.

I was putting the leftover pasta puttanesca in the fridge when my phone beeped. A text from Lonan: **Hey, meet me at the tree.**

I bit my lip, considering. I'd planned to put on a rated-G movie as a break from murder and monsters. And from my own raging lust, which had rekindled in spite of myself, since thinking of Lonan also made me think of the eargasm in the pool.

Another beep, another text: **r u there?** I sighed and slipped on a pair of shoes. Before heading out, I grabbed the last piece of garlic bread. *This way I won't be tempted to get close enough to inflict my garlic breath on him.*

Bobbin met me at the back door, leaping for my bread a few times on the way over to the tree. Lonan's top half was hidden in the leafy canopy as I approached, so I was startled to find him deep in conversation with a crow on the branch above him.

He finally turned to me with a broad grin. "He's seen Daniel!" he said. "Around the court some, and out in the wilds."

"And he's okay?"

"Yeah, he is." Lonan sounded almost as relieved as I was.

"When are we going to go get him?" I barely noticed the teeth scraping my fingers as Bobbin nabbed the garlic bread. The crow flew down to see if he could get a few crumbs from the dog's messy snack, and Lonan gestured for me to come closer.

"When isn't the question," he said in a low voice. "It's how. I keep telling you that we can't both be— How are we going to bring him back, if I'm already in his body?"

"**Y**ou can't scrunch really small in there?" I asked.

Lonan was shaking his head before I'd finished my question. "Not if you want Daniel to stay intact. That's kind of the whole point, isn't it?"

"Yeah," I said, deflated. Bobbin came over and snuffled my sandals, drooling garlicky bits onto my toes.

"Hey!" I scooped up the dog and waved his rotund form at Lonan. "Couldn't Daniel jump in here, like you did? He could be a corgin!"

Lonan frowned at Bobbin, getting close enough to peer into his eyes. The squozen dog obliged with a fragrant garlic belch right in Lonan's face. *Glad the business end's pointed away from me.*

"It might work." I could almost see gears turning in Lonan's head. "It should work. Bobbin's willing to try."

"Yay, thank you, Bobbin!" I kissed his muzzle and was rewarded with a French kiss with a garlicky dog tongue.

I gagged and put Bobbin down, swabbing my mouth with the hem of my shirt. I stole a glance at Lonan and saw he was fighting not to make a joke.

Then his eyes sobered and he said, "So, we have a vessel for Daniel. All we need to do is cross over and find Daniel again—not an easy task, by the way."

"Do we need a spell or what?"

"Not exactly." He studied me. "I know someone who might take us, but you should ask him. He's much more likely to say yes to you."

"Why? Who is it?"

"Just follow me."

He headed towards the cemetery and I stood frozen. "No way! Are you taking me to some ghost? I was totally joking that night I mentioned traveling with ghosts."

He grinned over his shoulder and hung a right to the garage. I ran to catch up and helped him push open the carriage doors. I peered into the dim interior, ready to run if a misty shape floated towards me.

Lonan stepped inside and placed a hand on Uncle Tam's car. "I think formal introductions are in order. Avery, this is a nykur."

"Duh, of course that's a Nykur. It says so on the steering wheel." I rolled my eyes. "But what are you—"

The side mirrors flipped forward of their own accord, gleaming like eyes on either side of a long gray muzzle. An exhalation of steam came out the grille, like a vaporous sigh.

I stumbled backwards, slamming the edge of the carriage house door with my shoulder. "That's not— He's not— What's going on?"

"A nykur is like a kelpie. Have you heard of those?" Lonan asked.

"They were both in the compendium. A bog horse or something?"

A short burst of steam this time, sounding ridiculously like a horse's snort. *The whiskey fuel, the music playing on its own, the way the car turns almost before I rotate the wheel—it all makes sense.* And yet, this news on top of all the other weird shit meant the world as a whole made less sense.

"Not quite a bog horse," Lonan said, chuckling. "They look like horses—feral ones—to lure people onto their backs. Take them for a wild ride."

I waited for him to continue, and when he didn't I added, "And drown them in the bog, right?"

"Not always. Sometimes they let the person go, with no more harm than their nerves rattled. At other times, they…seduce them instead."

He saw the "eww" forming on my lips and hastily added, "Nykurs can take a human form, too. Mostly, they're troublemakers. Corbin kind of have a rivalry going with them."

"Competing for young maidens, you mean?" If I could joke, I must have been getting over the shock. The Nykur's engine rumbled, a bass chuckle of appreciation. "So what's he doing in Uncle Tam's garage?"

"Good question. I can't talk to him directly in this form—" Lonan's voice was drowned out as the sound of static and scanning stations filled the garage.

The word "chain" emerged from the noise. Lonan and I exchanged a glance.

"I guess he's been sentenced here," Lonan said. The radio blared "yes" and I jumped.

I asked Lonan, "Why here and now? Because of your mission?"

"No, he seems attached to you or—your household. He'll have a strong desire to please you, so you should ask him about taking us to find Daniel."

A strong desire to please? "It was you, Nykur! The chocolate!" I blurted. The front of the car lowered, more like a bow than a hydraulic low-rider dip. "And did you move out of the garage to save me from the crows that day? How did you know I needed you?"

Nykur answered, "♫I know what you want,♫"with a sultry backbeat.

"If he's been assigned to you, he probably has an emotional connection to you," Lonan translated. "As in, he can read your thoughts and desires."

I glared at both of them. "What is it with you guys and eaves-dropping in my head? Don't you have anything better to do?"

Lonan chuckled, and Nykur rumbled another laugh at the same time.

"No, we don't," Lonan said. "We get kind of jaded in our world, so we come here for a little fun and variety."

"And sometimes torture and killing," I said. *Yeah, total buzzkill, but Lonan likes to downplay that part unless it suits his agenda.*

Lonan's grin faded. "Yeah. That, too. So, go ahead and ask him."

It took me a second to remember he'd said I should be the one to ask Nykur. Never in a million years could I ever have predicted I'd utter this question: "Nykur, can you take us into Faerie? We need to get the real owner of that body back, and Lonan says you might be able to."

Another mechanical sigh, and, "♫Maybe.♫"

"What does that mean?" I asked Lonan.

"He may have a geis on him, like he can't go back home until his sentence is up."

"What's a gesh? Is it like an ankle monitor?"

"No, a *geis*." He carefully pronounced it, but it still sounded like "gesh" to me. Lonan continued, "Like a compulsion. It could block him entirely at the border, or get him into trouble with the Queen."

"♫Bad news,♫" agreed Nykur.

"I wouldn't want him to go against the Queen," Lonan continued. "She's been known to condemn creatures to centuries of servitude on a whim. And that doesn't even take into account the ones she… let's just say you don't want to cross her."

"Oh," I said, trying to hide my disappointment. "We'll have to find some other way—"

"♫Do—Kkkkiiiiissshhhh—it.♫"

"You mean that, Nykur?" I asked. "You'll really do this for me?"

The car doors flew open, inviting us to step in, but Lonan spoke up. "Wait, we need to get a few things together first. You should have some St. John's wort with you, Avery, in case things go sour."

"No problem." I walked over to Uncle Tam's workbench and pulled out an old flour sack. "Salted bread cubes—well, bargain-priced croutons—and dried St. John's wort from the churchyard. I've stashed emergency kits all over the place."

Looking around, I snapped my fingers at Bobbin. His ears went up like a gremlin's as his brain registered CAR RIDE. With a joyous wriggle, he jumped in the car and squeezed into the backseat.

Lonan walked to the driver's door, but I beat him to it. He raised an eyebrow. "You're going to insist on driving? Not like there's GPS for this."

"Nykur's my man-horse-car," I argued.

Lonan sighed in defeat and said, "Unlike me, Nykur's used to crossing bodily. I guess we'll let him do his thing."

"♫Oh yeah.♫"

I gave Nykur's roof a smug pat and slid inside. Once Lonan settled and we latched our seatbelts, Nykur's engine started with a low rumble. *Hey, I didn't even need to use a key!* I guessed there was no point pretending he was a normal car now. Which got me wondering what else he could do.

"Hey, Nykur, what's for snacks and beverages on this flight?" I asked.

"♫Popcorn…Candy.♫"

The glove box popped open, banging Lonan's knee and making him scowl. But my drool started flowing at the bags of the caramel popcorn studded with hunks of dark chocolate, and mini bottles of imported sodas, inside.

"Sweet!" I nudged Lonan to make sure he'd noticed my lame pun.

He groaned and said, "Let's just go."

Nykur pulled smoothly out of the garage and headed through town, obeying all traffic signs and generally behaving like a law-abiding magical car. Since he didn't seem to need my help, I turned to Lonan.

"If the Queen sent Nykur here to serve out some kind of sentence, does that mean she had to let Uncle Tam know to expect an enchanted car on his doorstep? Or did Her Fae Majesty put a spell on him to blame Old Dude Brain for any fuzziness on how the car appeared?"

Instead of answering, Lonan asked, "Are you going to ask Tam what he knows about the Fae?" He laughed at my dubious expression. "Hey, you never know—you might spark a serious conversation where he warns you about the dangers of consorting with legendary creatures. Did he not include that in The Talk, along with the birds and the bees? How disappointing."

I snorted. "Duh, my mom is a nurse, so when I got The Talk—from her—it involved proper terms like coitus and oxytocin. No metaphors with bees and flowers, let alone pixies and flowers.

"And at no time has Uncle Tam felt the need to enlighten me on relations between humans—and I'm perfectly okay with that—or between humans and characters from fairy tales. But is that because he doesn't know, or because he's trying to protect me?"

"Then are you going to ask him?"

I took a beat to think that through before I answered. "Well…I mean, best-case scenario, he knows something that will help us, right?"

Lonan shrugged. "Don't you think that if the Queen had contact with some human who had the ability to stop this invasion, she would have just used him instead of sending me? Assuming they're on speaking terms, that is."

"True." I chewed my lip in thought. "I can't really find out what he knows without asking him, but if he's clueless it could land me back in the—back into mental health territory. Uncle Tam has always been leery of my medications, but I could see him getting on board if I start talking about body snatchers coming to take over the town.

"You have more experience talking to humans about the Fae—what do you think I should do?"

"If you're genuinely asking, I vote no. Say your best-case scenario is true, and he does want to help us? From my perspective, that's just one more human I have to worry about getting caught in the crossfire.

"If it's your worst-case scenario, the one where you get locked up or medicated to a drooling zombie state, then that still complicates things for me and my mission. I won't have you as backup, and Daniel's life could possibly fall under greater scrutiny. So, no. Not if you don't want to risk royally screwing things up for me—and your-self. "

"Yeah, you're probably right."

I popped open a soda and took a big gulp before I changed the subject. "So, what do we do once we get to Faerie? Will Daniel be waiting for us?"

"My cousin said Daniel's hiding out. He was at court for a time, and then—um, I guess you'd call it an orgy—before he disappeared into the wilds."

My head snapped back painfully into the seat's headrest. "*Daniel at an orgy?* That's not possible. So out of character, it's like finding out Mother Teresa ran a bioweapons lab. Unless Faerie is also Bizarro World?"

"Well, it is where the idea for Bizarro World came from—"

"Shut up!" I slugged Lonan in the arm. "Stop taking credit for all the cool things in my world. You can keep the blame for the wars and stuff, though."

He laughed. "Deal. But remember, Daniel's a guy, and it would be awfully hard for a guy to resist an orgy."

"Maybe for guys like you," I huffed. But I had to wonder: *would Daniel really say no to free, uncomplicated sex? Especially if he found himself in a world where all the rules and social codes making him neurotic don't apply?*

"You should prepare yourself for the possibility that Daniel might come back different, Avery." Lonan's words intruded on my thoughts. "Traits like paranoia and vengefulness are useful skills in my world, but only seem to cause trouble here. And to him, it may feel like he's been lost and abandoned there for a very long time."

"♪I'll be there for you.♪"

I gave the dashboard an affectionate pat. "I appreciate the sentiment, Nykur."

"As for you," I said, turning to Lonan, "give me some caramel corn if you're going to talk like that. I'll need to be perky when we find Daniel."

I munched away to try to fill that hollow sinking in my stomach from Lonan's warning. I wasn't as blasé as I was trying to sound. *If Daniel's one of the humans who comes back crazy, what happens then? Do I get a job at an institution so I can always be near his medicated self? Go live in a hermit cave with him?*

As if in response to my mental cue, Nykur took the turn for the narrow road leading to the Druid's Cave. "Hey, I'm not ready to set up house in a cave just yet, Nykur. Why are we going this way?" Nykur didn't answer, so I turned to Lonan.

"The border between the worlds is usually thinner in places like caverns," he said. "We can kind of push against them from the other side."

"Making Faerie mounds?" I asked.

He nodded and opened his mouth to speak, but Nykur's sharp turn into the gravel parking lot sent us both slipping and sliding across the seats. A thump and yelp from the back meant Bobbin had landed on the floor, but at least he hadn't been thrown out the window.

"Nykur—" Before I could scold him, the car's sudden acceleration stole my breath.

I gripped the steering wheel as the wheels hit a bump and we were airborne—and heading straight towards the cavern's opening. The jagged mantle passed so close it should have scraped the paint, but instead darkness enveloped us.

The overhead light switched on and I braced myself for the lurch of the wheels touching down again, but it never came. I hadn't realized I was holding my breath until it came out in a rush. "*Hoosh!* Did we make it through?"

"Yes," Lonan said, and turned towards me with a grin.

Under my gaze, Daniel's face transformed into some unearthly, idealized version of itself. The hair lengthened, black strands gathering into a feathered mane. So feathery-silky I wanted to bury my fingers in it, nuzzle against that impossibly chiseled jaw, run my tongue along his berry-ripe lips—

A twinge of pain as my knee caught between the seats made me realize I had climbed partway onto Lonan's lap. Only inches away from skin that smelled like jasmine, mandarin oranges, and marshmallow Peeps.

"♫You're a no good, dirty birdy.♫"

I had to agree with Nykur. "Looonan," I said in my most severe tone of voice.

He laughed, and his breath on my cheek was a desert wind, heady with spices.

"Sorry," he said. "It's like having phantom limbs, being without all my powers in your world. You can't blame me for wanting to stretch my wings, so to speak."

"I can, and I do," I grumped as I slid behind the wheel. "Knock that shit off."

He turned down the wattage on his smile a few notches, but kept the feathers.

"Is this what you look like in your natural form?" I asked.

"At times. My natural form is without form, really."

"So, you're like smoke? Mucosa? An amoeba?"

"No. And yes."

"Oh, so you're Mr. Mysterious again—" I stopped mid-rant. "What was that? Nykur, is it safe to use your headlights?"

"We want to keep a low profile," Lonan said hastily.

So we continued moving lightlessly through the dark. I stared intently, trying to see something in the blackness. And then it was like coming out the other end of a tunnel, into a light so bright it nearly triggered a migraine.

Beside me, Lonan gasped aloud. "Nykur, are you doing that?" he asked.

"♪No, no, no fooling.♪"

I asked, "Isn't this Faerie?"

Lonan shook his head. "This isn't quite what I expected, but you should take another look."

I studied the green hills, dotted with apple orchards close by and fringed with dark woods further away. Pleasant country that made me want to get out and skip and sing. Even Nykur's tires made a tuneful, rhythmic *dub-dub-dub-dub* on the road.

Hold on—we're traveling on a road paved with bricks. Yellow bricks. Holy shit! I blurted, "Is—tell me this isn't Oz."

"I read the book when it first came out, so it's been a while, but looks that way to me," Lonan said. "Is this how you pictured Faerie?"

"I hadn't really thought about it, but yeah, Oz works. Or maybe—" I stopped speaking as the colors outside swirled and blended, like water splashed on a chalk pastel drawing.

I held my breath as the scenery separated and flowed into a semblance of an Alpine valley. Except this one wasn't from the Alps—I recognized it as the area around Carson Pass where we hiked every August for the wildflowers. Snow clung to the knife-sharp ridges as Nykur tooled along a path nearly swallowed with a riot of blooms—lupines, columbine, mule ears, Indian paintbrush, lilies. The sound of a marmot whistle carried through the glass and I itched to run through the meadow and sing like a governess nun.

I actually had my hand on the door handle—until a spark of electricity zapped me through it. "Ow, Nykur! I just want to get out and see if it's real."

"♪You're wrong.♪"

"He says the fact you want out so badly should worry you," Lonan answered. "And I have to agree—he's protecting us the best he can from the full effect of Faerie."

"Oh. Wait, you can understand Nykur now?"

"Ever since we crossed the border. He's gotten close to Daniel a few times, but your friend learned quickly. He's slippery."

"You mean Daniel is out there?" I reached to roll down my window, but my finger sparked on the button. "Damnit! Please may I open the window, Nykur?"

"Nykur says opening the window isn't likely to help you find Daniel."

"Well, maybe Daniel doesn't know it's us looking for him. That's why I was going to stick my head out and yell." I tried again with the window and got a stronger zap for my trouble. *Not cool, Nykur! When we get back, I'm withholding your whiskey.*

A trumpet blared over the radio, like a baby blowing a raspberry.

"I have a better plan," Lonan said. "When you spoke that binding spell at the mineshaft, I could feel it was genuinely working. It was pulling Daniel to us. If you tried it here, where magic is stronger, it might pin him down long enough for us to let him know we're here to help."

"Okay—"

"Wait—Nykur says he doesn't think that's a good idea. It will get us noticed."

I think I like it better when Nykur can't argue with me. "What, then? We didn't come all this way only to go home without Daniel."

Lonan was silent, but his expression changed like it did when he was communing with the crows.

The Final Jeopardy music sounded—how did Nykur even find music from a TV show on the radio?—until Lonan said, "Nykur

couldn't come up with anything better, so he says go ahead and try. But his priority is your safety, and if things turn hairy he's going to run."

That's not going to cut it. "You're supposed to do what I want, Nykur, and I don't want to leave here unless Daniel comes home, too. Understood?"

I waited for an answer, but Lonan just shrugged.

"Fine," I said through gritted teeth. *Withholding whiskey won't be punishment enough if you make me lose Daniel again, Nykur—I'll figure out how to geld you.*

The car shivered and fishtailed. *Guess you heard that one loud and clear.*

"Here goes," I said.

Thread to me

Twine, twine, betwixt

Pull to thee

Twine, twine, the twain

Darkness swirled across the windshield, taking on the pearly hue of mist. Purple mist. With odd shapes in it, sweeping by so fast I couldn't identify them, so I continued.

Bind to me

Twine, twine, betwixt

Wed to thee

Twine, twine, the twain

Instead of darkness, gaps in the billowing mist revealed a new landscape. A parched wasteland with towers of rock, individual boulders stacked impossibly high. They seemed to lean over us in the lashing wind.

"Is this yours?" Lonan asked.

"No," I breathed, too intent on willing the rocks not to fall on us to say more.

"If things are changing outside, we're not unnoticed any longer. And likely not alone."

I opened my mouth to speak, but paused. *What is that up ahead? It's not… Is it moving?*

"Nykur says we need to go," Lonan said.

The car shifted under me. "Wait! I saw something. There!"

My hand struck the windshield as I tried to point. The shape I'd glimpsed grew closer. A figure—a human-looking figure—struggling against a strong wind. *They have mimes in Faerie?* No—not walking against a wind, pulling himself bodily against a tether. A tether that tugged on my hand.

"Daniel. It's Daniel."

The window still wouldn't work, and I mashed the button with my fist. "Nykur, don't be stupid! We're not in stealth mode anymore, and the faster we get Daniel, the sooner we can get home."

After a static-filled pause, like Nykur was pondering my words, my window cracked about four inches. A strange odor seeped into the car, like rotting meat and the most delicious fruity punch all blended into one. Shuddering, I put my mouth to the gap and yelled, "Daniel! It's Avery! Stop!"

Bobbin scrambled into my lap and began barking, sharp staccato blasts of joy. Finally, Daniel stopped walking and turned his head toward us. Nykur pulled up to him in an instant.

I started crying—Daniel looked like a raggedy mannequin. Parts of the velvet costume he was wearing hung in strips, as if giant claws had raked his chest. And when he tried to touch my fingers where they poked out the window, his hand went right through mine.

He pulled his arm back hastily, but not before I'd seen it was slightly transparent. *That's right—he doesn't have a body. It's here in the car with me.*

"Avery?" he said. "Is it really you?"

"Yes!" I said through fresh tears. "We came to save you."

He bent down to peer into the car, his face lighting up. "Bobbin! Hey, boy!" His eyes moved past us to the passenger seat, and anger and bitterness twisted his features. "You. This is all your fault!"

Lonan held up his hands—Daniel's hands—and said, "That's not true. If you hadn't fought the switch, we wouldn't be in this mess—"

Nykur's dash lights suddenly went haywire and the speakers blared air-raid sirens.

"They're coming!" Daniel and Lonan said together.

Nykur revved his engine, but I reached over and yanked the emergency brake. "No, Nykur! Give me one second."

Before I could say anything else, a screech like sheet metal tearing in a wind reverberated around us. And again, closer. Daniel's eyes held pure panic, and he turned to run.

"Daniel, get in the dog!" I screamed.

That threw him enough to hesitate. "Get in the what?"

"Get in the dog! Get in Bobbin, it's your only chance."

"That's crazy—"

"Just do it!" Lonan yelled over him.

With a touch to Bobbin's muzzle, Daniel's form flowed right in, like a cartoon food aroma. *Shiiit...*

But I didn't have time to trip out, because a dark cloud was approaching. It was close enough now to see that the mass was made up of misshapen, winged creatures.

"Go, Nykur!" Lonan smacked the dashboard and I let off the brake.

Now we were really flying—no doubt faster than a jet plane. And it seemed we'd left our new friends behind, until a series of impacts jarred the car. A sound like demon nails on a chalkboard shrieked over our heads. *Claws trying to cut the metal roof?*

Movement out of the corner of my eye made me whip my head around, and I came face to face with one of the creatures. *Is that a gargoyle? A naked mole rat? A devil from a tomb carving?*

Worse than all those things together.

Humongous fangs scraped on the glass next to me. "Aaagh!" I screamed. Lonan pulled me away from the window—now thankfully shut—and the view disappeared behind a wall of leathery wings and limbs. Hissing and muttering, they scrabbled for purchase on the hood, the windows, the roof.

I covered my face, barely aware of Lonan's arms around me and the shivering dog's body pressed against my side. Until a flare of light and the smell of ozone intruded, and I peeked through my fingers to see threads of electricity all over the outside of the car.

The monsters dropped away like scorched ticks—all but a really big one, which clung stubbornly to the windshield, even while it shuddered and smoked. I met its gaze, and despair thick as tar seeped into my mind. I struggled against the blackness, came up long enough to call Nykur's name.

Nykur rallied, targeting the fiend with a concentrated lightning ball. But it still didn't fall away like the others, and a voice sounded in my head: "*I see you, girl.*"

What was worse, I recognized that voice, and that dark gaze rimmed with a reddish glow. The crow who tried to attack me outside Uncle Tam's, before the other crows mobbed it. And Lonan's blanched face said he knew that voice, too.

"Siwennen!" Lonan snarled. Along with some other words I didn't catch, but they must have been a spell because finally the creature's claws lost their hold. Its form became part of the darkness as we continued unmolested.

After our launch back into the moonlit night, we idled in the parking lot for a few minutes to make sure nothing had followed us. I was grateful for a chance to calm my racing heart, but when I tried to ask Lonan about that creature I was met with stony silence.

And it continued as Nykur drove us home; he didn't even play regular music, let alone try to talk through the radio. But Daniel/Bobbin refused to leave my lap, burying his head in my armpit and shuddering every now and then. He started to fall asleep at one point, but jerked and whimpered his way into wakefulness again.

According to my phone, we'd been gone for eleven hours and it was now close to one AM. Uncle Tam had texted, wondering where I was, and I answered back "**r on r way.**" *I guess I should be grateful we didn't lose more time, or Uncle Tam would have sent out a search party.*

When we finally pulled up to Uncle Tam's, I stared aghast at Nykur, revealed under the porch light. Scores of scratches and dents marred his glossy finish. *Can he feel that? Does it hurt him when he's in this form?*

"Double ration of whiskey for you, Nykur, if I can find where Uncle Tam keeps it," I said. Muted music played, so briefly and weakly I couldn't identify the song.

"We all need to rest," Lonan said. He stooped to pick up Daniel, but the dog-boy growled and snapped. Lonan said casually instead, "Let him sleep with you tonight. Plenty of time for us to sort things out in the morning."

"Fine," I said. "But we're both going to want some answers."

He nodded and turned away. I tried again. "You knew that thing—the creature—didn't you, Lonan? And it knew you. And me, somehow."

Lonan didn't turn around, just nodded again and stepped through the gate. Daniel leaned against my leg and heaved a sigh before we tiredly stepped into the screen porch. Even after brushing my teeth twice, I still tasted ozone and burnt meat until I finally fell asleep.

I woke later that morning to find a pair of soulful brown eyes inches from my own. Bobbin's—Daniel's—head rested on the pillow next to mine. We stared at each other until I tentatively reached out a hand and petted his silky ears. Long lashes came down over his eyes and he sighed softly.

I remembered how, after we'd gotten in bed, Daniel had curled up against my back and heaved a long, shuddering breath. Like he could finally relax enough to sleep, after weeks of going without. We'd fostered an abandoned dog once, and it had done the exact same thing. *Home. Safe.*

"What happened to you, Daniel?" I whispered. "How long did it feel like you were lost?"

He rolled over and faced away from me, but scooted backwards so his spine pressed against my stomach.

"I wish there was some way we could talk. Maybe Lonan knows a spell?"

As if speaking the name had conjured him, Lonan's shape filled the screen door.

"Avery? You awake yet?" he whispered.

"Yeah, come on in." I sat up, and so did Bobbin. Er—Daniel. *This is getting way confusing—what do I call him now? I guess Daniel, when it's just us.*

Lonan and Daniel stared awkwardly at each other for a long moment, until Lonan cleared his throat and said, "Hope you enjoyed your lie-in, because we have a lot to do—"

"Do you need every waking moment to get ready?" I asked.

Lonan paused, trying to assess my mood. "Well…maybe not every moment, if you wanted to go swimming again. Or something." He gave me a saucy wink, and Daniel growled.

My cheeks warmed, and I shot Lonan a warning look. *The last thing I need is Lonan making Daniel think anything happened between us, without a chance to explain first.*

"Before we do anything else," I said, "you and Daniel need to talk about him getting his body back."

"Our original agreement was for me to have this body until the blue moon. I need it—no negotiation."

"Yes, I was listening all the other times you've explained it," I said. "But things went so wrong that I think Daniel deserves to be asked again. If he wants to be left in peace, we'll find some other way for you to do it."

"Is this about you spending time with Daniel?" Lonan asked. "Because in a week you can bed him all you want, guilt free. And not have to worry about monsters killing half the population while you're doing it."

What the hell? Why is Lonan being so mean, and bringing "bedding" into this conversation?

"That's not fair, Lonan." I dropped my hand from where it rested on Daniel's fur. "Yes, I want to spend time with Daniel, but this is about him. All I'm saying is you two should talk about it. You can communicate with him, can't you?"

Back to the boys' staring contest again. "Well?" I asked. "Can you or can't you?"

"Yes," Lonan gritted his teeth. "He's been telling me how much he hates me the entire time we've been talking."

I sighed. *Real productive, Daniel. Like that's going to get you what you want.* "Fine. Can we all agree that so far this has not gone as expected or promised, and move on? What does Daniel say about you staying in his body?"

Lonan's lips twisted in a bitter smile. "In a nutshell, he's against it."

"Can't you guys share?"

"I've told you a million times what would happen if we're both in here—"

"I meant, could you guys switch off? Call a truce and take turns with Daniel's body and Bobbin's?" *Gaah, so much testosterone and tension in my room. Maybe I should lock them both in Nykur's trunk and let them settle it themselves.* "And Bobbin should get a say, too."

"How do I know he'll give me the body back and not just keep it?" Lonan asked.

"He's probably thinking the same thing about you. You came to an agreement before, didn't you, with no guarantees? We're not going to get anywhere without a little trust."

They communed silently, and Lonan finally said, "Okay, we'll try trading places. But not here—I'll want to use a spell for the first trade, and we don't need to draw attention here. At least, not any more than we already have."

I glanced sharply at him, but Lonan didn't seem to be aware he'd confirmed my fear that we now had the attention of the creature from the night before.

"Both of you meet me up by the mineshaft in a few hours," Lonan said.

So, after killing a few hours with my shower and getting dressed (during which Daniel politely buried his head under the covers), and making a big batch of Daniel's favorite macaroni and cheese for brunch, we trudged up the hill to the mineshaft.

Lonan was waiting with a folding grill like the one I'd used. When I raised my eyebrows, he said, "Hey, I'm not above stealing good ideas. This is a lot more portable than a cauldron or a brazier."

"Do you have everything else?" I asked.

Lonan nodded. "I just need some of Bobbin's hair—I have Daniel's already."

Daniel stiffened and curled his lip into a snarl, but let Lonan snip a tuft of hair from Bobbin's tail. Then Lonan knelt by the embers and dropped the hairs in, muttering strange words all the while.

I wrinkled my nose at the stench of the singed hair, but watched closely. Maybe I could learn a trick to improve my own spell-casting. I almost missed it, but two glowing threads—one purple and one golden—rose above the smoke and intertwined before fading away.

"Was that it?" I asked.

Lonan looked up and said "Avery?" in a different voice.

My breath caught. "Daniel?"

I rushed into his arms, almost knocking over the grill. Tears started and I crushed him to me. For a moment I was perfectly happy.

But I didn't need the barking dog to tell me something was wrong—the hands squeezing my ass were a dead giveaway that Lonan was still in Daniel's body.

I yanked his head back by the hair. "Lonan, I swear to God you're the worst bastard. If you're trying to go back on our deal—"

He laughed and held his hands up in surrender. "Sorry, I couldn't resist. That spell was only to allow us to transfer—it doesn't actually do it."

I wanted to really punch him, but he'd probably just switch and let Daniel have the pain. "So do it now."

"Fine, fine." Lonan knelt next to the dog and held out his hand. "Shake, buddy."

Daniel hesitantly lifted a paw and set it in the palm of Lonan's hand. A brief flash of light, the same colors as the threads that appeared before, and it was done. This time, no mistaking it. It was absolutely Daniel who looked out at me, from his own eyes.

When it finally happened, the hug felt real. So did Daniel's tears wetting my hair. And for once, no smartass, snarky comments popped into my head. Just a rush of peace and joy, for Daniel and for my part in restoring him.

When I eventually stepped away, I looked to Lonan, eager for him to see this was worth it. But he rolled his doggy eyes exaggeratedly.

I glared at him for ruining the moment. "Can we get a little privacy, Lonan?" I asked.

He stood, staring pointedly at Daniel, before turning and heading down the trail.

"Did he say something else?" I asked.

"Yeah," Daniel replied. "He reminded me I'm not here to stay."

"We already knew that—you agreed, didn't you?"

Daniel studied me. "Avery, I don't know what happened between you while I was gone. But he is not a good guy."

"He's not a completely bad guy, either. He agreed to bring you back, didn't he? I didn't even need to use his name to compel him."
Well, not much, anyway.

"His name? You mean Lonan?" Daniel laughed bitterly—a sound I didn't remember him ever making. "That's not his name—he may as well have told you Bobbin's is Dog and yours is Girl. Lonan means blackbird."

But I asked him—no, come to think on it, I asked him what I could call him. That meant he'd been in charge the whole time. "Do you know his name?"

Daniel shook his head. "They're very careful. Their names hold great power over them, and they guard them like a dragon does gold. The only failsafe is an ancient magic which prevents blood relatives from using names against each other."

I stifled a giggle. Daniel'd always been a dork, but I'd never heard him use phrases like "guard them like a dragon does gold" so casually. Come to think on it, I'd never heard anyone but members of the Geek Club at school say things like that with perfect seriousness.

Daniel sank down to the dusty ground and patted a place beside him. "Catch me up on everything?" he asked.

I nodded. Our knees brushed together, and I found myself making it happen more often than it naturally would have as I talked. I wanted to touch him, revel in the fact he was really here. But too much contact seemed to make him edgy. *Am I the problem, or is he still overwhelmed and traumatized from Faerie?*

Finally all caught up, Daniel stood up and brushed his shorts off.

I quickly followed his lead. "What are you going to do now?" I asked.

"Go see my parents," he said.

"But I thought we could—"

"Look, Avery, I'm genuinely glad to see you, and I appreciate you sticking up for me, but I need to spend some time with my parents. It might be all I have."

I grabbed his arm as he started to walk away. "What do you mean?"

He removed my hand and said, "I haven't made up my mind to switch with Lonan again. But he said he's taking over again at ten o'clock tonight. Whether I want him to or not. Still think Lonan's not completely bad?"

"But you'd be—he said that makes people crazy, to have you both in there."

"He's willing to take the chance of me being permanently damaged. Lonan's obsessed with stopping his brother."

"*His brother?*" I called after his retreating figure. "What are you talking about?"

Daniel turned, walking backwards as he said, "Oh, he didn't tell you that thing on the windshield was his brother? They're the Faerie Queen's nephews."

And he was gone, leaving me standing with my mouth hanging open.

I packed up the grill once it cooled and walked back to Uncle Tam's.

Lonan came and scratched on the back door, but I told him, "Not now," and lifted him over the fence into the Dawes's yard. He didn't even bother to whine or fuss, and he wilted under my glare.

"If you hurt him, *Lonan*, I'll never let you rest. I don't care if I have to turn to dark magic—you will pay."

He nodded, head hanging, and went to lie under the bushes.

"But this is your chance to prove that Fae aren't all bad. That you have a generous side as well as a selfish one."

He blinked and I figured that meant he'd heard me. I went in search of a distraction.

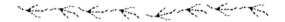

By nine-thirty I still hadn't succeeded in distracting myself, but Daniel and his parents came home. As the minutes ticked by, I tried texting Daniel's phone repeatedly.

plz, just trade lk u said

I never got an answer, so when a knock sounded on the back door a little after ten, I didn't know what to expect.

I yanked open the door and stared into Daniel's eyes. *Daniel's—or Lonan's?* Then I knew, and choked out, "Lonan?"

He nodded and I had to grab the doorjamb to keep myself from falling. But he stepped aside, and Bobbin came and leaned against my leg.

I knelt and grabbed his head, forced him to look at me. "Is that—Daniel, is that you?"

He licked my chin gently, and I sobbed into his fur.

14

Since they'd kept their word, I made good on mine and helped Lonan with his preparations. The six days that had seemed like plenty of time to fetch Daniel and get ready now seemed way too short. Especially since I was essentially on half-time with each of them.

They'd reluctantly worked out a system for trading, after I threw a tantrum about the worry they'd put me through. Daniel spent most of the sleeping hours in his body—Lonan said it would help re-establish the link between body and mind—plus six hours of waking time. That gave Lonan ten hours a day, more or less, to gather esoteric ingredients and practice the spell.

The day after the first switch, he showed me an ancient piece of tattooed hide—*I really hope it's not human skin*—and the spell it contained on its reverse.

"It's kind of rambly," Lonan said, "but it uses some ancient names for Faerie families, so I think it's legitimate."

Of course I took advantage of the mention of names to harass Lonan for lying to me. "So, Blackbird, what is your real name? Are you going to make me put a daisy chain on you again to get it?"

He heaved a mock-sigh. "A daisy chain alone isn't strong enough to make me tell you." He stepped closer, that all-too-familiar glint in his eyes, and whispered, "Maybe I'd let it slip in the throes of passion. Care to try?"

All that got him was a punch in the arm, just as it did the couple of times he tried to convince me he was Daniel so I'd kiss him. It never worked, though—I could always tell who was who.

Not that there was any kissing going on with Daniel. He'd been so prickly since he got back, not wanting me to touch him or fuss over him too much. Except being in Bobbin's body seemed to relax him enough, or maybe distance him enough, so he craved contact with me.

When Lonan and I got together one evening to discuss strategy and go over our checklist, Daniel lay pressed against my leg. His radar-dish ears followed our words closely.

"You still have plenty of bread and salt?" Lonan asked. Since even handling it left him with painful welts, I was in charge of that charm.

I nodded "And I got more bell necklaces from the New Age-y shop in town. Those'll work, right?"

"Yeah," he said. "I spent all morning searching for four-leafed clovers and we're up to nine of them now."

"How can that be? I thought they were really rare."

"Not all that rare—just powerful. Did you get a chance to try any more magic yourself? Apply those tips I gave you?"

"Yes—I tried that charm you wrote down like ten times, but nothing happened. The flower bulb just sat there like a pet rock. Then the Byrds' "Turn! Turn! Turn!" came on the radio"—*not going to fess up to singing along*—"and I turned around and it was blooming like crazy. Smelled like grape Kool-Aid."

"But did you do it?"

"I have no idea—but how else do you explain a dormant hyacinth bursting into bloom?"

"Hmm," he said. "So there's some magic there, but you'll have to keep working at it. Get some control before the blue moon."

"Consider it done." My sarcasm swooped right over his tired head.

He looked at the alarm clock—we were in Daniel's room—and rubbed a hand over his face tiredly. "Just enough time to run through my spell again before Daniel gets the body back for sleep time."

"Is the spell coming along?"

"I think so—it's not like I can try it out, since it only has power during a blue moon. Even with that, it feels like something's not quite right, like I'm missing some part."

Lonan had been fretting over how one edge of the skin was straight, like it had been cut. The other edges were uneven and frayed, and I had to agree it was suspicious, but it didn't start mid-line or mid-word like it was only a partial page.

"Where did you get that spell?" I asked. "Can you trust the source?"

"The Queen gave it to me before I left. She can't afford—politically—to publicly support my efforts, so helping me with the spell was the only thing she could do."

The Queen? Like, Aunt Queen? "What about your brother? Does he have a spell, too? Maybe the Queen helped both nephews, to cover all her bases."

I hadn't asked about him until now, and Lonan took his time before he answered, "Drake is my half-brother—same mother, different father. The Queen has no love for corbin like my father, but even less for wyverns like his."

"I read about wyverns, and they don't sound nearly as charming as corbin. So, if your mom's the Queen's sister, does that make you in line for the throne or something? Are you, like, a prince?"

"More like a minor lord. When the royals are so long-lived, it makes succession very complicated."

Long-lived? Not immortal? I didn't say it out loud, but it must have shown on my face because Lonan said, "Yes, Avery, we don't live forever, and we can be killed. Going to take a stab at it now that you hate me?" He said it jokingly, but a shadow in his eyes showed he was at least a little serious.

"I'm not going to— I don't hate you, Lonan. I like to think you would have done the right thing for Daniel without my pushing. And without that binding spell I tried to use—ow!"

That last part was because Daniel had launched himself off my lap, his nails raking my bare thighs in the process. The slashes didn't break the skin, but it looked like I'd been mauled.

Lonan stood and said, "It's time for Daniel and me to switch."

"I thought you said you had time to practice——" but they were already touching hand to paw. After the millisecond flash, they'd traded bodies.

"Daniel!" I said. "I thought before you go to sleep, we could——"

But without a word, Daniel picked up Lonan, put him in my arms, and shoved us both out the door so hard I stumbled to my knees as the door slammed behind us. Lonan growled as he hit the floor, barking his displeasure.

But my flash of anger quickly turned to tears. *Why am I always saying the wrong thing, doing the wrong thing, around Daniel now?* I couldn't help it if I sometimes forgot he was in the room and talked like he wasn't there. *Doesn't he know how hard I fought for him?*

I wiped away my tears and knocked softly. "Daniel? My bag is still in there and I need it——"

The door opened and before I could do more than part my lips to apologize, my bag was at my feet. Sighing, I turned to go—only to catch Lonan in the act of peeing in Daniel's sneakers.

"Lonan!" I hissed. "You might be the next one to wear those, you know. And stop antagonizing him."

Lonan did that after-pee scratching thing dogs do and trotted jauntily down the stairs. He followed me outside, and I let him. But I didn't go home—instead we went and sat in Nykur. My friendly neighborhood car-horse-man had an iced latte and a warm broccoli pastie waiting for me.

I bit into the treat, chewing it gloomily until I glanced over at Lonan and saw him covering his nose with his paws, an exaggerated look of terror in his eyes. I spewed dough and veggies all over Nykur's interior with my surprised guffaw. Lonan doggy-grinned and helpfully licked up the bits.

"What's going to protect me from *your* rank broccoli gas if you eat that?" I teased. "Though you definitely got the bad end of the bargain, since a dog's nose is so much more sensitive."

He sneezed explosively and I laughed again. "Thanks, Lonan, for trying to cheer me up. I've been trying to give Daniel his space, time to come around, but he acts like he's blaming me for something. Has he said anything to you?"

Lonan crawled on his belly across the seat and licked my hand. *Oh yeah, dogs don't talk.* I sighed and patted his head. *I need to get my mind off this stuff, or I'll drive myself crazy.*

No sooner had I thought it than the glove box popped open, bearing a travel set of checkers. I leaned over and grabbed it. "Up for a game of checkers, Lonan? You should be able to manage it with your paw or your nose." He managed well enough to beat me several times before we went to bed.

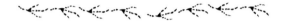

Lonan was gone when I woke up the next morning, and I decided I needed a break from him and Daniel. Besides, I'd promised the volunteer coordinator I'd take some photos of the restored faculty dining room at the Castle.

So, after a quick breakfast and check of my gear, I headed to the Castle. Usually no one was there on Mondays and I should have had the place to myself, but Mr. Forrest's car sat by the firehouse.

Oh well, he's pretty good about staying out of my way when I'm taking pictures. I parked next to the old van, only to be startled as Nykur followed me up the drive with his hazard lights flashing. *Is he trying to tell me something?*

I turned back to say, "Nykur? What's up? You know you can't follow me inside. Unless you turn human, or something."

The car visibly drooped and pulled to a stop at the curb. *No human form, then. Too bad—I'm kind of curious what he'd look like as a guy.*

"I'll only be an hour or so," I said. "We can go for a fun drive after." All I got out of him was a barrage of radio sounds, and I had no idea what they meant. I shrugged and kept walking.

Once inside, I headed over to the basement stairs, figuring Mr. Forrest might like to know I was here. But muffled voices echoed up the stairwell and I hesitated. *Maybe there's a tour or talk today?* No cars out front, but sometimes bus drivers dropped off a senior group and went to gas up.

Not a big deal, I've worked around tours and groups before. I'd better get upstairs and get as many shots as I can before they all go up there.

My jaw dropped as I turned into the dining room from the dim hallway. They'd done so much since I was last in here. Where the windows had once been boarded up and smeared with droppings from birds perching on the plywood, a stretch of floor-to-ceiling glass now gleamed.

Sunlight rippled on polished floorboards, glossily painted wainscoting and window trim, and curves of the elaborate brass chandelier. And on one wall, the *pièce de résistance*—the crumbling brick fireplace, refaced with a carved mantle and enameled tiles checkering the hearth.

All that was missing was chattering faculty in period dress along the length of the table, and the aroma of Mariah's cooking in the air.

Thinking of Mariah made me glance towards the doorway at the other end of the room. The police report said she was likely killed in the dining room, and her murderer used either the dumbwaiter or the narrow staircase to get her body down to the kitchen. *Before stuffing her in that alcove.*

I shivered. Now I could only see the shadows in the corners, not the light shining in.

Come on, Avery—you've been here a thousand times without anything happening in this room. Nothing to be scared of.

Not a good time for a series of thumps to come from the other side of the wall, but that's exactly what happened. I froze, not quite able to see the landing at the top of the stairs since the door was half-closed.

Is it just me, or does that squeaking sound exactly like protesting metal pulleys in an ancient dumbwaiter? My heart skipped a few beats before it leaped into overdrive. The smart thing to do would have been to quietly exit the building, before whoever—whatever—was using the dumbwaiter realized I was there. But I'd feel really stupid if it was just Mr. Forrest and I'd run out of here like a spooked rabbit.

So I tiptoed forward. The doors to the dumbwaiter stood open, further blocking my view. All I could see was a shadow flickering on the wall on the other side of the landing. A man-shaped shadow, but—were those wings?

Is Mr. Forrest bringing his pet cockatoo to work? It would explain the voices downstairs, and strange mutterings I'd heard in the elevator shaft before. I raised my hand to pull the door open.

Just then, the shadow changed as whoever was casting it bent over something at knee height. The angle made the dark wings sharper, more defined—and more impossible that this was a bird perched on a man's shoulder. *Too big, too centered over the four arms...*

Four arms?? I clapped a hand over my mouth and counted again. Yes, definitely four arms, but one torso, plus the distinctly bat-like wings.

Suddenly glad that I hadn't even had time to take the tripod off my back or unpack my camera bag, I backpedaled as fast as I could. My sneakers squeaked on the fresh varnish, and I gave up on a stealthy exit.

I turned and ran, my steps puffing dust from the rotting carpet in the hallway. A door slammed behind me, and I clattered down the stairs. If the thing had taken the kitchen stairs, it was now between me and the door I'd come in, so I headed into the old dormitory instead.

Footsteps pounded behind me as I burst out through the fire door, setting off the alarm. The sunlight blinded me for a moment as I stumbled on the brick steps, and I nearly face-planted when a car horn blared in front of me. But with a hand shading my eyes, I saw Nykur had come to my rescue.

I jumped in the open back door, landing on my stomach so I wouldn't crush my tripod. Nykur was already moving, bumping down the brick walkway and across the lawn before I'd struggled out of my tripod harness. I knelt on the seat and looked out the back window, searching for any pursuers.

There! In a ground-floor window, a figure was watching me. It looked like Mr. Forrest. *Oh, no—is he trapped with whatever manifested in the Castle?* But he raised a fist and shook it at me.

"*This is thrice—you're marked now, girl.*" The now-familiar sinister voice boomed in my head as Mr. Forrest's eyes flashed red.

I gasped and faced forward again. *Bang-bang-bang.* Dark objects bounced off the roof and windshield, and I screamed before risking another look behind us.

Littering the driveway, the street, were hundreds of black objects. A vast flock of blackbirds, struck down out of the sky. Staining the pavement like so many fallen plums.

Nykur stopped at the ice-cream place on the way home, but I didn't have the stomach for it and waved him on. Before I left the garage, I gave the car's roof a shaky pat and my hand came away with feathers stuck to the palm.

All those dead birds…a message meant for Lonan, aka Blackbird?

Daniel's car pulled into his driveway as I reached the back door, and I veered off to meet him. I couldn't tell yet if it was Daniel or Lonan, but when his lips thinned into an angry line I knew.

I stopped about ten feet away. "Daniel, can I talk to you for a sec?"

"What?" he said, not even bothering to hide his impatience.

It was too much, after what just happened. I sucked in a gasping sob and turned to go home. But I took only a few steps before rage overcame my tears.

"You know— Screw you, Daniel," I snarled as I got in his face. "What did I do that was so wrong? I went looking for you when no one else would—nobody but me even noticed you weren't you! And

I kept at it until I knew you were home safe. So here's your chance. Tell me—which part of me saving your ungrateful ass made you hate me?"

"You should have left me alone!" he yelled right back. "I was fine where I was, until you screwed it up with that spell."

I sputtered wordlessly, too surprised to have a comeback ready. Finally I said, "You didn't look fine when we found you! You were running scared."

"Because of you—you didn't know what you were messing with."

"But…my spell was supposed to help. What are you talking about?"

"You don't get it—until your misguided attempt, I was having a great time over there," he said. "When I first arrived in Faerie, one of Lonan's kin—a good one—recognized me and took me under his wing. He took me around to meet musicians. Parties, feasts, dances—a blur of pleasure."

Like those orgies Lonan mentioned? I never would have believed it, if this wasn't Daniel fessing up to it himself.

Daniel went on. "The best time of my life, until you used your binding spell and tried to kick Lonan out of my body. It broke the glamour of Faerie, so I saw everything for what it was—"

His voice caught before he could speak again. "Avery, all the time that I'd been indulging myself with—there were girls there, human ones. And guys, too. Kidnapped and brought over in their bodies, unwillingly. Some of the Fae got their kicks by bewitching them to do things to each other. Sexually, yeah, but also hurting and maiming, and making them think it was all—the best they'd ever felt. And then the Fae would wake them up and let them realize they'd just spooned out another person's eyeballs and slurped them up like maraschino cherries—"

His voice faded to a whisper. I lifted a hand to try to comfort him, but he recoiled.

"And the worst part is, I don't know if I did anything like that. I get these flashes of memory, and I think maybe… How am I supposed to live with that?"

But none of the things he saw were my fault—he kind of took that risk when he signed up. No way he could hold me responsible for the fine print.

"Daniel, I'm so sorry, I didn't know—"

He stormed past me, but turned to say, "If you had just let me be, Lonan would have come and found me once he'd finished here. I could have come home blissfully ignorant. One of the changelings that comes back better, instead of half-mad."

His anguish, his anger, crashed over me, leaving me gasping as he went in the house.

There's no making up for this—no greeting card for "Sorry I screwed up your Faerie vacation and made you see things you can't unsee." But he has to know, on some level, that I'm not responsible, right?

I started to follow Daniel, until a sharp bark at the fence caught my attention. Lonan stood with his paws on the fence, and his best "Let me talk to him" expression on his face. When he was sure I understood, he dropped out of sight and swung through the doggy door.

And I went to Uncle Tam's and cried myself into a nap.

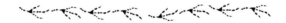

A persistent knocking woke me. I emerged from under my pillow, sweaty strands of hair plastered to my face. *Note to self: summer afternoons are not the best time of year to shut out the world with a pillow over your head.*

I groaned when I saw who it was outside the screen door. "Go away, Daniel."

"No, it's Lonan," he said. "Daniel's on sort of a time out. Can I talk to you?"

Damn, I am really out of it if I couldn't spot that was Lonan. I sighed. "Give me a minute to wash my face."

Feeling marginally better, I sank onto the back steps next to Lonan. He bumped my shoulder with his own, all buddy-buddy, but I just let it rock me without responding.

"The thing with Daniel earlier, that was pretty ugly," he said. "Are you okay?"

"Not really. How should I feel, with all that dumped on me?"

He fiddled with a hole in the sole of one shoe before he answered. "If it makes any difference, I talked to him."

I turned to him. "Did you know my binding spell would do that to Daniel?"

He held his hands out. "No way! I didn't think you had it in you to perform a decent spell, let alone one that could break the glamour of Faerie for Daniel."

"Um, thanks?" He ignored my sarcastic tone, so I asked, "What did you say to Daniel?"

"I told him how you'd thought of nothing but helping him. Taking Bobbin to the hospital—an absolute leap of faith. And coming after me, even as crazy as the evidence was, because you knew I was the key to getting Daniel back. That showed real loyalty. True devotion."

I snuck a sideways glance at Lonan. "Uncle Tam jokes that I was a terrier in a past life."

"He could be right. Craved any rats lately?"

"Uggh, no." I kicked his shin lightly. "So if you told Daniel all this, why isn't he here talking to me?"

Lonan's mischievous grin slipped. "Look, Avery, I don't think you get— Daniel is irrevocably changed from his time in Faerie. Once the glamour broke for him, he was thrown into a land where he didn't understand the rules. Not knowing who to trust—or whether he could even trust his own senses. Just a fight to keep it together and survive in hostile territory."

I thought about that for a minute and said in a small voice, "You make it sound like he's a refugee. Or a war veteran with PTSD."

"That's pretty apt. And he's going to need some time to readjust and feel safe again. In the meantime, he's going to lash out, make bad decisions. So cut him some slack, will you?"

"I can do that," I said. "And maybe we should be leaving Daniel out of our plans. Every time we talk about the Big Baddies, it must be like reopening a wound for him."

Lonan's dark eyebrows lowered in a V, like how kids draw birds in flight. "Avery, about that—I don't really need your help as much as I thought, either. Or at least, not enough to make it worth exposing you to more danger. It's better if you stay out of things until this is all over."

"You made a pretty convincing case for why I should help you before," I said skeptically. "What's changed—was it your brother coming after us in Faerie?"

I suddenly remembered I hadn't had a chance to tell him or Daniel about the weirdness at the Castle. "And speaking of your brother, could he—"

"We weren't speaking of my brother," Lonan said sharply. "And you'd be wise not to do anything else to draw his attention. Just let me do what I came here for, and you can get back to your normal life. With Daniel."

"But—" I started to say, only to find I was talking to his back as he walked away.

"Hey!" I hollered after him, but he ignored me. *Aauurgh!* If he'd been listening, I would have told him Daniel might have had the worst of it, but it was way too late for either of us to have a normal life again.

I stalked to the garage and took Nykur out for a drive. Afterwards, I fell asleep on the couch watching *Ancient Teenage Vampires in Love*. You know, just to put my own drama in perspective.

As promised, Daniel showed up in Uncle Tam's kitchen the next morning. Sheepish, and bearing his guitar. I let him stammer away at an apology while I sipped my coffee.

Uncle Tam came in and lifted Daniel into a hug, swinging him in his grasp like a bear with a salmon. I laughed, delighted that Daniel was now even more red-faced and sputtery.

"Where've you been keeping yourself, boy?" Uncle Tam let him down and clapped Daniel on the shoulder. "Nice to see you up close and personal, instead of in such a hurry that all you have time for is a wave."

Has Uncle Tam actually not seen Daniel in person since he got out of the hospital? Or when Lonan did, I guess. Come to think of it, we'd always met outside the house. The two had always been close, and maybe Lonan had been afraid Uncle Tam would spot him as a fraud.

"I've been around," Daniel said. "When do we get to jam again? I learned a few tricks since we last played."

"Tricks will only take you so far, m'boy. You need to have the art in you."

Daniel rolled his eyes and grinned, making it obvious they'd had this conversation before. "So, what is it you teach those students of yours? Tricks or art?"

"A little bit of both, as you well know." Uncle Tam winked and went to answer the door—his first student of the day.

"Should we go outside?" Daniel asked me.

"No, let's just go in the living room."

I shut the French doors so our voices wouldn't bother Uncle Tam in the music room next door. But after we settled uncomfortably on the couch, I regretted coming in here. I'd thought it would feel less awkward than the screen porch, with my bed offering the only seating. Instead, the broken-down cushions on the couch dragged us both into a dip in the middle. I had to use some fancy core-muscle moves to keep from entangling with Daniel.

He must have felt the awkward, too, because he cleared his throat and said, "You're still watching that vampire soap opera? How many times have you played those discs?"

"Making fun of my viewing habits is a curious way to say you're sorry."

He took my hand and forced my gaze to his. My façade of sulkiness fell away.

"Avery," he said, "instead of all this—this wrongness between us, tell me how it was supposed to be."

"Supposed to be?" I echoed, and held my breath.

"Yeah, like how it would have been if you'd gotten into town and I wasn't—gone. What would that have looked like?"

I rubbed my thumb across the fleshy part of his palm. "We would have been politely glad to see each other—at least in front of your parents. And Mom and Uncle Tam."

His eyes were only inches from mine as he let the couch dip bring us closer. "And once our parents weren't around?"

I chewed my lip before continuing. "After dark, we'd sneak to the barn and watch the owl bring dead voles to her puffball babies."

He raised an eyebrow, waiting me out. *Ugh! I already threw myself at Daniel once and that went over well—never mind that it was Lonan at the time— so why am I chickening out now? Here goes…* "And then—and then we'd lie back in the hay and I'd show you how much I missed you."

But he wasn't going to let me get away with a "fade to black" page break. "Show me how?"

I know Lonan said I should treat Daniel like he's different, but maybe this is a case where he craves normalcy. Like, how I would have treated him before.

I took a deep breath and threw a leg over his lap, the cushions sinking even further so I had to grab the back of the couch behind Daniel to keep from falling. I moved in for a kiss, but before there could be a hot melding of tongues, my pendant swung forward.

Clink. A distinct sound of metal hitting tooth enamel. He dumped me onto the floor as his hand flew to his mouth.

"Oh my God! Did I just chip your tooth?" I asked.

He felt around with his tongue and his fingertip. "I don't think so. It kind of hurt, but I don't feel anything different. Can you see anything?"

His parents had spent thousands of dollars on braces, and we both knew trouble awaited if we'd ruined the orthodontist's handiwork. I stood up, peering in his mouth as he turned side to side, his eyes wide with worry.

"It looks fine," I finally said, exhaling with relief.

He relaxed into the couch, and after a moment he said, "So, that was your big plan? Climb in my lap and clock me in the mouth? 'Cause I was expecting it to be hotter than that."

I laughed—way harder than his joke deserved—and sank onto the rug at the foot of the couch. "How 'bout I take my necklace off if we're going to try again?" I said.

In answer, he leaned forward and undid the clasp on my chain. Setting it on the side table, he began to rub my shoulders. And massaged the place at the base of my skull that he knew I loved. I settled back against the warmth of his legs and sighed.

Heat was spreading from his fingertips on my scalp to other points in my body. I reached to undo my top buttons. This time his hands barely brushed my shoulders as they moved down and forward, his rough skin snagging on the lace of my bra—

A sound at the French doors, and we jumped apart guiltily. *Uncle Tam would probably be cooler about catching us than our parents would, but still, it's so cliché to be caught petting on the couch.*

But instead of Uncle Tam, bat-wing ears and a brown snout filled a lower pane of glass in the door. A *skritch* sounded as Lonan pawed at the glass once more.

I started to get to my feet and let him in, but Daniel's hands on my shoulders shoved me down roughly. I rubbed my tailbone. "Ow! I was just going to see if it was something important—"

"Leave him," Daniel ordered in an icy tone I'd never heard before.

I turned around, the better to scowl at him. "Hey! Who died and made you boss?"

"Seriously, Avery—just decide where your loyalties lie. Him or me?"

It was too hard to scowl when my jaw wanted to drop, and the incredulous expression won out. "You think— Wait, was that an ultimatum? Where the hell did that come from?"

"I guess it was an ultimatum, but don't sound so surprised. Ever since I got back, it's obvious you're on way too friendly terms with the guy who stole my body. Keep in mind, if he gets you pregnant, the paternity test will show it's me."

A muffled growl came through the French doors just before I punched Daniel as hard as I could in the kneecap. He writhed in pain, his breath hissing in and out. Yeah, my fist didn't feel too hot, either, after hitting that knobby knee. *Screw cutting him some slack if he's going full asshole on me.*

I stood up, hands on my hips. "You're lucky I didn't punch you in the junk. That was really crossing the line, Daniel."

I took a few steps towards the door before turning back to say, "And for the record, this isn't me choosing Lonan, this is me *not* choosing you."

That would have been such a great exit line, but I made the mistake of looking at him. He seemed so deflated, so lost, that I relented. "You know what I wanted it to be like when I got into town? I wanted it to be simple—just us running into each other's arms and happily ever after. Not a complicated— This wrongness, like you said."

Daniel winced, but this time I think it was at the pain in my voice, not his throbbing knee. He hung his head in his hands, prompting me to speak softer. "Instead of the Disney fairytale, we got the Brothers Grimm-er version. It sucks, but we're going to have to deal with it."

And whatever he said next was going to tell me if we were going to deal with it together. The tension stretched, until he finally said, "You're right. I'm sorry I— That paternity test comment was a low blow."

I exhaled in relief. "Okay." Not forgiving him, exactly, but acknowledging his apology. "What now?"

He suddenly straightened, his posture of defeat and shame falling away. "Did you mean that? About how you wished it was simple, like love in a fairy tale?"

"Yes. Isn't it supposed to be easier? If it's meant to be?"

He nodded. "It could be easy. I could…make it easier for you."

He sounded so strangely euphoric now. *I'm going to get whiplash from all his mood swings. But if he's willing to try and make up, can I do any less?* "I'd like that."

"Will you come back and sit with me?"

I sat—but on the rug, not on the couch. He got up and walked to the door, and I thought he was going to let Lonan in after all. But he pushed in the lock on the doorknob and picked up his guitar case instead. In the hallway, the doggy ears drooped and Lonan sighed as he lay on the hardwood.

Daniel perched on the edge of the couch and took out his guitar. I hadn't heard him play anything since last summer, so my curiosity stirred. *Has he picked up some new music in Faerie, so something good actually came from his time there?* The tuning didn't sound any different.

Then he played some chords, and the notes were so beautiful they were almost visible. Like crystalline birds hovering in the air. "Wow," I breathed.

He grinned and launched into more show-offy playing before settling into a song. A slow, plaintive waltz. I swayed in time, eyes closed, relaxing into the rhythm. *Why were we even fighting? This is Daniel, the boy I've known and loved since forever.*

My eyes flew open as he started to sing.

If all the rivers turned to ice
And frost rode on the wind
If all the lands were covered in snow
I'd warm myself by the heat of your skin.

I'd never heard him like this. His voice, his words, filled every corner of me. Until I wasn't just me, I was an extension of him. With every note, the distinctions between us blurred. My every breath was *Daniel*.

If all the oceans boiled away
And ashes filled the skies
If all the lands were wasted and bare
I'd drink my fill from the love in your eyes.

I crawled across the floor, my eyes never leaving his. I needed to be closer to him, needed to get my skin against his. Somewhere far off, a dog howled, claws scrabbling against glass and wood. Daniel smiled and I was dazzled all over again.

If all the—

The doors burst open behind me in a hail of splinters and glass. A voice roared something unintelligible, something inhuman, and Daniel flew back as his guitar shattered.

As the last shrieks and twangs from the guitar strings stilled, I found myself flattened to the floor with a furry body stretched protectively across my back. I risked a look over my shoulder and, framed in the doorway, saw a figure of awesome fury.

Slitting my eyes against the blinding energy, the figure seemed to shrink until it was just the size of… "Uncle Tam?"

Uncle Tam's gaze darted to me when I spoke, but he went right back to glowering at Daniel. "Explain yourself, Daniel," he said through gritted teeth.

Daniel, pale and shaking, said, "I didn't—I had no idea it would be so strong here. It was just a love song back in Faerie."

In spite of Uncle Tam's interruption, Daniel's song still thrummed in my ears. What's more, his shame and fear burned through me like it was my own. When Uncle Tam took a few steps towards him, I grabbed a shard of glass and rolled to my feet, putting myself between Daniel and the threat.

"You stay away from him," I warned. Uncle Tam raised his hands but kept coming. "I mean it!" I slashed wildly with my glass dagger.

"Avery, just let me—" Uncle Tam started to say, but hastily backed up when I lunged at him, growling.

"Daniel," Uncle Tam tried, "fix this."

Waves of panic came from Daniel, and my own agitation rose. "I won't let anyone hurt Daniel! I'll die first!" A sensation like electricity crackling over my skin raised all the hairs on my body.

"Shit! I don't know what to do!" Daniel said. "God—she's bleeding! That glass—"

"I know, Daniel, but she needs you to stay calm," Uncle Tam said. "You're making it worse. Help her."

"Help her how?"

Uncle Tam's eyes went to my partly unbuttoned shirt. "If she'll let you, I need you to put her necklace back on her."

"Necklace?" Daniel repeated, bewildered. Then he scrabbled among the debris and came up with a gleam of gold in his hand.

"Avery?" He took a tentative step towards me. "Will you let me put this on you?"

"Of course, Daniel." I smiled. The electrical hum in my ears died and I felt only peace and love. "You can do anything you want with me."

My words made him flinch, but he raised his arms to clasp the gold chain around my neck. It settled onto my chest and a different kind of heat radiated through my veins. Complete clarity followed it, and I sank to my knees. *Was that love? That all-consuming feeling I had for Daniel just a few seconds ago?*

The shard of glass fell from my bloodied hand, and I cried out from the deferred pain. Lonan pressed himself against my leg, whimpering along with me.

I looked from Uncle Tam, who stood with his arms folded, to Daniel. Who refused to look at me. "What the— Was that a spell, Daniel? Did you put a spell on me?"

"Yeah," he said, so low that I almost didn't hear him. "But I didn't know— This isn't what I wanted to happen."

"Wasn't it?" Uncle Tam asked. Daniel, stricken, still wouldn't meet my eyes.

"But Uncle Tam, how did you know—" I said, before he interrupted me.

"Avery, go in the kitchen and fill a bowl with water. I'll be in to help you with that hand. But first, Daniel and I are going to have a little talk about using Fae magic in my house."

Now Daniel was sullen, like a kid caught out after curfew. When Lonan started to follow me, Daniel said, "If we're talking about Fae magic, *he* may as well stay in the room."

"The dog?" Uncle Tam's puzzlement lasted only a moment as he bent to peer closer at Lonan. When Lonan made a run for it, Uncle Tam grabbed him by the scruff. "Not a dog! A body thief, under my own nose!"

His roar was like when he'd blasted the doors, and I was terrified of him all over again. But when his fingers closed around Lonan's throat, I did my best to pry them off. My blood painted all of us red, but still I cried desperately, "Don't! Stop—don't hurt him!"

Lonan dropped to the ground, coughing, and Uncle Tam said, "I wasn't hurting him. I was bespelling him to speak."

"*Slainte*, Tam Lin," Lonan said. I froze in the midst of checking him for injuries.

Uncle Tam huffed. "You. And what are you doing here?"

"Wait," I said, "did he just call you Tam Lin? Like the fairy tale?"

Uncle Tam shrugged off my question—*what, did the spell turn me invisible, too?*—and said, "Answer me, corbin."

"The same reason you came back years ago. To stop my brother," Lonan said.

"They sent *you?*" Uncle Tam's voice dripped disbelief. "Because you did such a good job the last time? You'll likely get some poor girl killed again. Do you even think of Mariah?"

Silence lay heavy in the room, and Lonan hung his head. "I do," he whispered hoarsely. "I wanted another chance to make things right. I owe her that." He raised his head to look at me, brown eyes pleading. "Avery, there's a lot I couldn't tell you—"

"And you shouldn't be telling her any more," Uncle Tam interrupted. "Her involvement stops right now. Do you hear, both of you?" He looked to Lonan and Daniel, waiting for them each to nod. "I haven't spent years protecting her from the temptations of Faerie, only to have you two undo it with one misguided spell."

"And Avery," he continued, "get that bleeding stopped and—"

"I've had enough ordering and controlling today," I said. "You can all go to hell."

Nykur intercepted me at the back door, and I willingly climbed in. A cup of Kahlua gelato with chocolate cookie crumbles awaited me. *Finally, someone who actually cares about what I want and need.*

He also provided a jar of aromatic herbal ointment for my hand. And cottony bandages that looked like compressed spiderwebs.

"What is this," I asked, "some kind of Faerie first-aid kit? Are you sure it won't turn me into a frog or something?"

"♫It's good, good, good,♪" the radio crackled.

"You'll understand if I'm a little distrustful of magic at the moment," I said.

I rubbed some of the salve between my fingers. A faint tingling, but no warts or amphibian skin came from it. I spread a healthy dollop onto my palm and sighed as it numbed almost instantly. The webby bandages stuck all on their own, and I hoped this would be enough to keep the wound clean.

Now that the throbbing in my hand had stopped, I was unfortunately able to focus on other pain. Like thinking that Daniel had actually tried to turn me into some love zombie. Torn between anger that he'd do such a thing and sympathy for how broken he'd become, I found myself making excuses for him.

Like, he sounded sincere when he'd told Uncle Tam he didn't expect it to go like that. And he'd seemed so upset when it went wrong. But if he had been trying to spell me, where had that impulse come from? *Jealousy? Loneliness?*

I mean, Daniel must feel like no one understands what he went through, and it's true that I don't, not really. Lonan's advice to cut Daniel some slack came back to me and I decided to give Daniel the benefit of the doubt—for now. *But if he tries anything like that again, all bets are off.*

I sighed and settled further into the upholstery. There must have been some sleepytime herbs in the ointment, too, because I dozed off soon after. I awoke around midnight, reclined in my seat in the medicinal-smelling car. But my hand didn't hurt—unless it was being drowned out by the pangs of my full bladder.

Should I drive to the gas station and use their skanky facilities, or brave Uncle Tam and a lecture? My knee jigged in a pee-pee dance—*the house it is.*

As soon as I came through the back door, Uncle Tam called, "Avery?" from the kitchen.

"Be there in a sec!" I answered, already in the bathroom. *Ah, sweet relief.* I lingered afterwards, washing up and marveling at my newly healed hand, generally dawdling to avoid facing Uncle Tam.

But I couldn't put it off forever.

I walked into the kitchen, and Uncle Tam, Daniel, and Lonan looked up from a pile of scattered books and scrolls.

"Oh, yay. The gang's all here," I said. "Or are the Tooth Fairy and Snow White running late? Did Sleeping Beauty hit the snooze button?"

Uncle Tam sighed in annoyance, but Lonan let a doggy grin show his appreciation of my snark.

"We need to clear a few things up, young lady," Uncle Tam said.

"That's no lady, that's—" Uncle Tam quelled Lonan's Groucho Marx imitation with one look. But I was still mad enough about Uncle Tam trying to order me around earlier that The Glare didn't work on me.

"Fine," I said. "Should I start? I have lots of questions. Like, are you really the Tam Lin from the fairy encyclopedia? And what does my necklace have to do with all this? And how do you know Lonan? Where did Nykur—"

"Whoa, whoa," Uncle Tam said. "Slow down—I've every intention of answering your questions."

"I thought we weren't supposed to tell her anything else," Daniel said.

Daniel had The Glare turned on him as Uncle Tam said, "Some explanation is in order. Thanks to you two, she knows enough to put herself in danger. I've changed my mind; it's better that she know some things, so she's not left vulnerable."

"Excuse me?" I said. "So far, I'm the one who got Daniel out of danger, *and* who discovered the corbin."

Ignoring my outburst, Uncle Tam chose to answer my questions instead. "Yes, I am the Tam Lin the Queen took a fancy to all those centuries ago. I was your age when it happened, but I didn't grow any older while I was in Faerie. Only when I came home to our world again."

"When Lonan tried to stop the Big Baddies before?" I asked.

He shook his head. "That was the third time I returned. I came back the first time when the Queen and I had…when we were on a break, I suppose you could say. I came to London, with a few select corbin and nykurs, for a weeklong…holiday."

Lonan raised a paw to his muzzle and let out a cough that sounded like "debauch."

Uncle Tam continued like he hadn't been interrupted. "But I got a barmaid with child, so I stayed for a time and helped to raise the boy before the Queen found me and we made up. I lost track of my bloodline while I was in Faerie again, but I looked into it once I was back here in the thirties. Found your grandfather, the Avery Flynn you're named for."

"So you and I are actually related? You're like my great-great-great-great-great—"

"Great-grandfather many times over," he said with a grin. But then his smile faded. "That Avery was normal, but your father and yourself...you both have a tetch of the Sight, like me. A way about you that the Fae are both fascinated by and afeared of."

I had to suppress a grin—now that Uncle Tam's guard was down, his lilt and old-fashioned words were coloring his speech like crazy. "Why would they be afraid of me?"

"The way you get distracted—it's because you notice things that don't fit. You and I, we're constantly analyzing, looking for patterns. So, if one little bit of Faerie glamour is out of place, it's a blinking red neon sign to us. It was a valuable survival trait in my day, but causes all kinds of problems in modern human society.

"The Sight is both dangerous to the Fae, in case we out them, and fascinating to them because they can't fool us the way they do other humans."

"So Lonan was right?" I asked. "I am magical?"

Disappointment flickered in his eyes before he said, "No—that's just your necklace. I gave it to you after...after your father got involved with the Fae, and it helps filter your ability to notice things. The pendant also protects you from the Fae's attentions, since they keep tabs on Michael even when he's in our world. I couldn't risk him endangering you, too."

"Dad knows about the Fae? That explains his artwork, but not why you've let me think he's crazy or a druggie all these years. Why couldn't you explain it to me earlier?"

"He's made his choice, but I wanted to keep you out of the Fae's reach. In spite of my own history—or perhaps because of it—I've become convinced that humans are better off with no Fae interference. Like so many others, your father was ruined by his trips to Faerie—he came back different."

"Restless, and bitter," I said. Daniel felt my eyes on him and looked stricken. "So that's why things went bad. They fought all the time until my mom kicked him out."

"And straight back into his Fae lover's arms. He's been back and forth several times since then, leaving him unstable."

"All this time, Mom blamed it on drugs or drinking," I said sadly. She'd even been overly worried about me following in his footsteps, but so far my only addiction was those hazelnut chocolate bars.

"Addiction is as good a comparison as any. It's a torment—when you're in one land, you always long for the other. Never completely happy in either, no matter your ties to loved ones."

I thought of that perfect, Ozian meadow and how easy it would be to just lie in the flowers forever. Even knowing that would be a bad choice didn't stop a small twinge of longing. "But I've been to Faerie, and I don't feel like that," I said.

"Hmm, I'll want to hear the details of that trip to Faerie, young lady. You were lucky you had the pendant's protection, but it's not inexhaustible, Avery," Uncle Tam warned. "I've been recharging it with my own magic, but I have less and less to draw on as the years pass. I was never a magical creature myself—I just absorbed a lot of magic and knowledge from my time in Faerie.

"And giving the pendant to you in the first place may have backfired—it suppressed your Sight, but that seems to mean that when it came back, it came back stronger. Those bipolar episodes are when the magical defenses and the meds are struggling for dominance."

"So, instead of all those psychiatrist appointments, I should have been seeing a witch doctor or something?"

Uncle Tam gave me a token smile, but said, "You were barely ten years old, that time when they switched your meds. How much do you remember about your hospitalization?"

"Honestly…not much. They were trying me on so many different combinations of pills that the weeks before and after it are a blur now. All I remember is being scared, and angry, and helpless-feeling. And ashamed that there was something wrong with me."

He nodded. "Well, you'd already been put on some mild treatments by then, because your Sight and your young age meant you had trouble distinguishing between what was 'real' and what was glimpses you were getting of Fae activity. If your mom hadn't been so, um, prepared to look for mental illness after your dad's behaviors, she may have dismissed your stories as an overactive imagination.

"But as it was, she insisted you be put on some medications—and they did help, as much as I was against suppressing your gift in the first place. But then...she let you go visit your dad. Who, unbeknownst to your mother, had just come back from a long stint in Faerie, and brought his lover back with him."

I sat up straighter. "So...I met a Fae before Lonan?"

"Not really. Corriell was glamoured pretty heavily to be invisible, but you were aware on some level that something wasn't right. You'd likely only been exposed to weaker glamours before, and once faced with a stronger magic—and a Fae in person—your Sight surged to overcome your medications and protect you by revealing Corriell. It was only coincidence that they'd switched your meds right before then, and blamed your so-called 'break with reality' on that.

"I wasn't able to keep your mom from overmedicating you, since I couldn't explain what was really happening, but I gave you the pendant soon after. It helped filter out other instances of Fae glamour, so that you weren't triggered again so badly."

I scoffed. "Well, hey, thanks for that—but maybe I would have been better prepared for Fae-fighting if you'd just let me in on the big secret in the first place. With your way, I could have walked right into a fairy mound and been unable to See it—and unable to protect myself."

I let out a sigh, rubbing my eyes tiredly. I'd hit information overload, and Uncle Tam picked up on it.

"I think that's enough for now," he said. "Why don't you go to bed, Avery? Lonan and I are comparing notes on some spells for the full moon. Daniel, if you'd be so kind as to lend him your body once again, we'll make better progress."

I didn't wait to see if he agreed, just turned on my heel and went to bed.

As I was falling asleep, I felt a warm, furry body crawl under the sheet with me.

"Daniel?" I whispered. "Can you talk in Bobbin's body now, too?"

"Yeah," he said. "I won't bother you, but I wanted to say how sorry I am about—everything."

I didn't answer, but I pulled him in close, our breath synchronizing until we both fell asleep.

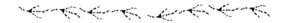

Raised voices woke me way too early the next morning. Still bleary-eyed, my hand reached for Daniel but felt only space beside me.

I followed the argument to the kitchen, and was greeted by the strange sight of a dog standing on the kitchen table pointing to a scroll.

"You see, right here, it says I need to speak the *dugh* section of this spell," Lonan was saying.

"But not for the blue moon, that changes everything—" Uncle Tam countered, before noticing I was standing there. His hair stood up in all directions, and even his beard was rumpled, like he'd been pulling on it in frustration. "You're up, then."

"Yeah," I said. *Like anyone could sleep through you two.* "Where's Daniel?"

"He took the body to get some rest," Lonan said. "I was up all night in it, but Bobbin was bright-eyed, so we switched again."

"What about you, Unc—Tam Lin? Did you sleep?"

"Call me Uncle Tam like usual—no need to make it more confusing than it already is. No, I didn't sleep. I'm trying to talk some sense into this pup."

Lonan's hackles rose, and the gruffness already present in his dog-channeled voice deepened to a growl. "I know what I'm doing and I don't need your help—"

I laughed and they both turned to me, startled. "Sorry," I said. "It's like watching Gandalf and Scrappy Doo argue. You're both ridiculous. Why don't you take a break?"

Uncle Tam looked offended, then sheepish. "You're right. We don't have much time before the blue moon, but we need to have clear heads for this. I'll go wash up."

He left Lonan and me in the kitchen, and Lonan got down off the table to stick his head in the fridge when I opened it.

"Do you have any bacon? Or ham? Something meaty-smoky for Bobbin?"

"Oh, it's for Bobbin? Not for you?"

"Yes—he's in here, I told you. And he says he'd settle for some of that blue cheese he can smell in the cheese drawer."

"No way, I'm not choking on dog farts for the rest of the day. He can have a little yogurt and some carrots."

Lonan made a long, drawn-out gagging noise but ate his treat anyway while I munched my cereal.

"What is it like with Bobbin in there? Does it throw him off every time you guys switch? He seemed kind of upset in the hospital after you left him for Daniel's body."

"He's honestly the most easy-going creature I've ever met. Bobbin's up for just about anything—life is just one big, joyous car ride for him. I would say he's a hairier version of The Dude, but The Dude's pretty hairy.

"And…I think he was upset because he thought Daniel would come back right away when I left his doggy body. But he doesn't hang onto disappointment or negative emotions very long."

I resolved to take Bobbin on more car rides, to make up for his hitchhikers and their agendas.

Lonan managed to look hangdog when I shut him out of the bathroom while I showered, and when I came out, he said, "Let's go do something fun, before Tam Lin sucks all the enjoyment out of the day."

"Hey! I like Uncle Tam. Watch what you say about him."

"Sorry—but you like him even when he's ordering you around? Because there's probably more of that in store. For me, too."

"Hmm, good point," I said. "Up for some ice cream?" Having ice cream right after breakfast seemed like a harmless way to rebel.

Lonan wriggled all over in delight. "Oh, yes—do they still have bacon caramel?"

We walked into town and sat outside the ice-cream shop at a table. Lonan kept up a running whispered commentary of wicked remarks about the passersby, making me laugh so hard that superfudge shake came out my nose. *Which is not nearly as fun as it sounds.*

While I was busy clearing chocolate from my nostrils, he must have slipped away. When I finally looked for him, the collar and leash hung slack from the table leg.

"Lonan!" I whisper-shouted. "We agreed you'd wear that in public."

I stood and spotted him a few doors down, by the bookstore. They had a bench out front with a bronze Mark Twain statue seated on it, in honor of Clemens's stint in the Gold Country as a journalist. A couple in their twenties were sharing the bench, eating breakfast pastries and making goo-goo eyes at each other. Obviously refueling for more macking.

Lonan sat at the foot of the statue, staring, waiting for them to notice him. *I should grab him, but he left half his bacon caramel cup to melt while he begs from strangers? There has to be more to it than this.*

After the couple finally spotted him and fed him bits of crust, Lonan put his diabolical plan into place. Maintaining eye contact with the happy couple all the while, he carefully positioned himself on Mark Twain's leg and started pumping like an oil derrick. Humped that bronze leg like it was his bitch, staring fixedly at the now-horrified couple.

I doubled over with laughter as they beat a hasty retreat. The woman dropped what was left of her bear claw and turned to pick it up, but the guy said, "Just leave it!" and dragged her away. Lonan abandoned his hump-fest and picked up the pastry, prancing back with it in his mouth.

I scooped him up and said, "That was simultaneously the most disgusting, uncomfortable, and hilarious thing I've ever seen. Like all great comedy should be. I love you!"

And of course, as soon as those last three words were out of my mouth, I turned around to see Daniel behind us. After an uncomfortable moment that wasn't funny at all, Daniel said, "Tam's looking for Lonan. We're supposed to switch again so he can try out some spell."

"Oh," I said, before setting Lonan down. Once they'd transferred, Lonan winked at me as he opened Daniel's car door.

"We'll just walk," Daniel said.

Lonan looked to me and I nodded. He shrugged. "Catch you guys later."

Daniel submitted to me putting the collar and leash on him without a word. I grabbed my bag and we headed back up the hill in silence.

When he finally spoke, Daniel picked up right in the middle of a conversation I didn't know we were having. "I probably lost the right to ask you this question with that stunt I pulled yesterday, but I want to know. Are you falling for Lonan?"

"What?" I stopped walking. "Is this because you heard me say 'I love you' to Lonan when he was trying to cheer me up? We were just screwing around, Daniel."

He sat, looking for all the world like a well-trained dog. But his gaze was too human. "You know, it never would have worked with you and me—at least, not the old me," he said.

"Wow—that's a lot of... How do you know it wouldn't have worked? You didn't give us much of a chance, and I made it clear I was totally in love with you."

He scrambled up a low stone wall so we were closer to the same level. "That's just it—I don't think you were in love with me."

"What?" I exploded. "How can you say that, after everything?"

"I think you were in love with the idea of me. Or with a version of me you thought you could bring out. Admit it—once you started seeing me as boyfriend material, you changed. *We* changed."

I spluttered. *There are so many things wrong with that, I don't know where to start. Did he take a Human Psych class in Faerie and now he thinks he's an expert?*

But Daniel continued, "Avery, what kind of picture did you have of us being together? Not that reunion scene—but if we'd been a couple, what did you dream about us doing after high school?"

That was an easier question. "We'd travel, probably. I'd take pictures while we hitchhiked all across Europe, South America, and the U.S. Maybe get some writing in. Connubial bliss—all that."

"And where do any of my wants and plans fit into that? Music, for example? College?"

"Well, music, you can do that anywhere. And you could study overseas…" That's all I had. "How did you picture it?"

"That's just it—when I pictured stuff like that, you weren't there. I mean, I didn't consciously think of it that way, but it's the truth."

Ouch—that one hurts. It sounds so final—like his feelings for me have totally changed, and mine are playing catch-up. "Was there someone else in your picture?"

"That's not what I meant—" He broke off in frustration. "It would just be easier if you weren't— I don't know how to say this without really hurting you."

So don't say it, I begged him with my eyes. But he seemed to have been working up his nerve and plowed on.

"Look, ever since we were kids, whenever I didn't want to do something, you'd drag me into it anyway and tell me it'd be good for me. Always pushing me—not just out of my comfort zone, but out of my tolerance zone. It got so it was easier to just go along with you, and then you stopped asking what I wanted altogether."

His words stung, but I owed him at least a few seconds of pondering. *Can he be right—even just a little bit?* I'd always been more daring, and prodded him to keep up, but it was for his own good. *For his own good*—that's what he'd just said I'd used as my excuse to bully him.

But that couldn't have been the basis of our entire relationship. We'd had lots of good memories, too. *Or at least, I think we did.*

I blurted, "What about us kissing in the barn? You weren't exactly lying there like a log while I macked on you."

He hung his head, ears flattening back in a classic dog-shame pose. "That was a mistake. I wanted to believe that if I threw myself into it, all the rough patches would just smooth over. And they did while we were kissing—but they came back once you'd left town. So I sent that text."

That's why this wrenching pain feels so familiar—it's just like getting that text all over again. And it doesn't seem like I have much say in it this time around, either.

"After you backed off, I thought if only you would talk to me—I could convince you to see things my way," I said. *Crap, I just confirmed what he's accusing me of.*

"Yeah, and I knew you might be able to. It was better to just cut you out of my life for a while."

But now my anger was overpowering the hurt. "Better for you? Daniel, you could have told me this before. Sure, nobody likes to have their flaws pointed out and I might not have listened right away. But if it meant not having you in my life, even as a friend, I would have changed things. Cutting me off was classic, passive-aggressive Daniel behavior. And not fair to either of us."

We parted ways at the gate to his yard, but as I took off his leash Daniel said, "Avery, I didn't get a chance to say—I wanted to warn you that you shouldn't blindly trust Lonan. And even Tam knows more than he's letting on—I heard things in Faerie that made me think he wasn't just a decoration on the Queen's arm. He had ambitions, too."

"Seriously? Now you have some kind of conspiracy theory about Uncle Tam? He's been trying to protect me."

"Protect you from who? Maybe you should ask."

"That should be 'whom,'" I shot back. *Oh, what a comeback, Avery— slay him with your grammar-liness.* "And maybe I will ask him," I muttered, but Daniel had already disappeared through the swinging dog door.

Lonan and Uncle Tam were back to arguing in the kitchen. I left them to it and flopped onto my bed. I meant to rest, but my brain took closing my eyes as an invitation to go into high gear instead.

I struggled to find a way through my own pain and defensiveness, but my mind had hit overload. It wasn't just the conversation with Daniel—it was all the things from the last few weeks. Learning about corbin, and Faerie, and monsters—and Uncle Tam being Tam Lin.

And Daniel raising the possibility that I hadn't either known or loved him well enough was just the icing on the cake left out in the rain.

Was I so caught up in a vision of us as a perfect couple that I missed the changes in Daniel? How else could I not know how serious he's gotten about his music? Serious enough that he'd been planning on spending time jamming with the Fae, before the switch with Lonan went wrong.

And wait just a minute—he planned that switch for right before I got into town. Just to avoid me?

I would have liked to think that if I'd known about the music, the volunteering at the hospital, the water polo tryouts, I would have been supportive of Daniel. *With a minimum of teasing.* After all, I'd thought I was helping by pushing him before. *When I was really just pushing him further away.*

On that depressing note, I managed to slip into a doze, but it wasn't a restful one, what with the occasional raised voice through the wall. Lonan and Uncle Tam needed a time out, but they'd both been so determined to keep me out of the blue moon plans that I wasn't sure if they would listen to me at this point. Until I eavesdropped on their argument and realized I was holding an important card in their reindeer games.

I slid into a chair at the kitchen table and waited for them to notice my extreme smugness.

Lonan spotted my smirk first and stopped mid-sentence. "I don't know what you're up to, Avery, but you can forget it."

"But you haven't even heard what I have to say."

Uncle Tam and Lonan exchanged aggravated looks. "Avery, we settled this already," Uncle Tam said. "You're staying out of the way, out of trouble."

I shrugged and dipped into the packet of cookies on the table. "Fine," I said, spewing crumbs. "But don't blame me when you miss your one opportunity to stop the Big Baddies because you're in the wrong place at the blue moon."

That got Lonan's attention, considering he'd just been arguing with Uncle Tam about that very thing.

"Not you, too," Uncle Tam groaned. "The Druid's Cave is where they tried to come through before. It's the most obvious place for them to try again because the borders are already weakened there."

I nodded agreeably, still smiling around a mouthful of chocolate chip cookie. "It *is* the obvious gateway," I said. "That's why it's the perfect decoy. But you're forgetting there's another place with a connection to Lonan and the last attempt."

"We don't have time for guessing games—" Uncle Tam started to say, but Lonan talked over him.

"So you think it's the Castle, too?"

"Ding-ding-ding," I said. "I think your brother, or one of his nefarious minions, has taken over Mr. Forrest."

I brought them up to speed with my freaky encounter at the Castle. "And he said I'm marked now—so I don't think you can keep me out of this, Uncle Tam. It's too late."

"Cack," Lonan muttered.

Uncle Tam barked a laugh, but I doubted he thought any of this was actually funny. "Change of plans," he said. "From now on, you're with me or Lonan at all times, Avery."

"Why am *I* being punished?" Lonan whined, but winked at me.

"Take this seriously, boy," Uncle Tam said. "We'll need to split up for the blue moon. Cover both possibilities. Which means we need to stop dilly-dallying about choosing a spell, so we have time to learn it and present a unified front."

Even though that sounded pretty decisive, arguing about which spell to use was exactly what they did for the next ten minutes. I'd had enough.

I blurted, "This is so lame! You guys are both full of threats about what could happen if we fail, and you can't even come together over which spell to use. Is it possible this is part of the Big Baddies' sinister plans? Divide and conquer?"

Uncle Tam's brow turned thunderous and he started to say, "You have no idea what's involved with magic—"

"So explain it to me," I said. "Look, Uncle Tam, I may not have any knowledge of spells and magic, but I do have a brain. A brain that you pointed out is highly analytical and able to see patterns and relationships where others don't. So, why not put it to use?"

He sputtered, but I didn't give him a chance to say anything before hammering home my argument. "Plus, you've said so many times that the best way for someone to understand something is for them to teach or explain it to others. Here's your chance to put your money where your motto is."

Uncle Tam stood there, frozen between looking angry and chagrined, but Lonan stood and clapped.

"That's my Avery," he crowed.

"Hey, don't patronize me," I said, turning on him. "You're perfectly willing to keep me in the dark when it suits you."

He raised his hands—and his eyebrows—in surrender and sat down without another word. In the silence of the room, a rhythmic whistling sound filled the space. It took a few seconds before I realized it was air passing through my highly flared nostrils. *Must maintain my righteous scowl*—a laugh won out.

Lonan joined in, and Uncle Tam gave a resigned shake of the head as we howled. "Hopeless," he said. "You two are as alike as pixies from the same pod."

Our mirth wound down and I sat next to Lonan. "Okay," I said, "now that's out of the way, you guys can tell me about these spells you have in mind."

Lonan dragged out the ancient scroll he'd been carrying around all week, and Uncle Tam showed me a spell taking up a few pages in his well-worn, handwritten journal.

"My spell is a much better choice," Uncle Tam said. "It's compiled from snippets I picked up in Faerie—pieces and poems with a history of success against the dark Fae. And notes from *A Compendium of the Faer Folke*."

Lonan shook his head. "But they were never meant to be used together as a whole—stringing them together may give you entirely unexpected results. This spell came from the Queen's own library."

"But there's some cut off the bottom," Uncle Tam insisted. "You can't know it's complete—"

"The answer's obvious," I said, breaking in on their millionth rehash of Team Scroll and Team Book. They both turned to me, matching expressions of fatigue and frustration on their faces. "Uncle Tam, you've already said we're going to have to split up. And Lonan, you told me instincts are really important.

"So, each of you use whichever spell fits you best. This isn't an either/or situation. I can't believe you didn't see that days ago."

Lonan's brows shot up from his scowl. "That's the… Why *didn't* we see it?"

"Because it's a crock of—" Uncle Tam said, but broke off when I stood up so suddenly my chair clattered to the floor. "What is it, Avery?"

"I'm not sure," I answered slowly. *Something about Uncle Tam doesn't look right.* Whenever he turned his head, there was just the barest glint of something catching the light. I touched the side of his head, and my hand came away sticky and stringy.

"Eww!" I tried to wipe off the webbing stuck to me, but it clung to my skin.

Lonan looked from me to Uncle Tam and sucked in a ragged breath. Like a bizarre beanie pulled too low, spidery webs wrapped around Uncle Tam's head, covering his eyes and ears in a filmy veil.

"What the hell is that?" I reached out to yank it off, but Lonan grabbed my arm.

"Don't touch it again!" he cried. "Do you have one of those kits in here—the bread cubes and St. John's wort?"

I pulled an old ice cream tub out of the freezer, cracking the lid to show my anti-Fae arsenal nestled inside.

Uncle Tam blanched. "You shouldn't leave food where the ants can get it."

"Since when do ants get in the freezer?"

Lonan stepped closer, bringing my attention back to the current dilemma. "Ignore anything he says at this point—he's just trying to divert you," he said. "Use a wand of St. John's wort to brush that stuff off."

"Okay," I said, "but first…" I darted my hand at Lonan's head, and came away with another stringy mess. "You have it, too, whatever it is."

"Stop using your hand before it spreads to you! Try the herbs on Tam Lin."

I rolled my eyes at his tone and did as he said. When the St. John's wort touched the strands on Uncle Tam's face, the webbing smoked faintly and shriveled away. The odor of burning hair or fingernails intensified as I applied the same method to Lonan.

"Uggh!" I coughed at the puff of smoke rising from my previously bewebbed palms. "What was that?"

Uncle Tam shook his head dazedly as Lonan answered, "It's a cloud veil—spun by spidery little creatures called lycorises. It looks like Tam had it first and it was spreading to me."

"Wait—are there spidery things on us?" I started slapping my clothing in a panic. "My truce with spiders only applies when they are not actually on my person."

"The lycoris is probably long gone. Once they've done their work, there's no reason for them to stay."

I paused in pulling off my T-shirt and tried to regain some no-spiders-on-me calm. "I still don't understand—what does a cloud veil do?"

"Exactly what you pointed out—it keeps the victims from seeing reason, from hearing sense. So instead they just argue in circles, unable to escape their illogical spiral."

I snorted a laugh and said, "Sounds like that hour of C-SPAN my poli sci teacher made us watch. You guys were really getting on my nerves—and each other's."

"Well, if I'd been in my own form, it wouldn't have affected me at all," Lonan said. "You humans are such easy targets for this kind of spell."

I drawled, "And yet, you didn't spot it on Uncle Tam before you were infected—a lowly human did."

"Well, you're not exactly defenseless, and Tam is known to be somewhat…"

"Opinionated?" Uncle Tam finished for him, back to his own glare-y self.

"Exactly," Lonan said blandly. "How would I notice the difference?"

After an awkward silence, they got back down to business—peacefully this time, leaving me to shuffle through the scrolls scattered on the table. Some looked truly ancient, feeling like mummified lambs or desert roadkill under my fingers. Not that I went around stroking either of those things, but if I did this was exactly what it'd feel like. And possibly smell like, too.

Hey, this one's tingly... I went back to a scroll I'd set aside. Sure enough, my fingers prickled when I touched it. And the writing and strange drawings seemed to shift under my gaze. I could have sworn it wasn't in English when I first noticed it, but now I could read the words as easily as my own name.

"What's this one?" I asked, waving it.

Uncle Tam barely paused in his pontificating, just long enough to glance at the page and say, "That's an expulsion spell. Not strong enough for this case."

I stared at it again. *Something about it seems more important than it looks at first glance.* The words were all about restoring balance. Anchoring things to their rightful place. "Still, don't you think it'd be useful to know this one, just in case?"

Lonan turned his attention to me and said, "Maybe you should learn it. It might be good practice for you."

I grinned, glad to feel like there might be something I could contribute, after all. The expulsion spell turned out to be a bust, though—it banished any Fae within a mile radius of the casting, making it useless if I wanted to keep Lonan around a while longer. *And I do want to spend more time with Lonan, to see if there's anything more to this chemistry.*

That thought made me go suddenly still.

Where did that come from? Am I falling for Lonan, like Daniel suspects? Because that just opened up all kinds of complications. *This isn't just lust, is it, or some kind of rebound thing from Daniel?* The honest answer was, this did have something to do with Daniel and our talk, because now I didn't feel like I needed to hold back for Daniel's sake. I'd been fighting my attraction to Lonan out of a misplaced sense of loyalty to a guy who didn't even want me that way.

But I don't want to make the mistake of not seeing things as they really are again. I studied Lonan from the corner of my eye, trying to see him with some objectivity. *What do I know about him as a person, not just as a corbin?* I ran through some traits in my head—he was really fun to be around, we had the same twisted sense of humor, and he was so open to new things. I mean, in that brief period after the coma, when I'd thought he was a "New and Improved!" Daniel, I couldn't have been more happy around him.

Not to mention Lonan's a really good kisser. Dang it, I was so determined not to go there! But I had to wonder—if I did sleep with him, would I just be another conquest once he was back in Faerie? Or did he want something more than that? *Do I?*

He felt my eyes on him and looked up. I don't know if the blood rushing to my face gave it away, but he seemed to guess just what I was thinking. One corner of his mouth lifted in a smile and the heat in his gaze melted my insides. *Maybe he's worth the complications…*

The sound of a throat clearing made us both jump. Uncle Tam glared at Lonan and said, "Avery, maybe you ought to go pick the last of the St. John's wort from across the street. We might want to have extra on hand to ward off more attacks."

"Um, yeah." I stood reluctantly, but I had to admit I was worried. "How did the lycoris thing even get to you, Uncle Tam?"

His brow furrowed, emphasizing his aged wrinkles. "I don't know. I admit I'm not as strong as I was, but I never thought I'd fall prey to such a ploy. We'll have to be extra-vigilant."

Lonan stood and followed me.

"Where are you going, boy?" Uncle Tam demanded.

"With Avery," he said innocently. "We decided she shouldn't be alone, didn't we? Unless you want to go. But I thought you'd want to get Daniel over here and catch him up on things."

Caught in his own web, Uncle Tam's only answer was a *harrumph.* I tried to hide my smug expression as we left, but judging by the glare burning into my back, I wasn't entirely successful.

St. John's wort didn't make Lonan blister like the bread and salt, but it did make him itchy, so he volunteered to hold the bag while I harvested. After we'd worked in companionable silence awhile, I asked over my shoulder, "Hey, do you think Uncle Tam is looking more tired lately? Showing his age? Well, not his real age, obviously."

Lonan didn't answer and I glanced behind me to find his eyes focused on my ass. *Okay, so these shorts go a little Daisy Duke when I bend over, but he's supposed to be keeping an eye out for danger.* "Hello? Lonan? Lonan!"

His gaze snapped guiltily to mine, and he actually blushed. "What?"

"If the bad guys decide to attack, they're not going to fly out my——"

"Okay, okay," he said. "What did you ask me a second ago?"

I repeated my question about Uncle Tam, and Lonan nodded. "I've noticed that, too. He's using up his remaining magic pretty quickly."

I hefted my pendant. "Using his magic to protect me, you mean. He probably lost a couple of years' worth busting in on Daniel's spell. Is that why he succumbed to the lycoris, you think? Because he's so much weaker now? And what does that mean for the blue moon?"

Lonan set down the bag we'd just filled and opened the other one. *Is he stalling? That can't be good.* "Lonan, if you know something, tell me. I'm tired of you all keeping me in the dark."

He sighed. "Fine, but I'm not sure this is mine to tell. When Tam Lin came to clean up my mess in the nineteen-thirties, he decided to stay permanently even though he would age like any other human.

"He'd become disillusioned with the Queen, her Court—all Fae. Said he'd lived well past his time and was determined to die in his homeworld. It's possible he wants this spell to be his last heroic act."

I dropped the bunches of herbs from my hands. "So…Uncle Tam doesn't expect to survive this? He's trying to go out in some stupid macho blaze of glory?"

Lonan nodded. "And I don't think even you can persuade him out of it."

"We'll see about that——"

"Avery, I don't claim to know all the reasons behind his staying here. But the love between him and the Queen, it was genuine. And she couldn't sway him in this."

"So their love was real and it still didn't make him want to live—but you don't think he'd do it for family?" I glared at Lonan, like it was him I needed to convince.

"That's just it—he thinks it's his fault your father was led astray. He believes you'd be better off without him around to draw the wrong kind of attention. He's determined to protect you."

"Then we'll have to do the same for him, won't we? Make sure nothing goes wrong and that he'll be fine. We all will."

I turned for home and froze with one foot in the air.

Teetering, I gripped Lonan's arm. "What about you?" I asked. "Are you willing to martyr yourself, too, to make up for Mariah?"

"No," he said softly. "I want to stay alive. For your sake." And he leaned in and kissed me. Like he meant it.

I was too busy processing his words to kiss him back. So by the time *He hasn't actually said the L word, but is that what he's working up to?* cycled through my brain, he was already pulling away.

"I'm sorry—I shouldn't have done that," Lonan said, avoiding my gaze. "I know you're with Daniel."

He turned for home, but I blurted, "Wait! There is no 'with' with Daniel."

I caught up and he said, "What do you mean?"

Put on the spot, I stammered, "I mean, I still love him, but things have changed—we've both changed. I don't think— It's complicated, okay?"

The corner of his mouth crept up. "Well, that clears things up. Good chat, Avery."

"Okay, give me a second to think and I'll try to explain better." I sorted through my jumbled thoughts and emotions, but they were one big, tangled yarn ball of guilt, infatuation, lust, hurt, joy, hope—I could go on and on. *But sometimes the best way to think things through is to talk them out.*

I took a deep breath. "I guess having the Sight didn't let me see what a mess Daniel and I were together. On the way back from ice cream, he laid it all on me—how I never listen to what he wants. I just shove my own needs and ideas down his throat."

"Whoa! Any truth to that?"

"Maybe. Sorta," I said in a small voice. I flung my hands out in frustration. "But…if he'd said something before this, I would've stopped. Not been such a bully about it. But now it's too late."

Lonan stepped closer and put his hands on my shoulders. "Hey, if that's how Daniel sees you, it's his loss. That's not what I see. Look, when I first came here and asked you to help me, it wasn't just for your magical potential.

"I saw right away that you were fiercely loyal to those you care about. Would do anything to help them. And yes, you do want your own way, but the flip side of that is decisiveness. If you were going to be fighting at my side, making split-second decisions was essential."

He tipped my chin up. Once he saw I was truly listening, he continued, "And I'm continually amazed by your mind—it's so incredibly flexible. If someone dares to say you can't do something, your brain immediately goes to work finding a way around—or through—that roadblock. I'm kind of jealous of how well you do that."

He kissed me again, his lips lingering softly on mine. A warm glow filled me, but another part of my brain was saying, *This is some intense shit, Avery, don't screw this up.*

But I must have had a self-destructive streak after all, because as soon as the kiss broke off, I joked, "So, this whole time, you've been into me for my mind?"

He shook his head and laughed, but he must have picked up on my need for breathing room and pulled me towards home without another word. Giving my ever-active—and somewhat skeptical—mind a chance to list all the reasons Lonan and I shouldn't be together.

We're literally from two different worlds—he's Fae royalty, for Crissakes, and doesn't even have his own body in this world. And he'll be leaving soon and I might never see him again.

It was that last one that got me; I couldn't stand to think he might be out of my life forever in just a few days. But he'd basically said I was his reason to stay, and that counted for a lot. *And I do want him to stay.*

I want him.

So, after we crossed through the cemetery, I dragged him into the dusty heat of the garage. "Before we go any further, tell me what that was, Lonan. Were you, like, declaring yourself or something?"

He wouldn't meet my eyes, but he smiled crookedly as he answered, "Not if it makes things complicated."

Okay, I guess the best way to get him to be truthful might be to offer up a truth of my own.

"You really wanna know how I spotted you weren't Daniel this whole time?"

He nodded, so I continued. "Because I was looking for *my* Daniel, and everything you did and said didn't fit. And once you both were using the body, I could tell who it was. Each and every time. Because I wasn't looking for Daniel anymore.

"I didn't know it, but I was already looking for Lonan. *My* Lonan."

He still didn't say anything, so I babbled on. "Look, I'm not saying for sure this is love—I don't believe in insta-love, like in books and movies—but there's *something* here. Something in you speaks to a part of me that I didn't even know was there.

"And I can't bear to think you could be out of my life in a few days and I never said any of this. So, what are we going to do about it?"

I held my breath long enough to start feeling dizzy before he responded by pinning me bodily against Nykur.

His tongue on mine was like Pop Rocks bursting with sparks; heat flared where his hands rested beneath my ribcage, and I knew he was helping things along with magic. But I didn't care—I didn't need a spell to want this. To want him.

I could have kissed him forever, but I gasped as his lips moved to my earlobe and my knees nearly gave way beneath me. When his fingers brushed my nipples and his hips ground into mine, suddenly kissing wasn't enough.

"Wait," I panted, placing my palms flat against his chest. "Not like this—not with Daniel's body. We can't—he's already made it clear he doesn't want it used this way. Not after what he's been through."

I wasn't sure if Lonan was listening, judging by the way he continued to nuzzle my neck. But then he said, "There's this old Fae saying of 'what Daniel doesn't know won't hurt him,' and I think it was made for situations just like this."

"No." I slipped away from Lonan and his temptations, letting some cooler air between us. "We've got to find another way."

Lonan groaned and rubbed his hands through his hair. "Yeah? How are we going to manage that? At the moment, Daniel's not the one suffering the consequences of…interruptus. I vote we keep going."

I shook my head, but gave him a grimace of sympathy. I was suffering the effects myself—in the absence of Lonan's magic as well as his kisses, I felt suddenly chilled.

Lonan slapped Nykur's roof in frustration, and the sound made me jump. A grumble of protest came from the radio, and that gave me an idea.

Placing my forehead against Nykur—*maybe it will transmit my thoughts better this way*—I struggled to find the right way to put my wishes.

Nykur, is there a way for me and Lonan to be together and not have Daniel's body in the equation? Right now, I mean—not after whatever goes down in the battle ahead?

Static, and then "♪I've got it.♪"

"Really, Nykur? There's a way?" I couldn't help jumping up and down like somebody had just offered me a sparkly pony.

"What?" Lonan asked.

Instead of answering him, I popped open the back door—revealing a vast backseat that would have made a limo proud.

I pulled Lonan in with me and we landed in a tangle on the plush upholstery. We sorted out our limbs and ended with me sprawled atop him in a *déjà vu* of when I jumped him in the cemetery that first time.

He must have realized it, too, because Lonan grinned and started to say, "Did you really think—"

But he lost all power of speech, eyes going wide, when I sat up and pulled my shirt and bra off. I leaned down to kiss him and a daze of taste and sensation overwhelmed me again—his hands, his lips, trailing heat I could almost see even with my eyes closed.

He paused in cupping my hip and questioned, "Avery? Did you change your mind?"

"This is just to tide us over, until we see what Nykur has in store," I murmured against the hollow of his throat. "I wished for a way for us to be together—what's the point of having a magic car if you don't use it for nefarious purposes? Anyway, I think he's got an idea."

The door had already closed behind us, and it felt like Nykur was moving at a pretty fast clip. *But not fast enough, if I'm going to resist my own screaming hormones any longer…*

A sudden turn threw me off Lonan, and I found myself turtled on the floor of the back seat. "Ack, where are we now?"

As Lonan helped me up, the ride got rougher, like we were offroad. And a look out the window showed that was exactly the case—we were on the old path leading to the closed-up mine. But Nykur continued past the clearing where I'd tried to expel Lonan, and went around the hillside to a hidden ledge.

Lonan and I exchanged puzzled glances—sure, it looked like there was a darkness under that ledge which hinted at an opening to the cavern, but it was way too small for Nykur. Then a squeezing compression pushed on me and before I could say more than "Nykur, what's— ," we all shrank down until that burrow was the size of a railroad tunnel.

Lonan must not have liked the sensation any better than I did, because he looked a little green in the dim light inside the cavern. But a few moments after we had crossed into what had to be a section of Lacuna, Lonan brightened and let out a delighted laugh that boomed in the, um, cavernous space.

"What's funny?" I asked, checking to see that all my parts had expanded back to normal size along with Nykur.

"It's perfect!" Lonan said. "Nykur, you're a genius—I take back all those jokes about bog horses being stupid."

"So let me in on the plan, you guys! Why are we here?"

Lonan put one arm around me and gave me a squeeze. "This place is exactly what we needed—it's still within the boundaries of Faerie for me in the caverns, but this is like a no-man's land since it's been tainted by the iron nearby. There are no Fae to notice us, so it should be perfectly safe for us here—and for Daniel's body, for a time."

"You say 'us' and 'Daniel's body' like those are separate—how?"

"I'll show you—don't worry, Nykur says the body can be safeguarded with your pendant, and he'll keep watch for any changes. Go ahead—put your necklace around my neck."

My hands went to the clasp of the gold chain, but I hesitated. *Do I trust Lonan enough to be without this protection, when he'll be at his full power here in Faerie?*

But then that cynical little voice in my head—yes, the one that's even snarkier than my normal head voice—piped up and asked, *So, you trust him enough to have sex, but that's where the trustiness ends? Good luck with the future of that relationship.*

I laughed aloud, and Lonan tilted his head quizzically. "Second thoughts?"

"Not really," I said, unhooking my necklace. Because the truth was, I did trust him. We wouldn't have gotten this far if I hadn't. And taking off my pendant—leaving me vulnerable—was the ultimate demonstration of that trust.

Once I'd put the necklace around his neck, Lonan crawled into the front and sat in the passenger seat. All I could see was the back of his head, and a wicked gaze in the mirror—before the eyes went blank.

As I opened my mouth to question what was happening, an amorphous violet shape flowed over the seat back and came to hover next to me. Under my disbelieving eyes, it fleshed out into a corbin—the real, one-hundred-percent-Lonan version of the creature I'd seen when we'd crossed into Faerie before.

That feathered mane he'd shown back then was now a full mantle, a cape of feathers over his shoulders and merging with his darkling hair. His face was more angular than Daniel's, but the glint in his purple eyes was all Lonan's. As my eyes roved over his lean torso *(why does a bird-like creature even need nipples?)* and then even lower, I realized he was naked.

Naked and ready, and also proving that Fae parts look much the same as the equivalent human parts.

He patted his lap, daring me with his gaze to climb aboard, and I laughed.

"Oh, I'm so there. But—do you have any—"

Before I could finish my question, a hail of objects rained down on us. I covered the back of my head and waited it out, giggling. Lonan picked one up and held it to the light filtering in from the cavern's glow. The word "Trojan" became visible, and I laughed at his expression as he took in the avalanche of condoms surrounding us.

"That's…intimidating," he said.

I grinned wickedly. "Or inspiring. Aren't you up for the challenge? Magically enhanced, and all?"

I shrieked as he rolled me onto my back and, for the next couple of hours, showed me exactly how up for the challenge he was.

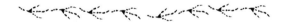

Later, when I sat up and looked for my clothes, I could only find my bra and Fruity Oaty Bar shirt. Lonan lay in a half-doze, one arm flung over his eyes.

"Hey—where are the rest of my clothes?" I asked.

He looked around and said, "Dunno. Guess you'll have to come back here and lie down until I have the energy to help you look."

He made a good attempt at a smolder, but it was obvious his heart—*and a more crucial, visible organ*—wasn't in it.

I kissed him on the forehead. "I wasn't expecting to want to do it that second time—my friend Kara said she was so sore after. But I barely felt any pain, just a little pinch. And then nothing but goodness. More magic?"

He pulled me down on him again and nuzzled into my hair. "Mmmhmm. Glad?"

"You weren't exaggerating when you said the eargasm was just a preview—wow." I surrendered to the afterglow and snuggled him for a few minutes.

I really was glad it hadn't hurt too bad—dreading that pain was what had stopped me when I'd come close to doing it before, not any residual prudishness. *All those novels with their first-time descriptions like "a sharp pain" and "a tearing inside" don't exactly make it sound appealing. More like just something to get through so you can move on to the good parts.*

Mmm, but those good parts—so worth it.

But we couldn't stay there forever, and I reluctantly sat up and said, "Lonan, we really should get home. The others will start to worry."

I leaned into the front seat to look for my shorts, and froze in place as I noticed a row of froggish faces pressed against Nykur's windshield. When I made eye contact, they laughed and pointed with their twiggy fingers.

"Um, Lonan?" I whispered. "We've got company."

He appeared at my shoulder and said in disgust, "Brownies. They're mostly harmless"

"But what are they doing here?" *And more importantly, how long have they been watching us?*

"Nykur says they got here when we were—" he held up a hand for a high five, but I narrowed my eyes at him, so he added hastily, "Well, he didn't want to interrupt us, when it was only brownies."

A flutter of wings caught my eye and I pointed to a swarm of tiny winged figures coming in for a landing on Nykur's hood. "And those?"

"Pixies. Also harmless. Mostly."

"But you said this cavern was tainted or something and nobody comes here."

"Didn't you? You made all the right noises and I just assumed…"

He trailed off, and when I continued to stare at him blankly, he waggled his feathery eyebrows at me suggestively. I played back the last thing I'd said, and the last thing he'd said.

"Oh my God! Lonan!" I punched him in the shoulder, but I doubt my fist made much of an impact through the layer of feathers. "For someone as old as you claim to be, you are so immature!"

He doubled over with laughter, and the pixies and brownies joined in with their own shrill chorus. I held out as long as I could before I laughed too; it was impossible to resist joining all that merriment. I mean, genuinely impossible, but it seemed like a benign-enough magic.

But then, cutting across the laughter, a tea-kettle shriek sounded in the distance. The brownies and pixies scattered, and Lonan and I exchanged worried looks.

"Time to go," he said before I could question him. Nykur was already on the move, and once again I was thrown to the floor by his sudden turn. But while I was down there, I spotted a glimpse of pink under the front seat and was able to reclaim my shorts and panties.

"Was that noise what I thought it was?" I asked as I pulled them on. "And hey, don't you need to get back into Daniel's body?"

Lonan nodded, and the purple vapor flowed over the seatback and into the body again. Which then turned to me and answered, "I don't think that was a wyvern, but it wasn't as friendly as the little folk who were there. Nykur said the cavern was stirring—something woke it, and the quickening magic was attracting too much attention." He grinned naughtily. "So that hookup will have to last you a while, since I don't think we can go back there safely again."

I rolled my eyes at him—*more Faerie mysteries, and he's fixated on when we'll get to do it again?*—before I put on my shoes. But when we kissed before getting out of Nykur's tinted-window sanctuary, I did find myself wondering wistfully about when the next time would be.

We stopped in the screen porch long enough for me to comb my hair; I thought about showering, but the impulse to smell Lonan on my skin a while longer won out.

Uncle Tam and Daniel were looking over more scrolls at the kitchen table as we came into the room. I nodded hello, feeling my cheeks heat self-consciously, and walked past them to get a glass out of the cupboard.

"So, once you're at the Druid's Cave," Daniel was saying, "then we'll need to—"

I turned to see why he'd stopped mid-sentence and found him staring intently at me. *He looks— Oh no, he suspects.* As my face heated, his nose rose in the air and sniffed twice. *Can he smell the sex on me?*

Daniel's head whipped around to look at Lonan, lips peeling back in a snarl as he launched his barrel-shaped body off the chair. Straight at Lonan.

"Daniel!" I didn't know if Daniel even heard me yelling his name over those ugly-sounding, frenzied growls. Flashing white teeth tore into Lonan's calf. Lonan tried to shake him off, but every snap of those jaws brought more blood and torn flesh.

Finally, I tackled the dog and his teeth sank into my hand. The recently healed palm ripped open, and now I was bleeding, too. It took Uncle Tam to pull Daniel off us, and he threw the dog into the cupboard under the kitchen sink.

"Someone tell me what the hell is going on!" Uncle Tam thundered over the muffled snarls and howls. "Is this another attack? A spell?"

"No, no." My voice cracked, but I didn't elaborate. Instead, I grabbed a few towels out of the drawer and knelt next to Lonan, trying to get a look at the damage. His leg was like fresh-ground hamburger, with flaps and chunks of skin hanging.

I swallowed back bile and tried to get a grip. *Okay, now's a good time to put all of Mom's lectures to use. What does she say to check for?* Whether the blood is pumping, like from an artery, or just seeping. If the bite's close to a tendon or the bone. *But—I can't tell—I'm not the nurse in the family!*

"Well?" Lonan said. "How bad is it?"

I looked up and he was trying to smile through gritted teeth, skin pale and pupils wide. *I know that's not good.*

Daniel had subsided to angry muttering in the cupboard, so I motioned for Uncle Tam to come look, too.

"Mmph," he said unhelpfully.

"I think you might need stitches, Lonan," I said, putting on my best nurse imitation. *Or a skin graft—shit!* "We need to get you to the hospital."

"No," said Uncle Tam.

I'd already started to stand, and Lonan and I stared at Uncle Tam in surprise.

In stereo, we said, "But—"

"If we take him to the hospital, they're legally obligated to report a dog bite. That one's bad enough to land Bobbin—Daniel—in quarantine. Maybe even doggy death row."

"So, what do we do?" I asked. "Call Mom and tell her to drive like hell out here?"

Uncle Tam shook his head. "We don't want to get her involved. But I've sewn up plenty of battle wounds and I can manage this one. Long as it doesn't fester, should be fine if you don't mind the scars."

"Fester?" Lonan squawked. "Are you crazy, Tam Lin? Swallow your pride. Send for the Queen's physician—you know she won't refuse you."

Judging by Uncle Tam's stubborn expression, that wasn't going to happen. "Can't you guys magic this all better?" I asked.

"No," Uncle Tam and Lonan said at the same time.

"It would take more magic than we can spare so close to the battle," Uncle Tam explained.

"Doesn't the rightful owner of that body get a say?" Daniel had worked his way out of the cupboard. "I didn't get a say in what led up to this."

Uncle Tam nodded grudgingly.

"Then you can put the stitches in, Tam. And you can stay in there and feel every single one, you corbin bastard."

Pandemonium as we all tried to talk at once, until Uncle Tam did his roaring thing again and shut us up.

"We have a little more than twenty-four hours before we're facing some serious opposition," Uncle Tam said, "and you three are fighting like children. There had better be a damn good reason for it."

Daniel snorted. "Well, either Lonan's up to the usual corbin tricks, or your precious little Avery is a slut. Maybe both."

Lonan tried to come after Daniel and ended up falling heavily against the table. Uncle Tam reined in his own anger to help him back into the chair.

And I spluttered, "I am not...and Lonan didn't trick me... You don't know what you're talking about!"

Daniel's smug expression disappeared as his face twisted into a sneer, so unnatural on a dog. "Oh, so you didn't just sleep with a guy you've known for only a few weeks—time he's spent in a stolen body? I must have misunderstood."

"That's rich, coming from a guy who admitted to taking full advantage of orgies in Faerie!"

"That is *my* body, Avery! It's not some plushie costume he puts on while he gets off. What if he got you pregnant?"

"That's not going to happen! We didn't use your body, okay? I was with *Lonan*." I hollered back.

Uncle Tam held up his hand, quelling Daniel's comeback. "Avery, I've always treated you like you have a good head on your shoulders. I thought that you'd outgrow your impulsiveness. And then you pull something like this and prove you're still a child. Our entire world is on the line and you couldn't keep your—your hormones in check."

I gasped, hurt to the core.

It's one thing to have an ex-almost-boyfriend call me a slut, but to also hear I've confirmed Uncle Tam's secret doubts?

Uncle Tam turned his fury on Lonan.

"And you, *boy*. Over the last week I'd started to think you'd changed, you'd grown. That you're finally taking things seriously. Recognizing the things you do in this world have consequences.

"But you're the same wastrel corbin, not caring how it affects others as long as you get what you want. I hope ruining Avery was worth it."

"Ruining?" I squawked. "Hey, you might be from some backwater era, Uncle Tam, but this is the twenty-first century."

"She's right." Lonan's voice was low and dangerous when he answered, "Avery doesn't deserve your censure, Tam Lin—you've done far worse in your time.

"And this war is not yet lost. The plan is going forward like we've talked about. Nothing has changed."

"*Everything's* changed!" Daniel cried. "You've said over and over that you're not able to cast your spell without a human body—a voice and hands. I hope all the practice you've done up to now is enough, because I want my body back until the blue moon."

Lonan shook his head. "I can't give you your body back at this stage, Daniel."

"Can't—or won't?" Daniel spat.

"Can't—really. Since I came here for a specific purpose, I'm under a geis to complete it. Our contract was different from the usual one where both parties are after some fun, and I'm connected to this body until after the blue moon. There's no way to change that, even if I wanted to."

All the hairs rose up on Daniel's back. "What? No. Tell him, Tam—he has to give it back."

Is Lonan telling the truth? Uncle Tam didn't speak, and that said it all.

Daniel turned to look at me, raw betrayal in those puppy dog eyes. "After all the warnings I gave you about what these Fae are really like, you chose to believe his charms over my truths.

"I hope his refusing to give back my body proves to you, once and for all, Avery, what kind of creature he is. He uses everyone. Including you. If you screwed him to try to keep him here, good luck with that. He got what he wanted."

My gaze darted to Lonan, who said, "Avery, it's not like that. This is too important—"

"I—I can't," I blurted, before running from the room. The screen door banged behind me, and I almost ran into Nykur's waiting bulk. He popped open a door, but I shook my head—*thanks, but I need to be alone*—and dodged into the cemetery.

I sank into the late afternoon shade of one of the larger ladys-tones. *Daniel hates me, Uncle Tam is beyond disappointed, and I may be just another conquest to Lonan. And I've brought it all on myself.*

L̶ater, when I heard Lonan call my name, I was tempted to hide from him. But his halting steps made me give in. *How is he even walking on that leg? More magic?*

"I'm over here," I called.

With a hiss of pain, he sat down next to me, handing me a sweating bottle of coconut water. Our easy intimacy from before— *was it really just hours ago?*—was gone, and I waited for him to speak first. My shoulders tightened with dread at every passing second.

Until he took my hand and said, "Avery, I'm sorry things turned out this way. But I don't regret lying with you—I couldn't possibly."

I exhaled, the heat of his body near mine striking me like the sun on a flower. But it wasn't his body, not really, and that brought up all kinds of confusing issues about our future. Questions I didn't want to bring up just yet, in case I didn't like the answer. *Or don't trust the answer.*

When I still didn't say anything, Lonan said in a falsetto, "Neither do I, Lonan, you're the best lover I've ever had. The snogging is so dreamy."

I barked a laugh in spite of myself. "Is that supposed to be me? That's pathetic—you sound like the pimply kid on *The Simpsons*. And considering you're the only real lover I've ever had, that's not exactly a ringing endorsement."

"But I'll take it. Unless you're sorry you slept with me?"

I sighed. "Honestly? I'm not sorry—not really. But you have to admit our timing was shit."

"That I'll concede. But we both knew it might be our only chance, and I'd do it all again." He paused. "Do you want to do it all again? Right now?"

I shook my head. "Not after the fallout back there. I don't think I could face that. Daniel and Uncle Tam must hate me—they're both so Team Human and they act like I'm cheering for the visiting Team Fae."

"I don't think they hate you. They're just having to make some adjustments in how they think about you. But that's good—relationships evolve."

"Yeah, but I think mine have *de*volved. Uncle Tam thinks I'm a hormone-fueled, irresponsible mess. And Daniel… He may never speak to me again."

Touching his forehead to mine, Lonan said, "Give it some time. Come back to the house and get some dinner."

"No way, I'm not ready. Could you—" I stopped, realizing I was about to ask the limping guy to fetch and carry for me. "Could you give me a few minutes?" I finished instead.

"Sure." He leaned over and kissed my ear softly. "Krrkennen," he breathed into it.

I shivered at the spiral of magic that accompanied his words. "What did you say? Is that some kind of kinky Fae talk?"

His mirth warmed my ear. "No. Krrkennen. Just thought giving you my name might lay to rest any doubts you may have that I'm not sincere."

He placed my pendant in my hand—I must have left it in Nykur—and painfully levered himself up. I didn't even offer to help, I was so shocked.

He gave me his name? But that's supposed to be some serious mojo! My veneer of heartache slipped as I realized the significance.

"See you in a bit…Krrkennen," I said. I didn't know if I got all the rolled r's in there like he did, but he smiled before making his way into the growing dusk.

Wow, this changes things. Or maybe solidifies them. Up until a minute ago, I did have doubts. *Like, is Lonan really going to be in my life after this blue moon? And will it be at Daniel's expense, if Lonan continues making excuses about keeping Daniel's body?*

But with one whispered word, Lonan had entrusted me with the power to compel him, to call him. Maybe to trust him enough to love him, with no holding back.

A footstep scuffed on the gravel path, and pure happiness welled up in me.

"Hey, I might have some ointment left over for that dog bite," I called as I stood and quick-stepped his direction. "But first, can I have that snog now?"

"I'd be delighted," a raspy voice answered. "But it will have to wait until I get you somewhere more private."

I froze in place as the figure stepped closer, revealing its cadaverous face. Eyes dark and hollow in the sockets, skin sagging and scabbed. A smell of rot and decay hit me as I recognized the houndstooth cap.

"Mr. Forrest?" I gasped.

"Close enough," he said, and raised his hand while muttering strange, twisted words.

Shit, is that a spell? My fingers tightened reflexively on the pendant still in my hand and—BAM! A bolt of energy knocked me right on my ass.

I sat, stunned, until the smell of seared flesh hit my nostrils, followed by an intense burning in my hand. I opened my fingers and a crumble of ash fell out, leaving just the shape of my pendant etched into my palm—it must have taken the brunt of whatever that spell was. Staring stupidly at the mark on my hand, I waited for my ears to stop ringing.

Before that could happen, a voice demanded, "What was that? Did my brother put a ward on you, girl?"

I looked up and Mr. Forrest's—*well, Drake's*—furious gaze met mine. *He's furious? That's nothing to the raginess I'm feeling.*

"No—but you'll wish you had a ward by the time I'm through with you."

He laughed at my comeback, but I had to keep him distracted—if he tried again, I'd be defenseless.

"No, really, what's next?" I asked, standing up. I wavered on my feet as my ears adjusted to being upright again. "Care to spill your villainous plan?"

He shrugged. "It's not terribly complicated—I kidnap you, my brother and the other two come running to save you, you all die before you even get a chance to stop me on the blue moon." He said it so matter-of-factly, like he was telling someone how to peel a banana.

"No, that's not how it's going to go," I retorted. "You'll be sorry you even messed with us. Your evil schemes will be foiled and we'll get our happily ever after."

"Oh, and how do you intend to do that?" he drawled.

"Um…"

Is it that obvious I don't really have a plan, other than to wait for someone to notice that spell and come rescue me? But he's just told me that's exactly what he wants them to do, so I'll need to try something else.

Drake tapped his foot, a patronizing smile twisting his lips.

Yeah, asshole, guess what—that just makes me more determined. If I use the binding spell, will it hold him in place long enough for Uncle Tam or Lonan to get here? Or what about the expulsion spell? *Wait, that casts out all the Fae in, like, a one-mile radius.* If only there was a way to make it specific to him.

Like using his name! *That should totally work. But…what is his true name?* "Drake" sounded way too simplified, like "Lonan" instead of Krrkennen.

Something about that name nagged at me. Lonan had said something, ending in *–ennen,* when his brother was attacking Nykur. Could that be a family name, pointing to Drake's real name? *It's worth a try—what else do I have in my arsenal, except the ability to annoy him to death?*

A triumphant grin crossed my features as I said, "Hey, bro—make like yo mama's prom dress and take off."

"What?" he asked, understandably confused. But not so confused that he couldn't raise his hand, ready to cast another spell.

"Siwennen," I said, putting all the force of my will behind the word. "Shut up."

His brow darkened and his mouth opened, ready to let me have it. Only nothing came out, giving me time to start the expulsion spell.

Water flows deeper than deep
So too does the cold.

Sap rises with the greenwood
So too does the blood.

While I spoke, poor Mr. Forrest looked like a science experiment gone wrong. His skin bubbled and seethed, and his eyes bugged out in terror as Siwennen fought to keep his hold inside the body.

Finally, a roiling cloud of smoke poured out of Mr. Forrest, half-solidifying into a dark, winged shape.

"Ha!" I pumped my fist in triumph—but too soon. With a roar that shook the trees, Siwennen flew right at me.

His burning red eyes, deadly claws—they pushed all coherent thought out of me. I desperately tried to dredge up the next lines of the expulsion spell, but—I had nothing.

Nothing but an instinctual raising of my hands as I screamed, "No! Go back to where you came from!"

When the final word echoed, a rushing sound like water escaping a broken dam roared outward from where I stood. Mr. Forrest crumpled beneath it, and the dark-winged shadow was swept away with the wave of energy, its roar growing fainter as it surged from the cemetery, leaving Mr. Forrest's body behind like flotsam or driftwood.

I stumbled to my knees. *Man, that was…draining.* I doubled over, laughing at my own pun, giddy with relief. Heady with power.

A groan from Mr. Forrest snapped me back to attention. *At least, I hope it's only the caretaker in there.*

"Mr. Forrest?" I called, surreptitiously checking my immediate vicinity for something to use as a weapon.

"Yes, it's me," he answered, sounding tired but fully human at last. "That nasty one is gone, then?"

"I hope so. How are you feeling?"

"That thing wore me like a pair of longjohns—how do you think?"

"I might be able to help," I said as I crossed over to him.

But as soon as I laid my hand on his arm, he screamed like I'd burned him. "No more magic!"

He tried to pull away, but I gritted my teeth and held on. I had to be sure that Drake wasn't anchored in there somehow. *This is the exact spot in a movie where they lull you into a false sense of security, and then the bad guy attacks again.*

But the magic still crackling through me said this was just a traumatized old man trembling beneath my hand, and I let him go. *If Drake has plans for another try, he's not using this host.*

His breath catching, Mr. Forrest stared at me with wide eyes and said, "Stay the hell away from me."

He fled the cemetery as fast as his abused body would let him.

"Mr. Forrest, wait! I don't think you should be running around yet," I called after him, but he disappeared into the lowering night.

At least he didn't seem totally cuckoo like before. *I hope he's one of the ones that can survive being taken over.*

I turned towards home, my steps quickening as I saw the lighted windows. *Wait until they hear what I did—I just saved the world! Singlehandedly!*

"Hey, you guys will never believe what happened," I called as I burst through the back door. "Lonan's brother tried to spell me—"

"Avery!" Uncle Tam's panicked voice rang from the kitchen. "Find Daniel—now!"

"What's going on?" I ran in there and skidded to a stop.

Daniel's body lay on the floor, empty-eyed and still but for the jerking motion of Uncle Tam's chest compressions. All I could do was stare in horror.

"Don't just stand there," Uncle Tam panted. "Go get Daniel—he went home. Lonan's gone and the body's empty—I can only keep this going so long."

I flew to Daniel's house, banging through their back door without knocking. By the light of the television screen, the Dawes's faces turned towards me in astonishment.

"Daniel! I need you!" Daniel raised his doggy head, but laid it down again once he saw it was me. *Idiot!*

"Avery, what on earth?" Mrs. Dawes said. "Daniel is over at your house, isn't he?"

"Uhhh—yeah, he is," I babbled. "I meant, Daniel needs Bobbin and sent me to get him."

I took a step towards the couch, but Daniel growled at me. Mrs. Dawes laid her hand protectively on his furred back. "I don't think Bobbin wants to go with you."

"But he has to, we need a dog for, um, doggy things," I said, stumbling for a convincing argument. *Shit, how long have I been over here already?* "Oh, screw it—Daniel, Lonan is gone from your body and if you don't come right now it will die! Get over to Uncle Tam's!"

Daniel's head whipped up and he stared for a microsecond before launching off the sofa. His little legs blurred as he ran out the door and down the slope.

I started after him, and behind me Mr. Dawes called out something, but I yelled, "We'll explain later!"

By the time I reached the kitchen, Uncle Tam had one hand on the dog and the other on Daniel's body as he chanted an incantation. A flash of golden light, and Daniel sucked in a wheezing breath. He sat up, coughing, and Bobbin pranced around him, barking his head off.

"Bobbin, it's okay," Daniel choked out, petting his dog until he quieted. "Jeez, Tam—did you have to crack my ribs?"

"Better than the alternative." Uncle Tam sat back on his heels, exhaustion written on his face.

"Daniel, I'm so glad you're safe," I said. He let me hug him for about one second before he pushed me off. *Oh, yeah, he's still mad at me.*

My smile wavered before I bustled to the fridge and said brightly, "You guys look like you could use some iced tea. And are you hungry? I have the most amazing news!"

Uncle Tam winced. "Dial it down a little, Avery, and give us a chance to catch our breath."

I didn't say anything else, but the mania and the hollowness left by the expulsion spell were still there—*so hungry!*—and I continued rummaging in the meat drawer.

"What happened with Lonan?" Daniel asked. "Did he finally decide to make this right? Wish he'd chosen a better way to do it."

"No, he just dropped to the floor, mid-sentence," Uncle Tam said. "I felt this wave of wild magic pass over, and it was like something tore him right out. Good thing I was here to see it happen and could take steps to save your body right away."

My hand froze as I spread mustard on a slice of bread. *Like something had torn Lonan right out of the body? Something like—an expulsion spell?* It couldn't be—I'd been careful to use Siwennen's name. To make sure only *he* was cast out of our world.

But what if it was me? Would other Fae have been affected? I clattered out of the kitchen and ran to the garage, throwing the door open.

Empty. *Nykur's gone, too.*

My steps back to the cottage were not the triumphant race they'd been when I returned from the cemetery. This time, I had to stop in the screen porch, doubled over as sobbing gasps seized my gut. *What have I done? I messed around with magic I don't fully understand and sent away Lonan and Nykur, that's what.* Got cocky and thought I could do everything myself. And only screwed things up.

Well, time to pay the proverbial piper. And see if Uncle Tam can fix any of this. I scrubbed the tears from my face and trudged into the kitchen.

Uncle Tam and Daniel looked at me with identical "what was that all about?" expressions.

"I think I know what happened," I said shakily. "I was trying to get rid of Drake, and it worked too well. My spell sent Lonan and Nykur away, too."

Uncle Tam looked at me intently. "That magic I felt—that was you? How can that be? Since when can you do spellcasting?"

Oh yeah, he doesn't know the whole story of how I tried to bring Daniel back. So I caught him up, starting with that fateful binding spell, and the way I could shape Faerie when we went there in Nykur. Plus smaller things, like the flower bulb blooming, and the things I hadn't put together until later, like the times I'd had phenomenal luck finding money on the ground when I needed it. Bringing us all the way up to Drake appearing in the cemetery and me sending him packing.

"So, can you bring Lonan back, Uncle Tam? Or help me do it?" I asked, touching his hand with my own shaking one.

But he stood up from his chair so suddenly that Daniel and I jumped. He paced furiously, muttering under his breath. I was able to catch "I'd nearly given up hope" and, "it could be time" before he lunged at me, grabbing my arm.

"Don't you see?" he demanded. "This could change everything!" The fanatical light in his eyes transformed his face into an unfamiliar mask.

"Uncle Tam, you're hurting my arm. And you're scaring me. What are you talking about?" He let me go abruptly and I rubbed the bruised spot on my forearm. *He's acting crazy—like my dad gets when he wigs out.*

"You're right," Uncle Tam said. "I could be getting ahead of myself. Like you said, we need to test you—some strong magic—see what you can do."

I shared a wide-eyed glance with Daniel, who didn't look like he knew what was going on, either. And was just as disturbed by this change in Uncle Tam.

"Um, I didn't say anything about testing me," I said. "I just want to make sure Lonan is okay."

Uncle Tam waved his hand dismissively as he went back to pacing. "We'll get to that. But first, we need to challenge your magic."

His eyes lit on the trash can full of bloody paper towels, still in the middle of the floor from when Daniel had attacked Lonan. "Perfect!" he said.

"What's perfect?" I asked, but Uncle Tam ignored me, grabbed the note pad by the phone, and began scribbling. He brought it over to me, shoved it in my face.

"This! Use this spell to heal Daniel's leg."

I took it from him gingerly and read through his crabbed handwriting. "This will heal Daniel?"

"No, *you* will! You've healed before—I should have realized. That salve Nykur gave you for your cut from the shard of glass, it should have only helped with the pain. But your hand was good as new a few hours later and we couldn't figure out why. But you'd magicked yourself better!" He beamed at me, like he was expecting me to get excited, too.

"If you say so," I said, humoring him. "If I try this spell and it doesn't work, it can't hurt Daniel, can it?"

Uncle Tam shook his head. "You'll let her try, won't you, Daniel?" he asked.

Daniel weighed his answer for an uncomfortably long time before lifting his pant leg. Nearly his entire calf was swaddled in bandages, and I winced in sympathy before pulling the bandage off so I could see what I was doing.

It was so much gorier than I'd remembered it. A few of Uncle Tam's serviceable stitches had ripped open (when Lonan fell?) and inside I could see all this graying connective tissue.

Fighting the heebie-jeebies, I picked up Uncle Tam's spell and read through it again. Super-simple, and über-creepy sounding on my tongue as I spoke it.

Blood to blood
Meat to meat
Skin to skin
Calls to each.

I stopped because I could feel a strange sensation under my hand. Without breaking contact, I peeked under my palm and saw that the deepest parts of the wound were knitting together. Nets of tissue were joining up and filling in.

Eww—as much as this was creeping the hell out of me, this was no time to be squeamish. I kept repeating my chant until the flesh sealed beneath my fingers and warmth returned to it. A pulse beat against my hand, stronger and stronger.

Another peek showed healthy (if hairless) skin and only a white, stitched scar. *Like it's years old instead of minutes.*

"Whoo-hoo!" I jumped up and did a little "I'm The Wo-Man" jig, with Bobbin frisking around my feet. Daniel stood to test out his leg, and once I saw it was all right I joined Bobbin for a gleeful lap around the kitchen.

Uncle Tam pulled me into his arms and danced a jaunty caper. "I knew you could do it!" he crowed. His hands trembled on my shoulders.

But his euphoria reminded me how weirdly intense—like, zealot-intense—he'd been just a few minutes ago and I decided maybe I shouldn't encourage him.

I pulled away and tried to sound casual as I asked, "How do we know it was me that healed Daniel, and not that spell? Maybe anyone could have done it."

Uncle Tam shook his head adamantly. "No, it was you. You're The One."

Whoa, did I hear capital letters in there? How did we get from "maybe you can do magic" to "you're The One?"

"But how can we be sure?" I persisted.

"Fine, you need convincing. I'm willing to bet you don't even need a spell."

Uncle Tam walked over to the knife block and pulled out his fillet knife. Then he sliced it into the fish-belly white flesh of his own wrist. I screamed as the blood flowed fast and red.

"Daniel, get the knife from him!" I called.

Daniel backpedaled, his eyes white around the edges and mouth open in horror. Stuck in some Faerie flashback, he could only stand in the corner, trembling.

I ran to Uncle Tam's side, ready to wrestle the knife from him, but he laid it down on the counter placidly, holding out his dripping arm. "Heal it, Avery. Do it. Prove to me you're The One."

"You're acting crazy, Uncle Tam!" I mopped at his arm with a paper towel, but he stilled my hands.

"Heal it," he said again. He nodded encouragingly when I looked in his eyes, his slight smile meant to be comforting. And it would have been comforting, if I wasn't so sure that Uncle Tam had somehow come completely unhinged.

"I—I can't," I said. "Not without— I'll use your spell again."

"No—just use your will. Your magic."

When I still hesitated, he picked up the knife again and dug into his arm until blood sprayed out. A splash of red with every beat of his heart. *Shit—that's what Mom said to look for, when it means arterial blood.*

Uncle Tam stood there, spraying gore like a demented fountain, waiting for me to heal him. I wasn't sure if an ambulance could get here in time, even if Daniel could stir himself to call 911. *No choice but to try and heal him, then.*

So I reached out, with my hand and my will, picturing the flesh and arteries knitting back together. The blood slowed to a trickle, and then stopped altogether. I kept at it until Uncle Tam gently pried away my hand and took the paper towel from me. Wiped his arm to show mended skin, with no trace of a wound.

"See," he said softly. Calmer now.

I burst into tears. "Don't ever do that again, Uncle Tam. You're supposed to be the one I can count on in this family, not another one of us crazies."

He put his arms around me, letting me sob into his shoulder. "I'm sorry, I went a little overboard, didn't I? But you don't know how long I've hoped for this—for *you*."

"You keep saying stuff like that—I need to know what you mean. Tell me the whole story," I said, wiping my nose on the paper towel before I realized it was all bloody. *Ick, ick, ick!* I washed my face in the sink before turning back to Uncle Tam. "I mean it—start talking."

"You deserve that much. Come sit down."

"Umm, I'm out," Daniel said. He still looked shell-shocked, and he wobbled on his feet as he headed towards the door. "Going home to rest."

I started to argue, but remembered he'd nearly died and could use some recovery time. "Don't forget to come up with some story for your parents, to explain about earlier."

He nodded, abandoning me. So it was just the two of us, drinking iced tea in the kitchen that smelled like a slaughterhouse, while Uncle Tam explained some things.

"Once upon a time, our world and Faerie overlapped quite a bit. That was the golden age of fairy tales—magic and the mundane intermingled freely. But at a cost—mankind could never quite advance beyond a feudal system because the Fae kept our population in check with their wars. Or their outright massacres. *Meddling.*

"But then a sorcerer—a man born with the power of wild magic— split the two worlds and imposed laws on their interactions. Closed the borders, so we could develop without interference. Humans could only go into Faerie under special circumstances, and the Fae couldn't come into our world without losing much of their powers.

"But the magic that rules them is weakening. Soon, it will be a free-for-all as the Fae come pouring into our world. Drake's attempt, although a genuine danger, was really just a symptom of that weakening—an attempt to establish a territory here, ahead of the masses."

"So it's not over?" I asked. "Sending Drake back didn't solve anything?" Then why the hell had Lonan spent so much time and energy trying to stop him? And then he'd gotten sent back to Faerie for no reason. *It's not fair.*

"Not in the long term, no. But once you learn how to use your magic, how to control it, you can change things. You can finish what Merlin started."

My glass of iced tea slipped out of my fingers, landing with a *clunk* on the tabletop. "Merlin? *The* Merlin? What are you talking about?"

"He's the one who separated the worlds. He was like you, but I think you're stronger. Strong enough to close the borders permanently."

"Oh, yeah, I'll just pick up where Merlin left off. No worries!" Now it was my turn to pace in an agitated fashion. "Come on, Uncle Tam, you can't say things like that without backing it up. What makes me so special? How could I be The One, when a few weeks ago I was just an ordinary girl?"

Next, he'll be telling me I'm actually a government experiment. Ha, or an alien.

"You're not an ordinary human, Avery," he said, as if he could read my mind and couldn't resist messing with me. But his expression was totally serious. "You never were."

I thumped down into my chair. "No more cryptic answers, Uncle Tam. Tell me everything, and tell me the truth."

He nodded. "Your birth was the result of a ritual—one joining the magic of Faerie to a human vessel. You have a Fae father as well as a human one."

"Oh, why didn't you just say so? That changes everything." Sarcasm dripping from my every pore, I rubbed my face in frustration.

"You asked, and I'm trying to tell you. Are you going to listen or not?" There was a spark of the old Uncle Tam.

I nodded and he continued, "The way you were conceived—it had all been arranged. I cast a spell to keep Michael quiet in his body, sort of in stasis. And a Fae stepped in, lying with your mother instead. So, you have two sires, and got gifts from both of them."

The gift of the heebie-jeebies, thinking about my mom being used like that? "And Mom? Did she know about any of this?"

"No—she didn't need to. Neither of them did. Your dad wasn't supposed to remember anything, but somehow he retained just enough to ask questions. And got sucked into Faerie politics."

Sounded more like he paid the price for someone else's politics—namely, Uncle Tam's and this other Fae's. "So, who's this other guy? My Fae father?"

"A wyvern. We needed to combine your dad's creative energy with a wilder magic. Wyverns tend towards the chaos, so Seisso was a good candidate."

"Seisso's not…he's not Drake's father?"

"No. We needed a more cooperative wyvern. One whose ambitions were more in line with our own."

Whew! I knew if Drake and I had shared a father, that didn't mean I was related to Lonan—but it would have been disturbing just the same. *Hell, this whole situation is disturbing no matter how you look at it.*

"So, what was the point of this whole thing? Why did you need someone to be born from this ritual? And if I'm part wyvern, am I a mutant hybrid?" I stared at my hand, trying to use my Sight to see if I had claws or something. *Nope—just dried blood under my fingernails. No big*

But Uncle Tam didn't seem to notice that I was teetering on the edge of freaking out, and he answered, "Do you remember when I made the distinction that I'm not magic myself, that I've just absorbed a lot by spending so much time in Faerie? Well, you *are* magic. It's just as much a part of you as—as your sarcasm, or your loyalty."

I bit my lip. "So I— We couldn't get rid of it, even if I wanted to?" *Not that I want to get rid of it before I've even had a chance to explore what it is, but it's nice to know the options.*

Uncle Tam growled, "Don't even think like that. All these years, I was convinced the ritual had failed. I didn't have it in me to try again, so I've been letting myself fade away. But now I can't afford to do that—you'll need me to train you. So you can finish our work."

I agreed that I needed training—*but is Uncle Tam the right one to do it?* I wasn't sure if I trusted him any longer. Not when he'd demonstrated that he was a "the ends justify the impregnating of an unsuspecting woman with Faeriespawn" kind of guy.

"How am I going to do training and everything else? School starts soon," I hedged.

"Oh, there's no sense in you wasting your time in school. I'll teach you what you need to know for your role in my plan."

"Drop out of school?" *Shyeah, right.* "Mom will never go for that, not in a million years—"

"She will. The right suggestion, with your magic to back it up, and she'll do anything you want her to."

I laughed. "Like not shopping for my clothes at Old Navy? That'd be great."

But Uncle Tam didn't laugh along with me. *Wait—he's serious? He actually thinks it'd be okay for me to spell my mom into letting me drop out of school?*

"Um, just to be clear, I'm not using magic on Mom," I said, standing.

"We can decide that later—"

"There's nothing to decide," I interrupted. "Look, I'm going to go take a shower, and then maybe call my dad. Okay? Since he knows about Faerie, too, I'd like to ask him to fill in some blanks. You and I can talk again later, once I've had a chance to process everything."

Uncle Tam nodded and I fled to my room, gathering a clean change of clothes. I breathed a sigh of relief once the bathroom door locked behind me. The sound of the water running was a welcome white noise, but before I undressed I remembered I'd used up the last of the body wash the last time I'd showered. I'd need to get a bar of soap from the linen closet.

I left the shower running and as I opened the cabinet in the hall, I caught the sound of Uncle Tam's voice in the kitchen. *Who's he talking to?* I pointed an ear in that direction and caught the name "Michael"—*did he call my dad, even though I said I was going to do it? Whoa, no reason yet to turn the paranoia up to eleven, Avery.* I tiptoed closer and listened some more.

"No, she's in the shower, but she'll be calling you soon," Uncle Tam was saying. "You need to think about what you're going to say to her—to put her doubts at ease."

Okay, so it's not paranoia if they're really talking about me. And Uncle Tam is coaching my dad on what to say?

"She's more powerful than even I hoped," he continued. "She healed me of a mortal wound, and it went even further—that arm is better than it's been in years. No arthritis, and it's muscled like it's thirty years younger than the rest of me. Only a few Fae are powerful enough to do something like that so casually. Merlin will be pleased his plan came to fruition so well."

I smiled—*it's still crazy to think Uncle Tam knows Merlin*—but then he said something that chilled me.

"A stroke of luck that her spell got rid of that corbin. He'd just be a distraction while I'm bringing her into line. Ironically, it was likely his spells and mischief that sparked her defenses, awakening her powers—but on a larger scale than when Corriell triggered them at your place." He paused; my dad must have asked him something. "Oh, no—he's likely dead or being tortured by now. Drake and his lot won't be happy their plans have been foiled, and I'm sure they took him as soon as he landed back in Faerie."

I covered my gasp before it could escape and give me away. *Drake has Lonan?* He'd already proven he was willing to attack his brother, since that attempt in the thirties nearly ended in Lonan's death. *Well, he's not going to succeed this time, if I have anything to say about it.*

I needed to get back into Faerie, to rescue Lonan this time. And Uncle Tam was worse than useless—he was keeping secrets and turning into Uncle Control Freak. *Well, I guess he needs a reminder just how loyal I can be—and how stubborn.*

I went ahead and showered real quick, since I needed Uncle Tam to think things were hunky-dory. But after I dressed, I hollered towards the kitchen, "Uncle Tam, I'm going to go check on Daniel, okay?"

I was already out the back door when he called, "All right. Don't take too long—you wanted to call your dad, remember."

I made a stop in the garage and picked up the emergency supplies I'd hidden in there—a basic first aid kit, augmented with St. John's wort and bread and salt. Then I continued to Daniel's and knocked on the front door.

"Oh, hi, Mrs. Dawes," I said when she opened the door. "Is Daniel around?"

"He's sleeping," she said, barring my way. "But since you're here, next time leave us out of your practical jokes. You didn't think it was in poor taste to yell something about Daniel's body dying, when he was just in a coma not too long ago? And to train Bobbin to run like that when you said it?"

"Um…"

"I should have listened to my gut instincts after what you pulled at the hospital, that maybe you shouldn't get to be in his life—"

"Mom," Daniel said behind her on the stairs. "Just leave it. I'll talk to her."

She left in a huff, and Daniel came out on the porch with me. He eyed the sack slung over my shoulder.

"You're going after Lonan, aren't you?" he asked.

"Yeah. Can I borrow your car? I don't want Uncle Tam to know where I'm going, so I can't take his truck to the Druid's Cave."

"Why are you even chasing after Lonan? If he's into you, he'll find his way back. If not, you'll know that I was right about him."

I wanted to hit Daniel right then, but that wasn't likely to get me his car. "You don't know the whole story." So I told him all the stuff Uncle Tam had said after Daniel'd left.

He studied me. "A wyvern, eh? I can see it."

I looked down at myself in horror. *Do I have those shadow wings and extra arms like Mr. Forrest did? Creepy, red, glowing eyes?* Then Daniel chuckled.

"You butthead!" I said.

"Well, we can't have the savior of mankind getting too full of herself." But then he got serious. "Actually, it kind of makes sense now. Especially what happened when I tried to get some sleep. I dreamt I was back in Faerie, and a wyvern offered me my heart's desire if I'd do what he asked."

"What? One of the baddies came to recruit you to the dark side? Like you'd ever consider that!"

Daniel didn't answer. The silence weighed heavier with every second. *Shit, is he actually considering helping them?* I backed away, gathering my magic.

"I told them no, Avery. Calm down."

I punched him, his T-shirt smoldering where my hand connected, probably from some of the magic leaking out of me. "Next time, lead with that! 'I wasn't tempted for a minute, Avery, and sent those losers packing' would have been good."

"But I was tempted," Daniel said. "They offered me all kinds of promises."

Holy shit! "Like what?"

"Putting you under a love spell, like I tried to do before." My eyes went wide and he laughed bitterly. "When they saw they were on the wrong track there, they offered to make you and Lonan suffer for a long, long time. And promised me power, a kingdom to rule over in Faerie, or legions of screaming fans at my sold-out concerts."

"So, which of those did you consider?"

"It doesn't matter," he said. "The important part is that they wanted me to bring you to the Castle—so I think that's where they're holed up. Stay away, Avery."

"Nope, going in." I patted my bag. "Got my trusty kit right here."

"You seriously think that's going to stop wyverns—"

"Helloo, wild magic girl here, scourge of the Fae," I said. "Can I borrow your car or not?" *But bravado may not be enough, and now would be a good time to be all gallant, Daniel, and offer to come with me.*

The question must have been on my face, because he said, "I can't—I'm not going with you, Avery. I'll stall Tam if he comes here looking for you, but no way am I going back to Faerie. Ever." But he fished his car keys out of his pocket and handed them over.

"Thanks." I stepped closer, arms raised, but he skittered away. "What, no hug?"

"Uh, no," he said with surprising vehemence. "You don't get it—"

Daniel broke off into a frustrated growl, and he suddenly had all my attention. *He's more than mad at me—he sounds...wounded.*

While I stood there, eyes wide in shock, he calmed down enough to add, "Let's just say that after what I went through in Faerie, it's going to be a long time before I let anyone in my personal space again."

I swallowed around the hairball of guilt clogging my throat. "Fair enough. But I hope, for your sake, we can talk some more about this later."

I'd only taken a few steps before his footsteps came up behind me. I turned quickly, half-afraid he'd changed his mind about delivering me to the bad guys. But instead, he carefully pulled me into his arms.

As I blinked away tears, he whispered, "I couldn't leave it like that. But yeah, we'll talk." It should have been comforting, but it actually kind of scared me—*he's hugging me like he doesn't think I'm coming back.* Daniel waved to me as I pulled out of the driveway, a very human silhouette against the homey glow of the porch light.

21

Daniel's car chugged along—its rattle-y ride couldn't have been more different than Nykur's smooth one. *Oh, I wish Nykur was here with me now.*

"What took you so long?" a deep voice asked next to me.

I squawked and jerked the wheel hard, and a guy's hand reached out and corrected before we landed in a ditch. I slammed on the brakes and brought the car to a stop. Turning to my passenger, I froze in astonishment.

He had a chiseled jaw, dark tousled curls, and a smile that could charm the pants off a girl. A T-shirt, with "Spare a Horse, Ride a Nykur" on it, strained over wide shoulders and etched pecs. *Makes all those Hollywood hotties and boy bands look like orcs.* Nykur let out a familiar bass laugh.

"Holy studmuffins," I breathed. "That is some good horse breeding."

Judging by the knowing curve of his lips and the wicked glint in his eyes, Nykur still had a direct line to my thoughts. *Even the naughty ones.* I reddened, and then annoyance flashed through me.

Hey, outta my head, Mr. Tall, Dark, and Horsesome. I'd meant to only push him out of my brain, but he hit the car door so hard it flew open.

I crawled across the seat and found Nykur lying in the weeds, laughing his ass off. "That was so worth it. But promise to be more gentle in the future."

"Sorry, I'm still learning how to use magic," I said.

In response, he merely pillowed his head on his hands seductively. I wanted to lie full-length on him, covering him with kisses... "Um, Nykur, am I suddenly a total nympho, or are you using your mojo on me?"

"A little bit of both?"

"Just get back in the car. I've got some rescuing to do. And I'm not getting in the middle of this corbin-nykur rivalry thing."

With a long-suffering sigh, he climbed back in. But he didn't turn down the volume on his pheromones until I glared at him. I started the car and pulled onto the empty road again.

"Okay, okay, so I was hoping you called me for some comforting," Nykur said. "But we'll keep it purely platonic for the rescue mission. Though Lonan's a fumbling virgin compared to my skills, if you'd only give me a chance—"

"Nykur, that's a great idea!" I said. He eagerly reached for me. "Not that! I was just thinking that if I could call you into our world, couldn't I do that with Lonan?"

He leaned back into the passenger seat. "You could, if he wasn't being held by Drake and his lot. Depending on how Drake is caging him, your calling his true name could have enough power behind it that Lonan would rip off his own arms trying to obey you. Just trying to make contact could tip them off that you're coming, and if he's still alive they might just kill him rather than risk you succeeding." At my horrified expression, he hastily added, "But I'm sure they've kept him alive. He's more valuable as leverage, right?"

"He is...but does Drake know that?" I pressed on the gas pedal and Daniel's car sped up slightly, before stuttering and slowing to half-speed. *Arrgh—at this rate, we might get there too late.* The Castle had never felt so far.

"Forget this jalopy," Nykur said. "Pull over. I can get us there quicker by taking us cross country."

I did as he said, parking in front of the mini-mart. When we got out, I turned to say something to him, but found I was facing a huge black horse instead.

"Um—I'd feel more comfortable with the car form." *Or maybe I could just hitch him to Daniel's car—he looks like he could pull a semi, no problem.*

Nykur stomped a hoof the size of a hubcap, whinnying impatiently. He tossed his head towards the Castle and gave me a significant look with one dark, liquid eye.

"O-kay," I said, approaching him gingerly. I climbed onto the back bumper of Daniel's car and used that to vault onto Nykur's back. I'd barely settled onto his heated hide before he took off. Straight into the brush, heading for the Castle as the crow flies.

A buckeye nut clonked me in the head as we bushwhacked, and I crouched lower over his back. *You so did that to get back at me, Nykur, I know it!* He rumbled beneath me in a horsey version of his laugh. And then he settled into his stride, crossing streets on thundering hooves, leaping fences into yards, before coming to a stop in front of the Castle's iron gates.

I swayed, breathing hard like I'd been the one galloping, when I'd actually only been working not to fall off. I studied Wilson Castle as I waited for my breath to slow. The hulking building lay quiet in the pool of its spotlights, slumbering in the summer night air.

"No sign of anyone here—is it a trick?" I asked.

Nykur bowed beneath me, sending me sliding off of him, but he caught me in his human arms as I stumbled.

"Sorry," he said. "Easier to talk this way. Take another look, though—use your Sight."

He turned me to face the Castle again and as I looked harder, it flickered under my gaze. I saw strobe-light glimpses of another castle in its place—one that soared higher than Wilson Castle's stumpy brick turrets. The more I concentrated on the other castle, the more it came into focus. Weird blue lights limned the windows, with shadows crawling across them occasionally. But even weirder were the flames snaking in the air above the shadow castle, like the northern lights had been juicing with steroids.

"What is with the sky?" I asked Nykur.

"That's the border. It's fraying in this spot, weakening all along its edge here."

"Like, unraveling? I wasn't expecting to actually be able to see that. Kinda freaky." I picked up my bag from where I'd dropped it. "Well, let's get this gate unlocked—shit! I don't have the keys. They're at Uncle Tam's—I didn't think to grab them."

"No worries," Nykur said. He stepped closer to the wrought-iron bars in the fence and placed his hands carefully. With a shriek of metal, he pulled the bars wide.

"Hey, how'd you do that?" I asked. "Isn't iron toxic to Fae?"

"I'm not the only nykur who can take on car form—we've evolved. And when you spend enough of your lifetime as animated steel, iron becomes no problem."

The opening he'd made was wide enough for me to slip through, but once I was on the other side it was obvious his solid bulk would never make it.

"Am I on my own from here?" Panic edged into my voice. Now that we were here, faced with that sinister castle, I didn't like the idea of entering it alone. *What if I can't do this by myself? Then they'll have Lonan and me.*

"I've got a few more tricks," Nykur said. He crouched, and in the blink of an eye was replaced by a sleek black hare. He hopped up to the fence and I reached through the mangled bars to pick him up.

"Aww, who da cootest wittle bun-bun," I teased, nuzzling his soft fur. He repaid me with a nip on my shoulder. "Ow!" I scruffed him, dangling him at arm's length, until he looked properly sorry.

"Behave," I said. "I'm just glad you're coming with me—I don't like the odds by myself, after all."

With one last cuddle, I lowered him to the ground. But as soon as his paws touched the earth, a red light arced all over his body. Screaming, Nykur tried to change into a horse, a man, the hare again—but the light only got brighter. Carrying with it the reek of burning flesh.

Oh my god, he's going to fry! I tried to gather my magic, to interrupt the circuit or whatever it was. But although it didn't have any effect on me, I wasn't able to stop it. Finally, when I saw him go into the hare form again, I picked him up and threw him back to the other side of the fence. The little body bounced on the pavement, smoke puffing from the ruined fur.

"Nykur!" I called repeatedly, until finally the hare's head lifted on a wobbly neck. "I'm coming."

But when I slipped an arm through and tried to follow it with my body, I met only resistance. I couldn't budge my torso through at all. "I can't get back through! Can you change into your human form, and let me know you're all right?"

He lifted himself onto his scorched paws and trembled with effort, but nothing else happened.

"Come close enough for me to touch you—maybe I can at least heal you."

Nykur panted as he dragged himself over to the fence, and my fingers buried themselves in his fur.

I chanted, over and over.

Blood to blood
Meat to meat
Skin to skin
Calls to each.

It was harder this time—*maybe because he's Fae?* It was like his cells were resisting me, sliding under my hand, recoiling from my magic. But finally they fell in line and my hand was touching warm skin.

Naked, manly thigh. "Nykur!" I whipped my hand away.

"Oh—sorry." He must have meant it, because leather pants clad his legs as he flushed. "Not feeling quite myself."

"Well, I nearly felt your…self," I said indignantly. "But I'm just glad you're better. I guess they know I'm here, and they want me to come alone. Not very reassuring."

He got to his feet shakily. "Maybe if you carry me—"

"No way," I said. "I'm not risking you again. I'll just have to go on my own."

He nodded reluctantly and reminded me to grab my bag. I gripped his hand for a moment, trying to draw whatever comfort I could, to take it with me. *It feels like I have to leave everyone behind just to move forward.* I was more rattled than I'd admit, too—lycoris webs were one thing, but seeing Nykur almost roasted made all this magical danger stuff real.

But I eventually started the slow trudge up the hill, alone. As I approached, a side door creaked open. I stopped, bracing myself for whatever emerged, but nothing happened.

In my Castle, it would have led into the basement. *But I should be careful expecting things here—I've already seen that expectations have a tendency to shape things in unexpected ways.* I took a deep breath and peered inside.

Yep—substitute these stone walls and elegant sconces with the familiar industrial, turn-of-the century fixtures, and it's laid out just like basement of Wilson Castle. Other doorways opened off this room, and a few windows set high in the opposite wall let in a dilute light from outside. Almost like a drowned palace, with the azure light of the torches flickering off a row of columns.

Chittering voices sounded at a great distance, but otherwise this room seemed to be empty. I took a wand of St. John's wort out of my bag and stepped forward—

Bam! I nearly jumped out of my skin as the door slammed behind me. I whirled, but there was no one there—only a blank wall where the door had been.

Okay, that's not entirely unexpected. Should have known Drake would do something like that. I sucked it up and explored the vast room, but there were no stairs—just the closed doors. *It looks like I'm going to have to open them—yay. But maybe don't think of anything when I do it, don't give them anything to use against me.*

An image of the Stay Puft marshmallow man came to mind and I laughed aloud.

No, Avery, don't do that! I got hold of myself and stood in front of one of the doors, deliberately blanking my mind. When I felt ready, I reached out and turned the knob.

A darkness seeped out. Full of scents and whispers not of my world. A thousand voices called my name. Wheedled. Begged. Smoky tendrils seeped into my skin, prying their way into my head.

They must have been looking for chinks in my armor, and a whiff of triumph meant they'd found one. Within the darkness, an inky, smeared figure stepped out. My mom, but with an expression of utter devotion on her face.

"Avery, let's go somewhere," she whispered. "Just you and me—no work, no distractions. Mother and daughter together for all time, like you've always wanted. Say yes."

I raised my hand, reaching towards her outstretched fingers, and stopped only inches away.

"You have got to be freaking kidding," I said. "Don't you know that's a teenager's worst nightmare? That might have held some appeal when I was eight, but no way do I want that now. Nice try."

When I laughed, the figure hissed angrily and dissolved. The door slammed shut and I moved on to the next one, with a spring in my step. *I've totally got this! Bring it on, Fae.*

In the next room, a boy turned to face me, joy lighting his face. *Daniel?* He smiled, in the sweet way Daniel used to. An innocence in his gaze, one lost forever from the real Daniel's eyes since his trip to Faerie.

And what's more, this boy looked at me with adoration. True love shining from him, only for me. *This is the Daniel I hoped to find this summer. The one who'd love me without complications.* And the baddies were offering him up to me on a platter.

"Avery, I've been waiting for you," Daniel said. "That other boy— it's one of their changeling tricks. It wasn't really me. I've been here the whole time, and if you come with me it will be everything we've ever imagined."

He opened his arms, making room for me in their circle. *All I have to do is take him up on it, and it would be so easy—all my fantasies from the last year come true. Happily ever after with the boy I've loved forever. The one I haven't let down.*

But how long would it be before my Sight showed the truth? That I'd given up Lonan—my world, even—for a love that had only been in my head. Nothing more than a phantom.

"Still no go," I said, and this figment faded away, too. Taking some of my confidence with it. *If I was genuinely tempted that time, what do they have in store for me next?* I hesitated before the next door, steeling myself before putting my hand on the handle.

The door swung open and showed a bright spotlight over a guy bound to a chair. Another man knelt before him, working furiously on the rope. As the door smacked the wall, he turned in a crouch, a pocketknife in his hand.

"Dad?" I said.

"Oh, honey, thank God it's you—I'm trying to get Lonan out of here. We need to cut these ropes."

My gaze went to the bound figure, with its mane of bedraggled feathers. But the eyes were closed, the head lolled in unconsciousness. *Is that really Lonan? Or is this another trick?*

"Please, help me, Avery," Dad said. "We don't have much time."

We have time to see if this is a con. "Yeah, Dad—but first, tell me, what did you give me for my third birthday?"

"What kind of question is that? There's no time for this!"

"Just answer the question." I concentrated on pink elephants, the Stay Puft man—anything but the stable he'd built for my toy horses. *Don't want to give them the answer to pull out of my brain.*

"I don't remember! A lot has happened since then. Do you want Lonan to die while you waste my time with this?"

The urgency in his voice made my heart race, even though my instincts told me this was false. "I don't want him to die at all. Try to remember, Dad. What was it?"

"A—a doll? No—a dollhouse." I turned to go. "Not a dollhouse—a horse house! A stable!"

Okay, that's right, but I'm still getting that prickly I-don't-quite-trust-him feeling. I faced my Dad again, warily. "How are you here?"

"I come back and forth a lot—and they took Corriell. My—my friend. They locked me in here and Lonan came awake long enough to tell me that you were somebody important. That we needed to get out of here before you came looking for him."

"He told you I'm important? Important how?"

"You have wild magic, and you can do things. Important things."

I narrowed my eyes. "Lonan told you that, did he? Which is strange, considering he doesn't know."

I lunged at the two of them, St. John's wort outstretched. The bound boy disappeared in a puff of smoke, but my dad was still there. Just as solid as the last time I'd seen him in our world. "Dad—it *is* you."

"Yes—and I'm sorry," he said as he clapped old-fashioned irons onto my wrists.

The cuffs burned into my skin, fusing with it before I could lift a finger. "What have you done?" I gasped as the burning settled into a dull throb.

"What he had to," a familiar voice said.

I turned and Drake stood behind me, gloating. *In his wyvern shape, if the bat wings, extra set of arms, and snaky scales are anything to go by. Ugh, and I guess I have that somewhere in my makeup, too.*

At the wave of his hand, the dark room illuminated to show an entire crowd of Fae around us, hemming us in like a mob. All shapes and sizes of creatures, united in their hungry focus on me. In reflex, I tried to gather my magic again, but all it did was fire up the cuffs on my wrists. *Yeowch!*

When the pain faded, a scent like crushed flowers caught my attention. I traced it to a pale body curled on the floor. My dad saw it at the same moment and ran to its side.

"Corriell," he murmured, gathering the slight form in his arms. The head flopped listlessly and I caught a glimpse of delicate, but decidedly male, features. *Whoa—Dad's lover is a guy? Obviously that got blocked out from when I met him the first time and triggered my magic.* After all the revelations of the last few days, it hardly even fazed me.

Dad felt my eyes on him and said, "I'm so sorry. I had to help ensnare you—they had my Corriell."

"And now they have your daughter," I growled. "And you've betrayed Uncle Tam, too—he called you, and you used that information to trap me." He winced, but continued to cradle his lover. *No help from that quarter.*

I asked Drake, "And Lonan? Did you ever have him?"

"Oh, yes—he's been my special guest since you sent him back. Thank you for that, by the way—it lessened the sting of my failure immensely."

The crowd parted to let two burly Fae through, dragging a shirtless, crowish boy between them. When they dropped Lonan to the floor, a loose cloud of dark feathers billowed up. Raw burns and wounds on his shoulders showed where more plumage had been plucked out, taking patches of skin with it. Like a blackbird escaped from the pie halfway through baking.

I couldn't make my feet walk over to see if he was alive or dead.

22

Lonan painfully lifted himself up on his forearms, looking around dazedly. His eyes fell on where I stood, helpless and speechless, and he shook his head.

"Avery," he rasped. "You shouldn't be here—I don't want you here."

I walked over to his side, expecting Drake to stop me, but no one kept me from kneeling next to Lonan.

"Aren't you the one who said I was loyal to those I care about? You should have known I'd come," I said softly as I tried to smooth what remained of his battered plumage.

Some feathers came out in my hand and I swallowed around a lump in my throat. He smiled through cracked lips, and his violet eyes cried out for me to Go!

Ha, nice try, but I didn't come all the way here to leave you behind, Lonan.

I started to help him sit up, fumbling with my bound hands, when a strange ripping sound from above made me hit the deck instead. The Fae mob cheered—*that can't be good*—and I looked up to see the writing flames of the border instead of a ceiling. *Is—is that normal, or is it getting worse?* There was more of a gap between the two edges, as if instead of a seam unraveling it was now a full-on tear.

"The blue moon is upon us!" Drake roared over the others.

How can that be? I still have another day! And then it hit me—the time differences between Faerie and home. *Not working in my favor, dammit.*

I stood and faced Lonan's brother, concentrating on getting up enough magical steam to overcome those cuffs. "Well, whoopty-frigging-doo for you, Drake, because I'm still not going to let you win."

But he laughed at me, moving in close. *Ugh, he's a close-talker on top of his other charming personality traits.*

"Your father asked that we give you a chance to step aside of your own free will, and I gave you three. I've more than fulfilled my bargain, and now comes my reward."

He grinned nastily, showing a mouth full of thorn-sharp teeth. "I like it better this way, anyhow. Slipping inside you like a poisoned barb…"

He placed his hands on either side of my head and I tried to jerk back, but he was too strong. He started turning all smoky, and I realized what he was going to do just a second too late—and my eyes, my mouth, my nose filled with a greasy seepage as Drake entered my body and made himself at home.

I still had some control—enough to let out a short scream before it was cut off—but I was losing my hold all too fast. One by one, I lost touch with my limbs, my tongue—even my heartbeat. Only sight and hearing remained, until I was boxed into a suffocating darkness, watching in horror as Drake raised my hands in triumph.

The crowd roared and bellowed in a crescendo of menace. One of the other Fae came forward to remove the shackles, and that's when things got really hairy.

Apparently, my magic went with the body. And in Drake's experienced hands, the very air around us vibrated with energy. The first thing he chose to do with it was to blast both Lonan and Corriell—red light arcing through them agonizingly, like with Nykur but a hundred times worse.

"Stop!" my dad cried. "You promised!" But all that got him was a dose for himself.

Dad's screams joined Lonan's and Corriell's and I tried to block them out, but Drake seemed to have deliberately left me a line to the eyes and ears. To torture me as well as them. I cringed, whimpering. Wished for it to end, yet was helpless to do anything about Drake's triumph flushing through my body.

Drake finally stopped, and Dad and Corriell lay limp and unmoving. Only Lonan managed to hold onto consciousness, a flare of "is that all you've got?" defiance in his eyes. *Shit—if he can still manage that, how can I do any less?*

I rallied, trying to grasp at any thread connecting me to my body, any last tendril of awareness. But it was like trying to gather pieces of straw while wearing oven mitts—they kept slipping through my clumsy, muffled grasp. With some experimentation, I discovered it helped if I visualized them as actual threads or ropes.

I kept at it until I had a few strands gathered, then crudely braided them together into a stronger cord. I gave an experimental tug, and felt like I had a left pinky finger again—just for a moment. Encouraged, I went back to building my lifeline, until I had a rope that looked as big around as my former wrist.

I checked on Drake, and he hadn't been idle while I was busy—he was currently muttering in some guttural language. The flames eating away at the border flared up in response to his spell, their roar louder than Drake's minions now. Chaos spilled out of the gap like a living thing.

Until Drake smacked himself in the face. He let the spell trail off in surprise as I tugged once more and my left hand (it was definitely mine again!) punched my body's left cheek. *Stop hitting yourself, Siwennen!* I wasn't sure if he could hear my cackle, but his growl of annoyance meant he knew I was responsible.

I had only a moment to gloat before the rope tore out of my hands and a pulsing redness surrounded my formless form. The walls shrank closer, drawing in until I curled into a tiny ball, trying to avoid contact with this raging electric current.

Wherever it touched "me," it burned away memories. Pieces of every experience that led up to me being me, flaking away like ash.

The first time I rode a pony. The time I found an abandoned nest of baby mice and tried to feed them but they died anyway. When Daniel and his parents moved in next door. My dad picking me up at the Amtrak station one spring break.

I grasped desperately at the dissolving memories, but they slipped away. Just enough of them remained for me to recognize they were gone, until there was only some core of my self huddling there, a remnant shaking and trembling. And still Drake's will burned me into char and dust.

Only the barest spark remained. Just enough to feel my attacker retreating, leaving me to fade away entirely. No longer even vaguely connected to my pirated body. A wisp of exhalation—

Nothing.

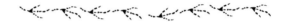

A pulse? Taking light-years to get out one spark. But still, it was something. It tried to remember what it was like to kindle. To breathe.

A flicker of blue. Then, an unfurling within the seed of light, as some determined scrap fought to survive.

It uncoiled like a serpent, spreading its bat wings, flexing its meaty arms. And then panted, half-slouched, like a monstrous butterfly fresh out of the cocoon. Until it raised a dragon-ish snout, scenting the traces of an enemy's presence. And came alive, roaring.

Waking the girl.

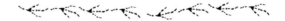

Nothingness, then BOOM—awareness. And disorientation, as I was able to see and hear again. Felt the air on my skin and the blood rushing through my veins. A moment of pure joy was all I got before Drake pushed back, damn him. His oozing darkness spread through my limbs again, trying to saturate my body with his essence so thoroughly that there'd be no coming back.

But that core of blue within me flared, and I found I could draw on it, shape with it. That slithery inner self was the embodiment of my magic. *May the best wyvern win, Cuz.* Between my human stubbornness and my new Fae powers, I was able to drive Drake into the very fringes of my body.

But the bastard just wouldn't let go—he scrabbled with his phantom, tearing claws, trying to hurt me enough to make me give up. A whisper insinuating how it would be so much easier to let him take over. *Let him make all the decisions and not have to feel like I'm always hurting others. Letting people down.*

But just like offering me forever with my mom, he'd gotten it wrong again. This ploy only reminded me that I wasn't the only one at stake here—Lonan was still a captive, my dad and his boyfriend might not have survived that last attack, and Uncle Tam needed me to set things right with the two worlds.

And the best way to not let them down is to keep trying, not to give in.

With an audible roar I thrust Drake away, using all my might. This time it worked, and I coughed up a gout of black smoke that was Drake. Red sparks spat within it as his anger mounted, and there was enough of a connection remaining that I knew he was going to finish Lonan once and for all.

Oh no, you don't! I reached out my hands and plunged them into the smoke, my own magic rushing to my bidding. Blue light engulfed the red as I forced him into physical shape again, a winged worm as long as my arm.

Drake writhed under my clawed hands and I squeezed, feeling delicate ribs shattering between my fingers. It sounded like a cat crunching on prey—something which would have grossed me out before, but only excited me more to hear. Now I rotated my grip, each hand moving tissue and flesh in opposing directions, feeling it tear beneath my scaly palms.

He shrieked and thrashed, bubbled as he tried to change form, but my grip was vise-tight. I only shifted it long enough to pull one of his frail wings off. *Like plucking a flower petal!*

I giggled as the wing fluttered to the ground and I pinched the other membrane, started to stretch it to the limit of its tendons—

"Avery!" A voice intruded on my fun. "Avery, stop! This isn't like you!"

Who would dare tell me to stop? I swiveled on my feet, wings unfurling behind me to balance the sudden movement. From a greater height than usual, I looked down into Lonan's desperate gaze.

"Krrkennen," I said, and he winced at my use of his real name.

But he forced a smile and nodded. "Yes, it's me. I don't know what's happened to change you, but this isn't the Avery I know. She is full of light and love and laughter—not pain."

"This," I said, Drake flopping limply in my hand as I gestured to my scaly self. "This is in me, too."

Lonan dragged himself up painfully into a seated position. "But it's not all of you—even here, in Faerie. You can choose your appearance, but your essential nature doesn't change. So that love and laughter is still in there. Prove it—please."

"And what about Drake? He would have destroyed me—and you—before moving on to let all this darkness loose in my world." I motioned at the snarling crowd still surrounding us—if anything, they were watching more avidly since I'd attacked Drake.

"So you're out to prove that you're like him? Or are you better than him?"

But Lonan doesn't know I have a wyvern father, with just as much influence on my nature as that man on the floor. Uncle Tam had made sure of it, made me into this…thing. So that I could fulfill my destiny and give the Fae what they deserved—exile.

But since when have I done whatever Uncle Tam wants? Or some Fae guy I've never even met? I'd always been truly, completely myself. *For better or for worse.*

With that realization, my bulk fell away. Scales scattered like glitter in a snow globe, leaving pink human skin behind. Only the wings stayed—because, hey, those were wicked cool.

Lonan smiled, and my own lips curved upwards. "Better?" I asked.

"Much," he breathed. "And Drake, is he…"

I gave him a shake and Lonan's brother mewled softly in protest. "Nope, still alive. Will he heal?"

"Not on his own." Lonan's tone said he knew I'd do the right thing there, too.

Dammit! Isn't it enough to be the better person, and not have to be the best Avery I can be? With a sigh, I directed my magic to heal Drake's broken body. As he mended, he assumed his human-sized form and hissed in anger. As a precaution, I grabbed the magical manacles from where they'd fallen and clapped them on one pair of his wrists.

"Just until I decide what to do with you," I said sweetly under his hateful gaze.

Then I moved on to Lonan, healing him even before my dad. Dad and I would have a lot to talk about, but seeing him held so tight in Corriell's arms made me think he couldn't have gone to the dark side completely. His lover's scent in the air was now like the sweetest of blooms, heady and comforting.

The crowd around us had broken into groups, talking softly to each other and casting measuring looks my way. A few even smiled—a sincere overture. But there were those who still sent dark glances shooting at me.

It looked like they were thwarted for now, but a group of wyverns suddenly launched into the air and proved me wrong. They darted towards the gap in the border, wings beating swiftly towards my world and all its waiting victims.

Oh, yeah—kind of forgot about the Faeriepocalypse. With a shake of my head, I raised a hand and swept them to the ground. They huddled, cowed, and none of the other creatures made a break for the rippling chaos above.

"What am I supposed to do about that?" I asked.

"Let me take Corriell through, and then close it like Tam said," Dad answered immediately. "Close it forever and leave these wretches to their fate."

"No!" Lonan cried. "You can't do that—Corriell will die if he's cut off from Faerie. And we need humans."

Howls of protest rose from the Fae, but he hollered over them, "It's true!"

Lonan leaned in close to me and said in a low voice, "They don't want you to know—the Fae can't create anything new. We never could, and humans are the only way change comes into our world.

"When the exchange is done within the rules, it benefits both of our kind. But without an influx of new ideas, of new people, the Fae will just fade away."

"Let them!" my father growled.

"Even your Corriell?" Lonan asked gently. "You know we're not all worthless or immoral. Avery, please, if you close off the borders permanently, you doom a lot of innocents."

Dad scoffed, but I noticed he wasn't exactly offering to give Corriell up. I looked back and forth between my Fae boyfriend, my dad, and his Fae boyfriend, not knowing who to trust. Drake's chains jangled as he raised a hand to get my attention.

"There is another alternative," he said. "Let the border unravel, and set yourself as ruler over both worlds."

I rolled my eyes at him, but he continued, "No, think on it—with your powers, you could establish laws to protect both humans and the Fae. You would control everything, see to it that we all thrive under your benevolent rule. I will be the first to bow to your commands."

Drake knelt before me, and with a rustle of wings and other strange limbs, much of the crowd followed his example. Sure, some of them were muttering resentfully, but others looked sincere. *Worshipful, even.*

The wyvern in me rose up again, basking in the tribute. But I was able to balance it with my human intellect, and I weighed Drake's suggestion. *Would that actually work? Could one person, magical or otherwise, solve thousands of years' worth of problems between the Fae and humans?*

Magic tingled along my skin in anticipation. But, fresh from being so intoxicated with power that I'd pulled a wing off my enemy, I had to wonder how long a benevolent rulership would last. *Before I grow corrupt with my own power, and shaping things to my will becomes more important than shaping them for the betterment of all.*

I glanced at Lonan and he was watching me, wearing a poker face. But when I winked at him, he broke out into a grin.

He kissed my hand, but I gently pulled it away. "Lonan…" I looked from him to my dad, and to all these creatures waiting for my decision. *No one will be truly happy with it—including me.*

"I'm obviously not going to follow Drake's suggestion of dual-world domination. But I can't in good conscience completely close off the border, either."

Biting my lip, I thought hard before I continued. "I'm going to re-establish the laws that Merlin formed. It may only be temporary until I have more information that sways me one way or the other, but I think we should use this as a chance to make peace with each other."

A clamor rose as everyone talked at once. Dad left Corriell's side to try to convince me to do what he said, Drake wanted me to rethink becoming a teenage totalitarian, and the other voices blurred into a sound of protest.

Only Lonan smiled sadly at me, grasping that my words meant he'd have to find his way back to me through the regular channels—no immediate happily-ever-after for us. But there would be one eventually, I was sure.

He waited while I stitched together the edges of the border seamlessly, following the threads of weakened laws and strengthening their weave. Too tired to think of anything completely new, I spoke only the refrain from the binding spell:

Twine, twine, betwixt
Twine, twine, the twain.

I could feel the changes rippling out throughout the fabric of the worlds, like shaking wrinkles from a quilt.

By the time I'd finished, most of the creatures had already wandered off. My dad was still here in Faerie—it was in my power to grant him some protection for his mind on this side of the border, since he no longer fit well in our world—but aside from his and Corriell's murmured conversation, the castle's vast hall lay quiet.

Flush with the satisfaction of a job well done, I took Lonan's hand and pulled him after me, back into the basement room.

"Where are we going?" he asked.

"Somewhere more private to say our goodbyes-for-now," I said.

"Oh? What did you have in mind?" He sounded excited, but also a little hesitant, like he no longer knew what to expect of my hybrid self.

"You'll see," I said in my best vamp voice.

I paused in front of one of the closed doors, gathering my thoughts, and threw it open. Music spilled out, along with happy screams and the rattle of roller coasters. The smell of fried foods and funnel cakes enveloped us, beckoning us inside.

We stepped forward, and Lonan took in the amusement park with puzzled awe. Then he read the flashing neon signs and laughed.

"Space Monkey Mountain? Mr. Toad's Sedate Ride? This is seriously where you want to spend our last few hours together, before we part for who knows how long?"

"Yep," I answered, jigging in place with glee. "Wait'll you taste the Peeps S'mores—they roll 'em in graham cracker and chocolate cookie crumbs before they go in the fryer. Come on!"

He shook his head at my little-kid impatience, so I pointed to another building. "Don't worry—there's some more mature fun in store, too."

The Honeymoon Mansion, a Gothic building draped in hot pink tulle, waited on the far side of the park. "It has a room just for us— with a ginormous bed and a bathtub built for two. Is that better?"

"I'd rather start with dessert." He leered and smacked my ass before racing down the yellow brick road. And he might have beaten me to the mansion, if the downdraft from my wyvern wings hadn't knocked him over before he could spread his own crow-ish ones.

EPILOGUE

How did girls in those vampire books and TV shows settle right back into the school year once they'd seen the entire spectrum of good and evil out there? However grateful I was that mean kids were the worst I had to deal with, it wasn't that easy for me.

For one thing, missing Lonan was an ache that always nagged at me. I wasn't going around wringing my hands over him, I wasn't going to curl up and go catatonic, but so many things could have been so much better if he was there. Not easier, but eased, if that makes sense.

As if it wasn't bad enough to have to pretend to be Little Miss Normal when my magic and emotions were barely under control, every weekend was spent at Uncle Tam's trying to get ready for my new role in Fae-human relations. His lessons included a meeting with the Faerie Queen, which didn't go well, as she seemed determined to put me in my place. She seemed especially put out—or was it nervous?—that I'd been able to send Nykur back to Faerie with the banishment spell, in spite of her geis that was meant to keep him in exile.

That bitch actually called me an "unnatural child" and a "bastard wyvern-spawn"—technically that last part was true, but I didn't like her tone. And I was all "you should be grateful you're not a refugee!" and Uncle Tam had to step in before another Fae got her wings pulled off.

So, we still had to work on my diplomacy skills.

The only bright spot was that, despite Mom's misgivings that a muscle car might prove too much for me, she let me drive Nykur to school. He was popular with gearheads of both genders, and strangely attractive to the giggly kind of girls.

So I wasn't surprised to see someone leaning against the car in the parking lot when school let out one day. *Great, another silly girl to ask if she can sit in the car and enjoy the "massage" feature, which is really just Nykur copping a feel of her parts.*

But as I got closer, I recognized Wolfgang from my yearbook class last year. Well, he'd been Todd then, but it was Wolfgang since he'd gone steampunk. That's why I'd thought he was a girl at first glance— his long, skirted neo-Victorian coat. I had no idea what he was after, but I just wanted to go home.

"Hey, Wolfgang," I said, setting my backpack on the car roof. "Can we catch up another time?"

He didn't say anything, so I turned toward him. Wolfgang rose up on his boot toes and placed a hand on either side of my head. My magic flared up in defense, but before I could focus it he kissed me.

My "what the hell?" was muffled against soft but practiced lips. Lips that tasted of cloves, but felt so familiar on mine that I relaxed into the kiss.

The rush of magic retreated, leaving behind a warm haze. "Lonan?" I breathed into his open mouth.

"Well, I certainly hope you don't go around kissing everyone like that," he said. "I went to a lot of trouble to trade with this Todd character so I could see you."

I wrapped my arms around him, in spite of the catcalls of "Ooo, steamy!" coming from the nearby football field.

"Only you, Krrkennen."

ACKNOWLEDGMENTS

It's been quite a journey to *Crow's Rest*, and I am so thankful for the company along the way! The cast of characters who helped bring *Crow's Rest* to life are:

The Spencer Hill Press "family" of authors and staff, including my fantabulous editor Owen Dean, who laughed in all the right places, and my first contact, Vikki Ciaffone, who upgraded a critique session into a book offer. Publicist-extraordinaire Jennifer Allis Provost deserves a mention too, as does Kate Kaynak (whose official title seems to be Grand Poobah of Spencer Hill Press) and all the SHP authors and editorial staff who cheer and support each other.

But before my writing got to the book stage, it passed through the inky hands of a number of critique partners, including Alison Kemper, Nancy Herman, Christina Mercer, Rachel Allen Dillon, Janelle Weiner, Karen McCoy, Laurie Dennison, Kate Coursey, The El Dorado Writers Guild, and various red-pen slashers on the Absolute Write Water Cooler Forum.

Support groups are essential for authors (especially debut authors, who get to learn the ins and outs of publishing while simultaneously suffering attacks of giddiness and doubts) so "thank you" to my fellow operatives at Operation Awesome, and to my bold Fearless Fifteeners colleagues. I'm also fortunate to fall within the borders of the California North/Central chapter of the Society of Children's Book Writers and Illustrators, and to be part of that stellar crowd of creative talents.

And then there are the Mermaids, who are the best support-group-in-a-pool I could ask for. And, of course, other family and friends figured into this, but I'll leave them nameless to make it easier on the Witness Protection Program later on. But you know who you are.

There are probably even more people who I should thank, but their names have been overwritten on my brain by other things. Probably useless things, like how many toes a chicken has, but that doesn't mean you're any less important—just that the chicken-toes thing came along later and knocked you out of the memory banks temporarily. Please forgive the momentary lapse and buy my book anyway, even if it's just to draw a moustache on my author photo.

ABOUT THE AUTHOR

Angelica R. Jackson, in keeping with her scattered Gemini nature, has published articles on gardening, natural history, web design, travel, hiking, and local history. Other interests include pets, reading, green living, and cooking for food allergies (the latter not necessarily by choice, but she's come to terms with it). Ongoing projects include short fiction, poetry, novels, art photography, and children's picture books. In 2012, she started Pens for Paws Auction, which features critiques and swag from agents and authors to raise money for a no-kill, cage-free cat sanctuary where she volunteers, Fat Kitty City. She's also been involved with capturing the restoration efforts for Preston Castle in photographs and can sometimes be found haunting its hallways.

CAMERON PARK
JUL 0 6 2015 Mn